MARIA FRANKLAND

The Last Cuckoo

When Ghosts Live on in Stepfamilies

AUTONOMY PRESS

First published by Autonomy Press 2020

Copyright © 2020 by Maria Frankland

All rights reserved. No part of this publication may be reproduced, stored or transmitted in any form or by any means, electronic, mechanical, photocopying, recording, scanning, or otherwise without written permission from the publisher. It is illegal to copy this book, post it to a website, or distribute it by any other means without permission.

This novel is entirely a work of fiction. The names, characters and incidents portrayed in it are the work of the author's imagination. Any resemblance to actual persons, living or dead, events or localities is entirely coincidental.

Maria Frankland asserts the moral right to be identified as the author of this work.

First edition

ISBN: 978-1-9162-2480-3

Cover art by Darran Holmes

This book was professionally typeset on Reedsy. Find out more at reedsy.com

This book is dedicated to anyone who has found themselves in a dark place within their own family.

To join Maria Frankland's 'keep in touch' list, and receive a free collection of short stories, visit www.autonomypress.co.uk

Prologue

Your hair wafts in the breeze through the open door. You lie, still as a rock, your eyes partially closed. Blood trails from your ear to the floor.

Then I notice the line of your neck. And know for certain, that you're no longer here.

Chapter One

"*Come on*, Jamie." I can hear the irritation in Iain's tone. I'm pissing him off now. It's the fifth time he's called me but I can't face going downstairs. Not yet.

Claudia's down there, your prodigal stepdaughter-to-be, in on 'the action.' Hypocrite. And God knows who else. People talk in low voices, which drift in and out of the house.

"Can I come up Jamie?" Cate calls. "Just for a chat. I want to make sure you're ok."

"I'm not decent. I'm fine." I know she's your mate Mum, but Cate's *always* done my head in. She speaks to me like I'm still a little boy. She's been pretty good to me though. Filled the freezer up a bit. Everyone keeps asking if I'm eating ok. In fact, it's one of the first things they ask.

Anyway, you wouldn't recognise me today. I've had my hair cut, yep, even without you nagging me, and Dad's helped me find a suit. I had to pay for it though. He's skint, as usual. We both know he's been a bit of a waste of space for the last few years, but since you've gone, he's not been too bad. He keeps ringing me.

So now, I'm sat, in front of your mirrored wardrobes, suited and booted, looking like a pleb, all in black, right down to my tie. I reckon you'd be impressed – I've even had a shower.

It could be just another day. The light is getting in between your blinds and traffic is still passing by. I sometimes wonder how the world can keep going without you. I've been dreading today. I've got to hold up and get through it. Then it'll get better. People will probably start to leave me alone. I remember you saying after Grandma died that you didn't get a minute's peace. Then once the funeral was over, everyone expected you to get over it. I can't remember Grandma. I wish I could.

"Jamie, if you don't come now, we'll be late."

Iain's voice makes me jump this time. *So what if we're late.* You were always late anyway Mum. I kind of wonder what Iain's doing here. He could have just met us at the crematorium, instead of coming to the house and getting on my case. It's not as if you got married or he actually lived here, and Claudia has never been overly fond of either of us – maybe I will never see them again after today.

I stand, too quickly, feel dizzy and have to sit back down again. Your painting swims in front of my eyes. Bracelet Bay, South Wales. We had a right laugh there. When things were different. It's a lifetime ago now. You've painted it so clearly – I can almost smell the sea. I'm going to drive down there, I reckon. When this is all over. I could really do with buggering off somewhere.

"Jamie!" It's Cate again.

"Ok. Coming." Deep breath. I can do this. I open your bedroom door and walk across the landing. You wouldn't tell me off for having my shoes on. They're new, after all. I look down the stairs, knowing I can't put it off any longer. I'll have to go down them. Several pairs of eyes are on me as I enter the living room. There are sympathy cards everywhere. I can't stand looking at them – they're all coming down later. And it stinks of, well I don't know – I think it's the flowers.

"She's here," someone says. I don't want to look out of the window, but I can't avoid it. You are here. *Are you really in – there?* Your coffin is covered in white flowers, lilies, I think. You used to like them. Flowered letters spell out A-N-N-A in the window. I feel dizzy again.

I catch my breath as I stare at the hearse.

"Come on lad." I feel Iain's hand on my shoulder and for a moment I feel grateful for it. "Let's give her the send-off she deserves."

I stand, staring at your coffin from the pavement. This isn't happening. You're not *really* in there. A tear drips off my chin and lands with a splash onto my shoe. Another one follows. I haven't cried so much since I was a kid.

"We're in that one." Iain squeezes my arm as he steers me towards the huge black car behind yours. I follow, obediently. I get in first, then Iain, then Claudia. There's a pane of glass between us and the driver. All I can see is a fat neck with a cap plonked on top of it. Mine and Iain's knees are touching. I pull mine to the left. I don't look at him.

Claudia's staring out of the window, probably eyeing up Jake from next door. I think he's the only reason she ever came to our house. *What the hell is she doing in this car anyway?* It's not *her* mum that's died. She's not family and doesn't care. She's got her own mum to go back to. Sadistic Stacey. Apparently, they used to laugh all the time about you. Claudia and Stacey, that is. You kept well away from Iain's ex. I'd hear stories about her nastiness and shudder. She sounds like a right cow. Claudia never gave you a chance either. I can understand Iain being here, in this car, if I'm honest. I suppose you were engaged. But not *her*. I glance across; she's trying to appear 'sad' but her eyes are bone dry. She's all blonde hair and big tits – I should fancy her, but I don't. Not one bit. *Beauty is only skin deep*, you used to say. And you were right.

All the neighbours are gawking as we pull out of the street, some are dressed as though they'll follow us on. Your brother and sister are meeting us there.

"Why are Sarah and Cate in their own cars?" I turn to Iain. "There's room for them in here – they were Mum's best friends." I hold back

CHAPTER ONE

from saying that they've more right to be in here than Claudia.

"Cate's bringing you back later," Iain explains, sniffing, "and Sarah's picked us up. She's going to drop Claudia off at her mum's and me back at home. So we needed cars there."

"Oh. Right." I hope Cate's not going to do my head in when she brings me back. Not today.

"Unless you want me to come back with you?" Iain adds, tugging a disgusting looking hanky from his pocket. "I don't mind. You might not want to be on your own tonight."

"*I* might want to stay with you Dad." I hate that stupid, whining voice of Claudia's. At twenty-three, she's only a year younger than me but reminds me of a spoilt ten-year-old.

"I'll be alright on my own thanks," I say quickly.

I can't take my eyes off your coffin. I wonder if it's your head or feet pointing towards me. *What a waste.* Why did it have to happen? Your car turns left at the ring road and I feel panicky as another car cuts in before us. It is immediately behind you. Then another car changes lanes. By the time we've joined the dual carriageway, we're three cars behind you. I'm fuming. Why won't they move? Can't they see that we're with you? I sit forwards in my seat, willing them to shift lanes. I'm never going to see you again. I need our car to stay behind yours. It's really pissing me off.

"Easy mate." Iain's got his hand on my shoulder again. I shrug it off. It could be any journey really. We pass my old school, then your art gallery and the café we used to go to. Before I know it, we're driving into the crematorium's entrance. 'Welcome,' says the sign. *Welcome!* I'd rather be anywhere than here! Gravestones are lit in the sunshine, and branches, covered in flowers, bow over the drive through which our cars pass. You'd always liked May. It would have been your birthday a week ago. That was a hard day. You'd be pleased with the weather. *A perfect day*, you would say. Except it's not. It's the worst day of my life.

There are too many people to count as we approach the entrance. A queue snakes from the doors and is way back beyond the length of the building. Everyone is staring at your coffin, dabbing their eyes as it is slid, out of the car, onto a trolley. Iain passes me a tissue. I realise that I'm crying again. I'm led towards you, with Iain, where Uncle Simon and Cate's husband, David, are waiting. Your Godson Tom, and my cousin, who I never see, ever, Paul, makes the sixth pallbearer. We assemble ourselves according to height. Iain and I find ourselves at the front. This is all wrong. You should be still alive, enjoying a gin and tonic in the garden. I can't believe this is happening.

Somewhere over the Rainbow is playing. Iain picked this one. He said I could pick the song at the end. You were to have Eva Cassidy at your wedding when you walked down the aisle apparently. So you're having her down this aisle instead.

Iain's in bits. I've never seen him like this before. I know I've had my run-ins with him, but I think he loved you. Claudia's making a performance out of comforting him. I wonder again why she's walking in with us, taking a place in the front row. A ghost of a smirk plays on her lips – I think she's enjoying being at the fore of the attention. Dust dances in the slivers of light that are finding their way in through the gloom of the chapel.

I turn in response to a squeeze of my shoulder. It's Auntie Liz, right behind me. So she's in the second row and Claudia's at the front. *She's your bloody sister.* Wrong. Wrong. Wrong. The room is stuffed to capacity and the break-out area behind is full too. So many people love you. But it's *my* life where the mum-shaped hole has been left. I'm numb as I stare at your coffin, wondering how many minutes I have left with you in the same room before you are taken away forever. My head swoons again. I haven't eaten anything really, just a couple of bites of toast. I need to sit but must remain standing with everyone else as the Vicar steps up to the lectern at the front.

CHAPTER ONE

"You ok mate?" Iain whispers.

"Um, yeah. I think so."

We say the *Lord's Prayer*. I don't believe in all that crap, but you did, so I join in. I can remember the words from when you used to make me go to church with you. Then everyone sings a hymn. *Amazing Grace*. I don't join in. I can't. No way can I *sing*. I stare at your coffin, trying to picture your face and pretend that you're still alive. I study your picture on my service sheet. Brown eyes that everyone says I've got and a smile that had no idea of where you'd be within a year of the photograph being taken. You'd just had your hair cut above your shoulders and moaned for a week about it being too short.

"We are here to celebrate the life of Anna Louise Hardaker," begins the vicar.

Celebrate! I feel like shouting. *What have we got to celebrate!* It's as bad as the welcome sign on the gate.

He goes on to give an outline of your life, acknowledging that its duration has been at least halved. Who expects to die at the age of forty-three? He talks about how loved you were, all the things you achieved in your career as an artist and how it wasn't *what* you had in your life that mattered, but *who*.

Everyone looks at me as my phone beeps loudly with a text. As I rush to turn it off, I notice it's Alex, my mate from work, seeing how I am.

Then Uncle Si gets up. He looks like shit and I wonder how he's going to hold it together.

"My big sister Anna," he begins. "She drove me insane when we were kids. She and Elizabeth were always in league with one another, with their roller boots, secrets and dance routines to Wham songs." There's an echo of laughter around the chapel. "I always felt left out and would do what I could to disrupt their sisterly friendship. I was just the irritating little brother.

What I didn't appreciate at the time was how much she adored me. My relationship with her was like having a second mother." He stares at your coffin. "She took me swimming, stuck up for me at school and let me tag along when she did her paper round or when she was hanging around with her mates." His voice cracks. "As we grew older, she would pick me up when I got dumped and she helped me believe in myself. Then as is often the case with families, our lives started to go in opposite directions. She got married and had my awesome nephew Jamie. I had one or two disastrous relationships, but my sister was always there for me. She and Jamie would show me again and again that family is where it is at and where it will always be. I could tell her anything and she never judged me. Never. But she was so much more than just mine and Liz's sister. She was an amazing mother to Jamie, as well as a friend to many, teacher, artist and fiancée to Iain."

I'm in bits watching him. I feel like I can't breathe.

"If something needed doing, she got it done and, if someone needed help, she made sure they got it. She was a gifted artist and her work, I'm sure, will go on and on. For all the times when we were kids, when I used to laugh at her, shout at her or just feel utterly irritated by her, all that's left to say now is *Anna, my incredible sister. I've been so lucky to have you as a friend and inspiration.* I will personally ensure that Jamie is always taken care of and that your memory lives forever. I love you sis."

I need you back Mum. I need for all this to have never happened and for you to be back at home. How am I ever going to cope without you here? Auntie Liz has moved to the front of her pew and has an arm on my shoulder, draped around the front of my neck. She smells a bit like you – you must wear the same perfume. Suddenly it's all over and the final song plays. *Angels.* It's my song to you. I cry harder at the line *whether I'm right or wrong.* No matter what a shite I was, especially as a teenager, you were always there for me. I'm the first to arrive at your coffin, spreading my arms up and down its length and kissing the wood like a div. You'd laugh at me, that I'm capable of such behaviour, but there it is. Other people walk to you and pay similar respects. Some 'tap' the coffin's surface, some kiss it, others bow their heads. Everyone loved you, especially me. I look away when the curtain starts to close around you. I can't bear it. I feel like jumping in there with you but instead, trudge from the room.

"Dad! What are *you* doing here?" He stands, smoking a cigarette in the porch. I'm one of the first out, after shrugging everyone off who tried to talk to me or hug me on my way out.

"I had to come son." He sinks onto a bench as someone lines up the A-N-N-A arrangement on the floor. This must mean they are about to burn you. I guess it's better than you being buried. I definitely couldn't stand watching you being lowered into the ground.

"Does *Katherine* know you're here?" I can't imagine she'd be best pleased, my 'wicked' stepmother. You weren't exactly her favourite person, were you Mum?

"No. And she doesn't need to know. She's jealous enough of your mum as it is."

"She's dead," I say, flatly. "Nothing much to be jealous about."

"What are *you* doing here?" Iain's behind me, echoing my question to Dad.

"I was married to Anna for ten years. How could I *not* come? I've as much right as anyone to be here." His voice is high pitch, challenging.

"Fair enough. Just no trouble, eh?"

"I won't come to the wake," Dad says. "I'll get lynched. I'll ring you tomorrow son."

I bet you never thought Dad would turn up, did you Mum? He's right about getting lynched though. Over the years, he's had a run in with just about everyone you know.

I watch Dad walk away. I sit on the bench beside the flowers. Iain sits beside me. I don't want to talk to him so I pull my phone out. There are several notifications on the welcome screen; well-wishers who haven't been able to make the funeral. One of them is obviously an old one, it must be, it's *your* Twitter handle. It's bad timing, whatever it is.

***@artistanna123 has tweeted for the first time in a while.*

Chapter Two

Iain, me, Liz and Simon stand in a line, shaking hands with people as they file into the hotel lounge. It's like being royal or something. I notice Sarah and Cate making their way down the line and hope they don't try to hug me. I watch as Sarah hugs Iain, dread pooling in my stomach. *If she thinks she's getting hold of me like that.* Bloody hell. She's whispering something into his ear and he's holding her hand. The longer they stay like this, the more uncomfortable I feel. Just when I'm about to say *what the hell are you both playing at,* they let go of one another and the procession down our line continues. Everyone says how sorry they are, there's lots of comments about me supposedly looking like you and how proud you'd be of me. *What's there to be proud of?* I'm barely holding it together. I'm getting fed up of saying thank you to people. I want a beer. It's not long until Iain's sorted it.

"Sit yourself down lad. Have a rest."

The beer doesn't touch the sides. You'd be lecturing me for drinking on an empty stomach. It certainly does the trick. I feel calmer straight away.

"Another?" Iain's on his way back to the bar before I've had the chance to answer. People keep clapping me on the back or squeezing my arm as they pass me. I guess they don't really know what to say. To be honest, I've never known what to say either, when someone dies.

"You ok?" Claudia slides into the chair opposite me.

I'm shocked. I don't usually get care and concern from Claudia. I guess we got on to a certain extent in the beginning when you and Iain were planning 'fun' activities to try and help us all bond. But all that went out of the window when she became jealous of me.

"I've had better days."

"I'm surprised your dad turned up."

"He was married to her."

"Thought she hated him." She purses her lips around a straw.

"She's dead Claudia. Leave it. It's none of your business anyway."

"He looks like a waste of space."

"Get lost." It's the day of your funeral and she really can't leave it, can she? Her *concern*, if that's what it had been, had not lasted long.

"What are you two bickering about. Today of all days." Iain places another bottle of Bud in front of me.

"Cheers mate. I'm off to sit somewhere else though." Today's about *you* Mum. I don't want everyone to remember it as the day I punched Claudia. I notice that my cousin, Paul is sat on his own. I make my way over to him.

This is the first time I've been to a funeral; everyone is darkly dressed and speaks in a quiet voice to start with. You would have wanted them to have a few drinks and enjoy the pie and chips that have been put on. Eventually they do. I force a bit of food down and stand at the bar to get another Bud. Iain, once again, swoops in to buy it for me. Then he tells me that this is where you should have been having your wedding reception. I feel gutted for you both. Also gutted with myself for being pissed off and jealous of him.

You were on your own for a while after you broke up with Dad. You said you needed to put *yourself back together again*. At first, I thought you might take him back, but I saw you become stronger and happier as the weeks, then months went by.

Then you started having evenings out. You'd be done up like a dog's dinner, more than if you were just going out with Cate or someone. You were a strange sort of happy all the time and always disappearing to speak on your phone. It came as no surprise when you told me you had a *boyfriend* you wanted me to meet. *Boyfriend!* It wasn't like you were a spring chicken Mum! I was reasonably interested when I found out his daughter was a year younger than me. *Who wouldn't be?*

I could tell you were nervous when you brought Iain over to meet me. I probably made that worse by threatening to say *so which one's this then!* Lol. I was unusually on my best behaviour, even if I did think he was a bit of a weirdo. *Trying too hard*, I reckoned at the time. Wanted his feet under the table. I couldn't really be arsed getting to know him. Who knew if you'd even stay together? I don't think I ever got to know him really. The only time he bothered with me, in all the time he was around, was to give me grief.

The hardest thing about it all was Dad. I knew I had to let him know you had a *boyfriend,* and I know he gave you some right shit over it afterwards – shouting down the phone at you and everything. Betty even saw him parked at the end of the road, spying on you. God knows why – he was with Katherine by then. He used to grill me about you both all the time. *Has he stayed over yet? What does he drive? How often is she seeing him?* And on and on and on. *Awkward.*

Looking towards the door, I imagine you walking into the hotel function room, wearing your big wedding dress. You always used to moan about weight, wrinkles, bad hair days, spots, you name it, but to me, you were lovely, and I'm not just saying that because you were my mum. I just didn't appreciate you enough when you were alive.

"If she'd stayed with me, it would never have happened. She would still be here." Iain and I turn around. Dad's back, looking like he's had a few and he's glaring at Iain.

"Be civil or leave Phil."

"Just saying," Dad goes on. "She should never have been balancing on that banister like she was. Whatever happened to make her fall wouldn't have done if she'd have stayed with me."

"What do you mean, *make her fall?* She had a bloody accident." Iain is squaring up to him now, not for the first time. You'd be well stressed if you were here.

Auntie Liz saves the day, shepherding Dad towards the exit. I stay with Iain. I can't put my finger on the expression Dad is wearing when he looks back at us before disappearing outside, but I hope I never see it again. It's a mixture of sadness, regret and fury.

They say a funeral brings closure. Supposedly allowing a new beginning when the goodbyes have been said. Everyone can remember the person, cry about them and recall funny stories. If only you were here to listen to them Mum. I'd forgotten about the time you left me at the *wrong* birthday party. Someone else is talking about how you couldn't sing and always made a fool of yourself on the karaoke. I then hear a couple of your schoolfriends recounting an episode from your teens with some boy or other. Each tale is followed by silence. People, your friends and family, lost in their thoughts. Again and again, repeats of *what a waste* and *she should still be with us.* I don't join in. I just listen. I want to be on my own really, but it is cool to hear how loved you are, how popular and how everyone trusted and respected you. It really is an utter waste.

Chapter Three

I'm sitting in the garden at your bistro table. I'm relieved the funeral is over and done with. My head feels fuzzy, partly due to all the Bud I drank yesterday and because I'm not sleeping. You know how much I usually love my shut eye. *Sleep through an earthquake, that one*, you'd tell anyone who'd listen. It's only half nine but it's warm already. You've always said Spring was your favourite time of year. A time of new beginnings. Your funeral hasn't brought closure – and it certainly can't bring a new beginning. You've gone and I'm feeling like my right arm has been cut off. I can't focus, can't relax and I don't know what to do next. I feel sick all the time. I need to get out of here.

Without locking the back door, I head off. I don't know where I'm going but I don't want to go back into the house. I pass people on the path by the stream. I notice how they smile and even laugh. What's there to laugh about? I feel like I will never laugh again. Some say *good morning* to me. *Good!* I want to shout at them, *my mother is bloody dead.*

I haven't been to the park in ages, but this is where I find myself. I sink onto a bench, hoping to assemble my jumbled thoughts and find some light in my misery. There's a woman pushing herself back and forth on a swing. A boy, most likely her son, sits on the swing beside her. Looking somewhat embarrassed. He's about ten. That's probably around the age you stopped taking me to the park. By the time I was a teenager, you'd even started letting me go into town. I can remember my thirteenth birthday like it was yesterday. You and Dad were splitting up. You said that I was all that mattered. That it was me and you against the world and you would always be my best friend. I already had a best friend and remember thinking I didn't need another. I told you that I just wanted you to be my mum and you laughed.

Same with my dad. He tries to be my mate too – that's when I see him. Although I've seen more of him in the time since you've died than I have in the last year. Katherine has even been up to the house – I can't imagine you'd be right happy about that Mum. I can't believe she's supposedly still jealous. He sure ruffled Iain's feathers yesterday when he returned to the wake. I'm not sure what he was getting at. *If she'd stayed with me, it would never have happened.* Maybe because Dad used to do the decorating – I don't know. You've always said that he turns like a riptide when he's got a drink inside him.

I decide to walk a bit and find myself on the footpath by the river. Whenever I'm out of the house, I don't want to go back. You're everywhere. Maybe I should sort your stuff out, but I wouldn't know where to start. And that would be really, you know, like admitting you're never coming back. It's strange, not having you around to speak to. *How's your day been?* You'd always ask me. *Have you eaten? Have you this? Have you that?* You'd do my head in mostly but now I'd give anything for you to ring, moaning that my dinner's in the microwave and I should have let you know where I am. No one cares now. Not even Dad. Not like you did. He knows I'm old enough to sort my own dinner and my own life.

You didn't used to want me to leave home, well, not until recently anyway. Iain had been the first one to make it clear I'd be in the way. He was pretty up front about it. Like *are you not wanting to get your own place lad?* I might still not stay in the house – I haven't decided yet. So yeah, there you have it Mum. I'm a bit lost. I don't know where I'm going or what I'm doing. I just wish I could talk to you.

CHAPTER THREE

I trudge home via the supermarket. I haven't got much money left out of my wage – I'm not sure what I'll do when it's gone. I reckon I'll have to ask Dad or Iain to help. I've been signed off with *depression*, so who knows? They might carry on paying me my full wage.

I haven't been in a supermarket for years either. Life might be shit but I've still got to eat. I drag one of those stupid baskets on wheels behind me. I imagine your disapproval as I chuck in the necessities; pizza, crisps, biscuits, Nutella, Coke, sausages. I'm sure people are staring at me as I walk around. *That's the lad who's lost his mother,* they'll be whispering. *Wonder how he's coping.* You always said that everyone knows everyone else's knicker size in this community. No one speaks to me now. It's as though a death in the family is something they can catch.

I'm pleased when I get to the checkout and find Meghan there, who I've fancied for ages. She smiles at me as I unload my basket. "I'm sorry to hear about your mum." She pauses her scanning and looks at me. "She was really nice. How are you doing?"

"I'm not sure really." And I'm not. I feel disorientated. I can hear your voice Mum. *Ask her out! Ask her out!*

"If ever you need someone to talk to." Meghan holds out the 'contactless' card reader. "Give me a shout."

"That'd be great – thanks. Maybe we could go for a drink sometime?" She's not going to turn down a 'date' invitation from someone whose mum has just died.

"Sounds like a plan." She scribbles her number on the back of my receipt.

I feel like I can hear you mum. *That's my boy.* Or maybe I'm going mad. Maybe you're up there, in heaven, or wherever you believe people go, pulling some strings. But as I leave the supermarket, I feel ten times better than when I arrived, so that's something.

I still can't face going home so decide to stop at the local for a coke, killing some time by mooching about on my phone. Facebook has gone mental. I can't believe how many posts are on your wall. I 'like' a few of them but can't be arsed going through them all. Most of them say the same thing anyway. *Thinking of Iain and Jamie. So sorry for your loss. In shock. We all miss you Anna.* Lots of people have posted photos of you. Carefree pictures of you dressed up, out with friends. You sometimes asked me if you looked OK before you went out. I'd shrug and say '*s'pose so*.' Now, as tears blur my eyes again, I realise I should have told you how great you looked Mum.

I scroll back to pictures of you when you first met Dad. You looked right happy together, I can't believe how things changed between you. In the end, you couldn't stand being in the same room. I remember one evening when he was having a go at you for eating something that was *his* from the fridge and you shouted back at him that he was sat on *your* sofa. Me, I was stuck in the middle. I'm not going to dwell on that though – I can't handle it.

Fury creeps up my spine as I realise Claudia's been crawling all over your Facebook page, 'liking' posts and broadcasting about how she's looking after her dad. Whilst I know she cares about Iain, it's the way she felt about you that I can't let go of. I click through to Iain's page. Then *hers*. Same. She's right in there, lapping up the attention. She didn't even try with you, Mum. You might not have picked up on her frequent snide remarks when we were all together. But I did. Always going on about not getting *enough* of whatever, or not taken to the *right* places on holiday. She'd try to stop you and Iain sitting together and she'd talk constantly about times before her parents broke up. She'd look at you to check you were listening and you let her talk. I guess you had to.

I remember that long car journey when we were on our way back from Edinburgh. You and Iain were in the front – Me and Claudia were in the back, but she spent nearly the entire time sat on the edge of the seat, so her head was between your two front seats, talking, talking, talking. It was a conversation that you and I couldn't have joined in with – it was all about their past. *Dad, do you remember when we went on holiday with Grandma and Grandad and Mum was scared of the swans? Or what about the time I wouldn't go to sleep when we lived at the cottage and you threatened me with that school trip. I remember Auntie Vanessa's wedding when you tripped up when you were dancing with Mum.* I wondered if she'd ever come up for air.

I looked at Iain. He was laughing along with her, probably not noticing you with your head turned squarely to the window, possibly trying to drown out her voice in your right ear. She's got one of those voices. It's kind of moany, like she's hankering after something, but it's also loud and she talks over people. She didn't leave a stone unturned throughout that journey. *How long had you and Mum been together when you proposed?* She asked Iain. Then, *what stones were in her engagement ring – where is it now?* And on and on and on. You and I looked at each other in the passenger mirror. You must have felt like telling her to shut up, especially when she started going on about her parent's engagement.

Iain reached across the gearstick for your hand, which may have made Claudia change tack and call time on the nicey-nicey. *I remember when you came home one Christmas, Dad. You were drunk and you threw up all over the floor. Or, what about the time you lost your temper and chucked that fork to the floor.* She turned to me. *It bounced up and hit me on the head. Look, have you seen my scar? I had to lie to people about how it had happened.*

"You know I felt bad about that," Iain replied.

Grow a pair, you spineless pillock! She could say what she wanted to him and he just soaked it all up, like a flannel.

"I bet you didn't know about that, did you Anna? My dad's rotten temper when I was little."

"We all grow up," Iain started to say, "And – "

"Take the next exit," you'd said suddenly. "Me and Jamie are going home."

"I thought you were staying at my house?" But thankfully, he pulled into the inside lane. In another twenty minutes, we'd be free of Claudia.

"*Our* house." Claudia was smiling.

"I've just remembered that I've got stuff to do." Three-and-a-half hours of Claudia's constant drivel had obviously finished you off.

Claudia leaned further forwards. "Don't worry Dad. We'll have a right nice night. We'll get a takeaway and watch a film."

The illumination of my phone screen averts my attention.

@artistanna123 *is following you.*

Eh? That's your Twitter handle again Mum. I rub my eyes. Maybe the tiredness has caught up with me. Maybe it's an old notification. I click on it. No, it's just been made. *Weird.* There must be a glitch in the system. You probably 'followed' me ages ago and for some reason the notification's only just come through. It's not as if I'm on Twitter much. I feel a little unnerved by it though.

I slip my phone into my pocket. I drain the last of my coke and contemplate getting something to eat but it's dead in this pub. I suppose I'll have to go home. I can't put it off forever. We used to walk together Mum, when I was younger, I mean, enjoying being nosy, glancing into people's windows from the outside. You said *if you're not nosy, you don't get to know nowt.* I don't see the rooms anymore. I only see families.

I feel so alone as I walk up our path, bracing myself for the empty house. Normally it would smell of clean laundry, candles and dinner being prepared. As I push the door open, there's the slightest whiff of our former life, the plug-in air freshener and hint of your perfume. Then as I walk into the lounge, I gag at the stench of lilies. They were OK when they first arrived after the funeral date was announced, but

CHAPTER THREE

now that they've opened, they stink. I wrench them all from their vases, march back out the front door and dump them into the garden recycle bin.

Then I storm back in and gather up the sympathy cards. At first, they were a comfort but now I can't stand looking at them anymore. I start doing the same with the framed photographs. They're all over the place. But suddenly, breathless, I stop and put them back. My chest feels tight Mum. I feel awful. I sink to my knees onto the rug you bought when you started decorating a couple of months ago and rest my head on the floor. Tears are leaking from my eyes again. I've never cried much but now, I can't stop.

I don't know how long I'm down here but think I might have fallen asleep. When I open my eyes, there's a hungry growl in my belly and the room is dark. Dragging myself into a seated position, I get a sense of panic and foreboding. My breath catches in my throat as I rise and snap the light on. I get a horrid sense of not being alone and even check outside the windows before closing all the curtains.

I walk into the kitchen to sort my pizza out, wishing for the millionth time you were still here. I glance around the kitchen where your essence fills every corner. Family photos, many of me, have spilled from the lounge, onto the kitchen unit where they sit amongst candles, silly pot bird things, vases you've painted yourself and framed pictures of quotes like *bless this house with love and laughter*. Yeah right. There's a picture you painted of me at five, blowing bubbles through a wand. All sweet and innocent. I wonder if I'll ever stop thinking about you.

As I sit, chewing my pizza, I pull my phone from my pocket in response to an unusual beeping. *Maybe it's Meghan!* It's a Twitter notification. I blink. *Nah, this can't be right.* What sicko has done this? I stare at my phone. The screen simply says:

Anna Hardaker has tweeted for the first time in a while. Find out what she has said.

Chapter Four

I wake, shivering in the night. After my bit of pizza and a hot chocolate, sleep found me easily. For a while, anyway. I reach over to the chest of drawers for my phone. *Did I imagine it?* I wait a couple of moments for Twitter to load up, then click through from the notification to your so-called tweet. It's still there, large as life.

@artistanna123 I can't believe how many people turned up yesterday. I felt so loved. It was as perfect as these things can be. The music, the flowers, the speeches, everything #cuckoo #beforemytime

What the fuck Mum? And yes, I'm swearing now. I'm seriously spooked. It's 3:25. I click the bedside lamp on. *How did that tweet get here?* I blink then look at it again, right beside the photo of you with your newly cut hair. It's the professional photo you had done, especially taken to put on all your promotional stuff, and social media.

Even though it's May, I need to pull an extra blanket from the drawer in my divan to stop me shaking. I need a pee, but I don't want to leave my bedroom in the dark. I might still see you, balancing on the banister, trying to reach where you couldn't. I wish – *Stop it!* I reach for my phone again, feeling slightly better with the light on. It's still there. Your tweet, I mean. I really haven't imagined it. Written at 10:47pm. Some twisted arsehole has even liked it. *All the best for the future,* it says underneath. *Glad your big day went well.* Whoever it is **@aspireadam2018** obviously thinks it was your wedding day. *How* *did it get here?* I click through to your profile. You're following ninety-eight people. You've got fifty-eight followers. You'd only just gone on Twitter. Wanted it to promote your gallery a bit, you said. I look down your list of followers. Most of them look like 'artsy' people. Apart from Iain, Claudia and Auntie Liz. What the hell, Stacey is following you too. *Iain's ex-wife.* I want to delete her, but I can't. I don't know the log in for your account, but I will find a way.

I lie in my comfy double bed, watching an hour tick by. When I was little, I would creep along the landing to your room.

What is it Jamie? You'd call out. *Don't you feel well?* God do I wish I could do that now.

I'm having bad dreams Mum, I'd reply, the sound of your voice making everything alright. Then you'd either let me climb in with you or, as I grew older, you'd tuck me back into my own bed. Whether it was a nightmare, a worry or illness, you were always there. And now, you're not.

I must have fallen asleep eventually as I'm woken by a sodding bird making a right racket. I get out of bed, close my window and lie back down, hoping for more sleep to find me. It doesn't. Eventually I go downstairs and make a coffee in your *Life begins at 40* mug. I guess I'm allowed to use it now – I wasn't allowed to touch it before. I take it into the hallway and decide to tackle the three-day accumulation of post. I drop onto the third stair, placing the mug at the side of me and drag the pile onto my lap. You always used to bollock me for wandering around in my boxers, but I can do what I like now. The first couple of letters are sympathy cards. The first one's addressed to *Jamie and family – what bloody family!* I've only really got Dad now, when he bothers to answer the phone to me. The card's from someone I've never heard of.

The second one's from some people I vaguely remember, Jenny and Craig – they've addressed it to Jamie and Iain, like we belong together or something. Now that you've gone, maybe I'll never see Iain again. We haven't spoken since the funeral. There's a Council Tax reminder, a gas statement and something to do with your car insurance. I glance out of the window at your soft-top cream Mini – your pride and joy. I can drive your car any time I want to now. It's not all that cool for a lad my age, in fact, I used to duck down when I was out with you. However it can shift – much faster than mine. The girls seem to like it too. Maybe I'll flog it and get another. I feel guilty immediately for thinking such a thought. But what else am I supposed to do with it?

There's a cheque for an art order followed by a TV licence bill. I don't know what to do with all of this. Obviously, I've never lived on my own before. I'm going to have to sort stuff out now, I guess. Let them know you've gone. I'm not sure how I'm going to manage the bills. Whether or not I can stay in this house if I wanted to. Then there's your business. I need help.

"Dad, can you come over? I don't know what to do." I'm surprised when he answers the phone on the second ring.

"With what?" His voice has an impatient edge. The weight inside me sags further. He never sounds glad to hear from me. I'm always such an inconvenience.

"Stuff. You know. Bills and that."

"I can't give you anything son. You know I'm skint."

"I'm not asking for money." You always moaned about this Mum. You couldn't even get maintenance out of him when I was still at school. "I need to sort Mum's stuff out and I don't know where to start."

He goes quiet for a moment then in a different tone, replies. "There's definitely stuff for you to sort. The will, for one thing." He sounds brighter. "I'll be with you shortly son. I'll just get a shower."

I get dressed and force a bit of toast down whilst I'm waiting. My appetite is shot. You'd be well on my case Mum. I've needed to put a belt on my jeans. As I drink my tea, I try to chase away thoughts of that tweet. I decide I'm not going to mention it to Dad. There's obviously some mistake and it will go away soon enough. Tweets don't last very long before they're swallowed up amongst the others.

Katherine's with him when he gets here. I'm taken aback to see her standing there when I answer the door, it's only since you've died that it's ever happened. However, I obviously invite them in. It's only after I've made them a brew and I'm thinking about it and to use one of your sayings Mum, you'd be *spinning in your grave* if you could see them both sipping coffee in your kitchen. If Katherine ever had any opportunity to have a dig about *you*, she would always take it. It did my head in sometimes. If Dad ever had to talk to you, she went quiet and maybe insecure. She seems happy today though, perched on your bar stool, drinking your coffee. She doesn't need to be insecure anymore. You've gone.

The first time I met Katherine was in a pub. *Surprise, surprise.* I don't think Dad meant for us to meet but she'd come looking for him. Apparently, he'd promised to be home two hours earlier. Obviously, he'd not changed!

"Listen love," he'd said, in that awful tone of voice when he's irritated with someone. "We're not married yet you know. I had enough of all that shit when I was with this one's mother." He gestured towards me.

Her face hardened. "So this is your *son*, is it?"

"Yep. Katherine, Jamie. Jamie, Katherine."

I nodded at her.

She looked at me with cold eyes. "I've heard lots about you." She stood up stiffly and walked over to the bar.

"What's that supposed to mean?" I stared at the back of her.

"Take no notice," Dad swallowed the last of his pint. "Mine's a pint," he called across the bar. "She's seen her arse this week. Must be PMT or the menopause or summat."

"You must look like your mother." Katherine plonked a pint in front of Dad. I'd finished my drink too, but she hadn't bothered to offer me one. "You don't look anything like your dad."

I wasn't sure how to reply to that, so I stood up instead. "I'm off to get myself a drink."

I sneaked a look towards them whilst I was waiting at the bar. They looked like they were having words. He was pointing at her as he spoke, and her face was screwed up with anger as she replied to him. Even from here, I could see all the veins popping out in her neck. They shut up real quick when I returned to the table. Katherine took her phone from her bag and busied herself with that, whilst she drank her wine. I thought she was a miserable cow and wanted her to 'do one.' I didn't even feel I could talk to Dad with her around. I didn't like her at that first meeting and I've never liked her since.

As time went on, I realised she didn't want me to be on my own with Dad. I've never been sure why. She always had to be there. Maybe she felt scared of what he'd say, or what I'd say, or maybe she was just that jealous, she couldn't stand the thought of him wanting to spend time with anyone but *her*.

Chapter Five

I pull out the file where you kept all your important stuff and hand it to Dad. After a few moments, he lets out a long whistle. "You've nowt to worry about son. Did you know she had life insurance?"

Katherine looks over his shoulder. "How much?"

"Blow me. Two hundred grand."

"What does that mean?" I'm interested now!

"It means you're quids in son. She's left you a hundred and twenty grand of it and that pillock, Iain, eighty. He's got his own money, what's she leaving *him* money for?"

I tug the document from him. It says here that Iain's to book a cruise. *The one they'd talked about.* There's a message next to my name too. I'm to keep working and not just rely on your money. Build a career of my own. Something inside me feels warm. I like how you're *still* caring about me, even though you're not here.

"Wait a minute." Dad's reading something else now. "The mortgage. Bloody hell. It's going to get paid off. The house is yours." His face darkens. "Although strictly speaking, it should be mine. I paid a share in here too. I think we should have a chat about that son."

Katherine's looking around, possibly thinking the same thing. I remember when Dad lived here. He was always drunk. He would roll in when he felt like it and spend most of the time shouting at you. I hated him for a time and was often scared of him. We get on fairly well now, considering.

"And there's more." He's looking excited. "There's a note here about a will. It's kept at a solicitors - Rowlings, Finn and Mason. You'd better get in touch with them and find out what's in it. There's her business and all that to sort too. You're going to come out of this pretty well Jamie."

"I'd much rather have my mother here."

"You should get some of this Phil." Katherine pouts as she reassembles herself on the bar stool. "You were here long enough."

"Ah, I'm sure Jamie will see me right, won't you son." He ruffles my hair then steps back and puts his arm around Katherine. "Right. You need to ring the solicitor, the life insurance and the mortgage company for starters. See what figure you're looking at."

"Whoa." My head is spinning. "I think I'd better ring Iain. Tell him about the life insurance."

"No chance." Dad's face clouds over. "They'd not got married yet – thank God. He'll have to fight you if he wants more than what he's got."

"Depends what she's put in her will," Katherine says. "It might be that you've got to contest it, Phil. Make sure *you* get what you should be entitled to.

"Well there's only one way to find out what she's put in it." Dad thrusts his phone at me. "And yes love, I'll get some advice on the will."

"There's no need Dad. Really." I'm sorry Mum. It's only the day before yesterday when we laid you to rest and now, we're trying to work out what you were worth. I feel weird as I dial the number that Dad is reading out to me.

A few minutes later, I pass the phone back to him. "They were really nice. They're apparently in the process of getting things together to send out to everyone involved in Mum's will."

"How do they know she's died?"

CHAPTER FIVE

"Iain's apparently already sent them the death certificate. I just need to wait to hear."

"Bloody Iain." Dad's voice drips with sarcasm. Then it softens as he says, "keep us posted son. Right. Life insurance next." He passes his phone back to me. "Let's get this ball rolling too."

After press *one* for this, *three* for that and listening to the awful music for an eternity, I finally get through to a human being. However, it is better than listening to Dad and Katherine hissing at each other about *money* and *entitlement*.

"They're going to send me a claim form," I say, fifteen minutes later.

Dad's still rifling through your paperwork. "So there's the house to sort, the business, her van." His voice is strange. He's doing that *talking through his nose* thing that he does when he's fired up about something.

"Dad can we leave it for now? I know it all needs sorting out, but I'll do it gradually. It's all feeling like too much." I dump my cup in the sink. "Let me see what the will says, fill in the life insurance form and then we can take it from there."

"Well you don't have to do it on your own. Katherine and I are always here for you mate. Your mum's gone but you've still got us, you know that, don't you?" He touches Katherine's shoulder as he speaks. The sun belts into our yellow kitchen, shining on what looks like happiness in his face. I should maybe feel a bit happier too. I've chased him around for years, trying to spend time with him. Make him proud of me. Get him to notice me. And now, he's here. He wants to help me. *Every cloud* and all that.

"I must use the facilities." He puts his cup in the sink too and strides from the kitchen. It feels odd. Dad, in our house again. He stopped coming here completely after you met Iain. Before that, he'd turn up at least once a month, either to call you names or to beg you to take him back. Even after he'd met Katherine.

"So, it sounds like the world's about to be your lobster," Katherine smiles. I'm not sure whether it's a statement or a question. "What are you going to do with all that money?"

"I don't know yet. I need to get my head around everything first, it feels really weird."

"Maybe we could all have a nice family holiday. That might do us good."

I look at her. She actually means it. I feel guilty Mum. *You* were my family. I hope she's not going to try and take your place.

"So how are you feeling, you know, generally?" She obviously senses my reluctance to talk about holidays. She's OK, I suppose, *sometimes*, in very small doses, but I don't want to bare my soul to her. She's got her own sons anyway. She can leave me alone. I'm too old to be mollycoddled.

"I'll be fine," I say. "I just wish people would stop saying things like, *time heals* and all that crap. Or *she's watching over you* or *she's gone to a better place.*"

"It'll get easier," Katherine says gently, surprising me. "I promise. And your dad won't let you go through it on your own."

I hope she means it, and that she'll let him. If I'm honest, I could do with Dad around at the moment.

The upstairs floor at the front of the house creaks. Your bedroom. Without saying anything to Katherine, I walk away from her and ascend the stairs.

"What are you doing Dad?"

He's sat on your bed, rummaging through your jewellery box.

"Just looking for something." He glances around the walls. "Blimey she's changed it in here, hasn't she? Purple. Yuck."

"What are you looking for?"

"Something that's rightly mine."

"What?"

"Her rings. *I* bought them."

CHAPTER FIVE

"What rings? Dad. I don't think-"

"Ah-ha!" He pulls out what he's looking for. There, in a tiny polythene bag are what looks like three rings, an array of yellow gold and diamonds. I vaguely remember you wearing them. "There's a few quid here, I reckon." Dad holds the bag aloft before dropping it into the pocket of his shirt and patting it. "I bet there's more stuff I bought her, in here. He continues his rummaging as Katherine appears in the doorway.

"What are you doing?"

"That's what I was asking him," I say, as Katherine strides towards your open wardrobe door.

"What are you going to do with this lot?" She's leafing through your clothes like she's in Primark. "Gosh, she had a lot of clothes, didn't she?"

Mum. If you could see them now. Dad, sifting through your jewellery box and Katherine through your wardrobe – you'd have an absolute fit. *I don't know what to do.*

"You'll have to bag it all up and take it to a charity shop," says Dad.

I can hardly bear the thought of that. I stride towards Katherine and slam the wardrobe door. "I'll get around to sorting her things. Iain might want to go through them too."

Dad scowls at the sound of his name. But at least he closes your jewellery box. I'm shaking Mum. I don't know why. I feel like a wuss for not standing up for you more. Well, it's just that it's Dad and you know how it is.

Katherine's running her hands down a trouser suit that's hanging from the outside of one of the mirrored doors. I think I can remember you wearing it the day before you died. "If only I was a size smaller," she says. Dad stays quiet.

"Come on. Let's go downstairs," I suggest. It doesn't feel right being in your bedroom. They glance at each other and Dad gets to his feet.

However, instead of heading back to the stairs, he's turned right into the spare bedroom, which was your studio. I haven't been in there since you died. I haven't been able to face it.

There isn't space in here for the three of us amidst easels, packages and half-finished canvasses. The whiff of acrylic paint sends that all-too-familiar heat stabbing at the back of my eyes. A tear escapes as my gaze falls onto another picture that you painted of me. I'm eight and I'm standing with my back to you, throwing pebbles into the sea. It's a great painting. Maybe you were right when you said once that the work of artistic people often isn't appreciated until after they're dead.

As if he can read my thoughts, Dad pipes up. "What are you going to do with this lot? It might be worth a few quid." *God, is that all he thinks about?*

"I don't know yet." I might have a go at it myself. Painting, I mean. You'd like that Mum. Me, following in your footsteps. Might make up for things – for all the times I was a dick.

"What about her gallery?" Dad glances out of the window, the light making his blonde hair look even blonder. He almost looks like he has a halo. "Oh bloody hell, what does *she* want?" I follow his gaze to see Betty making her way across the road. You'd be breathing a sigh of relief Mum. "Don't answer it," Dad hisses as the doorbell goes.

"I'll have to. She'll have seen you at the window." Without giving him the chance to stop me, I take the stairs, two at a time, to the front door.

"Just checking you're OK," Betty whispers. "I saw at the upstairs window that you've got *company*."

"I'm OK, I guess."

She's always looked out for you Mum. She was the first one over here when I ran out into the street that day, shouting for help. She's nearly eighty and it must have given her a terrible shock, to see you lying there like that. But she got me a brandy and didn't flinch as the

CHAPTER FIVE

paramedics did what they had to do. And then the undertakers, who carried you in a body bag towards a black estate car. It's a sight that will never leave me. *My mum's in there*, I kept thinking. How can a person, so full of life, now be so *dead*? I'd been totally numb, barely able to speak, just going through the motions and trying to answer their questions. Betty had taken charge until Iain got here.

She steps forwards now and puts her hand on my shoulder. A tear escapes again. We're standing in the spot where you finished up Mum. Betty and I look up to see Dad and Katherine silhouetted in the space at the top of the stairs.

"Can I ask," Betty's tone changes as she clears her throat, "what you were doing in Anna's room?" There's a severity in her usual twinkly Welsh lilt. "I do not think she would wish for you to be in there."

"Well she's not here, is she?" Dad's voice is equally stony as he descends the stairs.

"No, but I am." Betty's always disliked Dad. I know she saw things, heard things. We've never talked about it though.

"It's none of your business love. It never was." Dad's at the bottom of the stairs now, his six-foot towering over Betty's four-and-a-half. She doesn't waiver. She might be tiny but I wouldn't want to be on the wrong side of her.

"He's supporting his son." Katherine steps out now from behind Dad.

"That may well be," Betty looks at Katherine, coldly, "but I know for a fact that Anna would not want *either* of you going through the personal things in her bedroom or her study."

"Haven't you got anything better to do than curtain twitch?" Dad takes another step towards her. If they were the same height, their faces would nearly be touching.

Betty still doesn't flinch. A few uncomfortable

moments pass. "You're quite the man, aren't you Phil? I might be a little old lady, but you don't intimidate me." More agonising silence.

"We'd better go Phil." Katherine's voice cuts through the tension at last.

I watch Dad step away from Betty, his angular features hard and set. I've seen that expression lots of times Mum, often when he had hold of you. I don't think he would have ever hurt you, but he liked to give the impression that he would.

"Ring me if you need anything son." He backs towards the door but doesn't leave before taking a parting shot at Betty. "You need to keep your nasty nose out."

Chapter Six

"Come on then Martha Mini." My voice sounds strange in the silence of the car. I haven't spoken to anyone since the confrontation yesterday with Dad and Betty and I'm keen for human contact and normality. "You're taking me back to work today. You might be a Mini but you're a lot better than my battered heap of a Renault Clio which has rust holding it together." I narrowly miss hitting the wheelie bin as I reverse from the drive whilst waving at Betty. You'd be fizzing Mum, if you were looking out of the window.

This car suited you but it's too 'girly' for me. I do feel a bit as though I'm doing something wrong, driving it, but if it's not driven, it will seize up or something. I really think I'll flog it, though I'm not ready to yet. You lent me it a few times after I first passed my test when you didn't need it. "Look after her," you would say. "You know how much I love Martha Mini." I used to find it strange that you would always give your cars alliterative car names. There was Percy Peugeot, Fiona Fiesta and Bertie Beetle. *Mad.*

I can't mope around the house anymore; I must get my brain into something else. It's nearly five weeks since you died. It took them bloody ages to sort the death certificate. Because it was *unexpected,* there was a post-mortem *and* an investigation *and* a coroner's hearing. It was a relief when they finally acknowledged you'd fallen; it was an accident and we could lay you to rest at last.

It's good to get out of my joggers and to get trousers and a shirt back on. I've got my running gear in the seat beside me for when I've finished. I haven't been for a run since you died – I haven't had the energy.

I enjoy the drive to work and resist the urge to put the top down in the early June sunshine. It's hardly appropriate for me to arrive at work on my first day back with the top down and my tunes blaring. I fire up the radio instead. It's where you left it the last time you drove. Heart FM. One of your favourite songs is on. Whitney Houston, I think. You once said this song's about being pregnant. You used to talk to me about some right stuff Mum! *The greatest love of all is happening inside of me ...* I can't listen to it. I thump the CD function. Not much better. Bloody Adele. *Hello. It's me.* It gives me the heebie-jeebies. I drive the remainder of the journey in silence.

The car park at work is nearly full when I arrive. It's well after nine – I never have been able to get here on time. I reverse into one of the last empty spaces then sit for a few moments staring at the imposing insurance building. As I try to steady my breathing, it dawns on me that no one would bat an eyelid if I had another month off. Maybe I'm betraying you by going back to work so soon. This time, six weeks ago, you were still alive. I glance around the interior of your car. There's a hair bobble twisted around the gearstick and in the passenger footwell, your high heels are poised for a getaway they'll never make. There's a whiff of your perfume in here too. I was going to get you it for Christmas, but Iain beat me to it. *Daisy Dream.* It was bloody expensive anyway. I got you a charm for your Pandora bracelet instead. It was a paintbrush. You were well pleased. I'm not sure where your Pandora bracelet is. I haven't seen it since you died.

You loved Christmas and always made it brilliant. The house would smell of the tree, candles and that hot mulled wine you liked. Christmas definitely got better after Dad left. He was then no longer able to spoil it after getting drunk. He's my dad and I love him but how he was – shit! A tear plops onto the steering wheel. *Pull yourself together man!*

My thoughts turn back to last Christmas – your final Christmas. We'd spent it at Iain's brother's house with his family. They're all pretty sound. It was quite a good laugh. Then Claudia turned up.

"This is Nathan," she'd announced, as she walked in with some chiselled and tanned bloke on her arm. I clocked his Hugo Boss coat and designer jeans and wished I'd made more of an effort. One by one, she introduced him to everyone. "Nathan, this is my Grandma. Uncle David, meet Nathan. Auntie Vanessa, this is who I've been telling you about." I saw the anticipation on your face, ready to say hello to him. But she passed over you and introduced him to her other uncle. Then she ignored me too and started towards the living room with Nathan in pursuit. I saw the hurt in your face but without speaking, you followed them into the living room. So did I.

I watched on as Claudia made her introductions in there, then began holding court with stories of how she and Nathan met, and where they were planning a holiday. Quietly, you sidled up to Nathan and held out your hand. "I'm Anna. I'm engaged to Claudia's dad. That's my son, Jamie." She pointed towards me.

"Oh yes, he replied. "Good to put faces to names. I've heard lots about you both."

"What's that supposed to mean?" I strode to your side, ready to defend.

You hissed "leave it" into my ear and headed back to the kitchen.

There was an atmosphere all evening. Whenever Claudia could have a dig about either of us in conversation, she took it. "Yeah. It's good to have Nathan around," I heard her telling her cousin. "At least someone gives a shit. My dad's more interested in other people's kids than me."

I looked at Iain when she said that. *Tell her to shut her face*, I thought but he just laughed and said something about me always being in my room when he came around.

She continued her 'pity party' with her cousin for a while, wallowing in misery about how she'd been shunted as a teenager between her parent's two homes and how Iain had neglected her since meeting you. *You should try having my dad!* I had thought to myself.

The next morning, Claudia was yelling *it's Christmas* all around the house before it was even nine o' clock. Then the silly cow tried tugging my duvet off me from where I was laid on the sofa. I had no clothes on, apart from my boxers, and I felt like decking her.

"Get off. Leave me alone."

"Move off our sofa then. I want to sit down."

"Piss off."

"Dad! Have you heard what he said to me?"

"Pack it in, both of you, you're acting like a couple of children, not adults in their twenties!"

You handed me a coffee and the usual Christmas card with a hundred quid in. "Cheers Mum, I'll go to the sales with that." I wished there was another room I could sit in – not really wishing to watch as Claudia began tackling the enormous mound of presents beside the tree. She stopped and watched as you opened your two gifts.

"Who bought you that?" She stared at the large bottle of Daisy Dream perfume.

"I did," said Iain. "Why?"

"You haven't bought *me* any perfume. In fact, you *never* have."

"I'm off to check on the bacon." Iain got to his feet and walked towards the kitchen.

"Grow up Claudia," I said.

"Breakfast's ready," Iain called.

Claudia, as always, was the first to dig in, piling her plate up with bacon, sausage, beans and egg. For someone so slim, she could really eat. I hoped there'd be enough left for everyone else. Then she stood, blocking the space, so no one else could get near whilst she put some bacon into a slice of bread.

"Move out of the way Claudia," Iain finally said. "Other people might want breakfast too."

"Yeah. But I *live* here."

"Half live here," you scowled at her. "Just think. We could all be at our house next Christmas. We'll be married this time next year."

She flounced past you.

You wanted to get off to Auntie Liz's house where we'd been invited for dinner so you could help a bit. Claudia said we *weren't allowed* to leave until midday, when Stacey was due to collect her on her way back from somewhere.

"You can't leave me alone on Christmas Day," she whined to Iain. You'd have told me where to go Mum, if I'd tried to call the shots like that. "I want collecting at five, OK? You won't be late, will you?"

I wonder what Christmas Day this year will hold. It's going to be bloody awful without you but at least I won't have to be anyway near Claudia.

Gingerly, I head towards the revolving door of Ingleton's Insurance. Boring insurance for boring people. The buzz of the open plan office stills as I walk in.

"Ey-up Jamie," Sam from Accounts calls out as I make my way towards my desk. The room is thick with sympathy I don't want and my face burns as I dump my rucksack next to my chair. I've barely sat down when Nicole, my manager, appears. "How are you doing Jamie?"

"Alright, I guess." I look around. *Everyone* is looking. I wish they'd all bugger off.

Maybe she senses my fury. "Get yourself settled," she says, "then pop along to my office in ten minutes." She tucks her hair behind her ears.

"I'll have a coffee waiting. How do you have it?"

"White. Two Sugars. Thanks."

As I wait for my computer to fire up, Jack emerges from nowhere, slapping my back as he passes me. "I'm sorry about your mum mate."

"Thanks." My voice is flat.

Claire from Contracts leans over her side of the desk partition. "We've all been thinking about you Jamie. Are you sure you're ok? To be back, I mean. I thought you'd be off a while longer. You've got a sick note, haven't you?"

"I just need to get back to normal." I feel guilty saying this Mum. Without you here, I'm never going to be normal again. I haven't even brought anything for lunch. Normally, you'd make me a butty. My work colleagues used to laugh at me, call me a *mummy's boy*, especially when you cut them into triangles! When I was small, I remember you putting notes in with my sandwiches. You really loved me then, didn't you Mum, and when it really mattered, I –

"Jamie." Nicole is beside me again, her hand on my arm. "Come with me." I've tears flooding down my face and everyone is staring at me. *Shit. Shit. Shit.* I follow her into her office just off our open plan bit. "Sit down," she says, pulling up a chair next to me and passing me a tissue. It stinks of sodding lilies in here too. I can't get away from them. I'm transported back a few days to the day of your funeral. Nicole crosses one of her shapely legs over the other and leans towards me. "Jamie," she says again. I could right fancy her, but I know she's married. "I think it's too soon for you to be back at work."

"I'm fine." I dab furiously at my face with the tissue. I've got a lump in my throat the size of a marrow. I can't stop these bloody tears. *What an idiot!*

"You're not fine and no one would expect you to be." She strokes my arm, sending little electrical pulses cascading through my body. "What you're going through – it takes time. You're on full pay Jamie. You're covered by a sick note. Go home."

"I can't. I'm going crazy. I need to keep busy." My voice doesn't sound like my own. I'm making a right pillock of myself. There's snot and tears and drool all over my face. I look up and see the whole office watching. Nicole follows my gaze then closes the blinds.

"You're not ready yet. Have you thought about bereavement counselling?"

I shake my head. "I don't need a shrink."

"It's not a shrink. They'll just provide a space to help you talk through your loss. You've been through a lot, especially being the one who actually *found* your mum."

"I don't need a space. I'll be ok." I stare at her purple-painted toenails. They remind me of the colour of Easter egg foil wrapping.

"Well, if you change your mind, you must talk to your GP about counselling."

I'm beaten. She's right. I just want to get out of here. I should never have come. But I've got to do the walk of shame past everyone. "You could do me one favour," I sniff, raising my eyes from the floor.

"Anything," she replies.

"Would you mind bringing my rucksack from the side of my desk, so I can leave by the fire escape? I can't face walking past everyone."

"Of course."

I wait, still feeling foolish until she returns.

"Take all the time you need." She holds the door open. "We've got everything covered."

"Thanks. And I'm sorry."

"You've got absolutely nothing to be sorry about."

Ahh, but I have. *I failed you Mum.* I blink as I walk back across the car park. For a few seconds, I see you, sat in the driving seat. I think I'm hallucinating. It's the stress. Your dark hair gleams in the light and you turn, watching my approach. Of course, when I get there, the car is empty, but it's given me a start. I don't want to get in, but I've got to.

I drive to the nearest Mackie-D's and stride into the toilets. Emerging in my running gear, I dump my bag in the boot of the mini and I'm away. Suddenly, an energy has fired inside me. I don't know which direction I'm running in and I don't care. I haven't run since, well, before you died, so I'm a bit out of condition but it feels damn good to run again. The knot in my belly unravels and my arms swing at my sides. My breath is deep and rhythmic. My whole body is saturated by clean, fresh oxygen and I feel lighter than I have in weeks. The air rushes towards me as I pound the pavement in time to my breath. *God, how I've missed this!* I run and run, losing all my shit as I go. You can't be down when your body is filled with endorphins. At least that's what *you* always told me Mum. You loved running too. I imagine I see you on the opposite side of the road, running in the other direction, all pink and purple and with a bandana wrapped around your head. You always looked a sight when you were out running.

I thought you were an embarrassment but most of my mates thought you were cool. I remember Max saying "she doesn't look old enough to be you mum, pal, more like your sister. My mum, she's got grey hair." My other mate Callum added, saying his mum wouldn't dream of keeping fit in any way whatsoever. She preferred to flop in an armchair after work and watch Corrie.

The woman at the other side of the road keeps running. I wish, more than anything in the world, that it had been you. The likeness has stopped me in my tracks as I watch her retreating form. All energy seeps from me and my shitty feelings return. You always said that everyone has a double somewhere and I think I've just seen yours. I return to the car. I just want to crawl under my duvet and never come out.

Chapter Seven

Sleep seems to permit itself to me in the daytime more than at night. I pass out for over four hours. Cider is my first thought on waking, so after a sandwich, I head to the supermarket to pick some up.

On the way out back out of the store, I notice Meghan, weighed down with an armful of shopping bags. "Let me help."

"My mum and her bloody shopping lists," she groans. I've tried ringing her for a lift but she's not answering."

I swallow my envy at Meghan's mention of her mum. "Where do you live?" Having fancied her for ages, I know full well where she lives but I can hardly let her know that. She'll think I'm a weirdo. She flicks her dark hair over one shoulder as she bends over two of her shopping bags. I can see right down her top. I force my gaze upwards to look into her eyes instead. "I'll take you in the car if you want?"

"Just around the corner. Not far. If you could give me a lift, that would be awesome. I'll make you a brew if you like?"

Result! I gather the other three bags and lead her towards the car.

"This is a seriously cool car," Meghan gets into the passenger seat.

"It's my mum's. It's a bit girly for me. I'm probably going to get rid of it."

Meghan's eyes widen as she looks at me. "Yeah." She pauses for a moment. "I guess you'll get everything that belonged to your mum. In fact my mum's *always* saying she'd be worth more dead than alive."

I'm taken aback by Meghan's shit comment but I'll let it go. "I'd rather have *her* back though."

"I know." She cups her hand over where mine rests on the gearstick. Just for two or three seconds but long enough to send waves of pleasure shooting through me.

"So has she left you *everything?*"

I notice her looking at my wallet which I've shoved in the ashtray area.

"I'm not sure yet. I'm in the middle of sorting everything. It's a bit of a nightmare."

"I bet it is."

"It's here." She gestures to a small but modern looking house, covered with hanging baskets.

"That looks like a very girlie house too."

"My mum likes her flowers. I wouldn't be bothered. It's just me and her now."

"Where's your dad?"

A cloud crosses her face. "He died. Four years ago. So I know what you're going through."

We're part of a club no one ever wants to join. *The Dead Parents' Society.* "I'm really sorry to hear that. What did he die from?" I warm to her a bit more.

"Cancer. Here she is now." A VW Polo pulls up beside us and an older version of Meghan gets out. "Mum-Jamie. Jamie-Mum. Jamie helped me cart all that shopping back since you left me to it."

"Sorry love. I needed something new to wear. We've got that barbecue this evening for your Auntie's birthday. *Remember?*"

"Oh no! I'd forgotten all about it."

"Well we'd better get this lot in and get a move on. We've just over an hour to get ready. It starts at half six."

"But I'd invited Jamie round. He's just lost his mum."

From her use of past tense, I know it's off. I'm pissed off but try to hold the smile on my face.

"Sorry love," her mum says to me. "Some other time? Sorry to hear about your mum."

"Definitely," Meghan adds. "Cheers for giving me a hand."

"Anytime." As I walk away, I know things have moved on. I've evolved from being some lad she occasionally says hello to, even if she is only interested in my money. *She's* got things that *I'm* interested in so it's win-win. Jake next door would approve of my philosophy.

I manoeuvre your car back down our drive and prepare myself for the slap of silence that will hit me as soon as the door is pushed open. Normally the TV or music would be blaring out, you'd be singing in the shower or I'd hear echoes of your conversation with Iain from a corner of the house. Your noise used to piss me off sometimes. Now I'd do anything to hear it again. I open a cider and head upstairs.

I feel more human as I shower, however, I wish I could wash away some of this 'heaviness' within me. This *dragged down* feeling won't go away. I'm scrubbed, shaved, brushed and I've even had earbuds in my ears, but I still feel unclean. I gasp as I leave the bathroom.

There, on the banister, you're balancing, covered in paint, wearing cut-off jeans and one of Dad's old shirts. Your feet are bare and your face is expressionless. You look straight at me. I step back and slam the bathroom door, feeling my heart bang inside my chest for several moments. When I open the door again, there's nothing there. *A trick of the light*, you would say when I was a kid and thought I'd seen or heard something in the night. I always had a stupid imagination. However, it's unnerved me Mum. *You're everywhere.* I'm still toying with the idea of moving to a new house to escape it all, even though it will kill me to leave the memories of where I grew up.

I pull on joggers and a t-shirt in my room whilst gulping the rest of my cider. It calms me down a bit. I lie on my bed, wondering what the hell I'm going to do. Whilst staring at the movement of the tree outside my window, my phone makes me jump.

"It's me. How are you doing son?"

Dad hardly ever rings me. I've spent *years* chasing him down. It used to make you angry. And he's calling me *son* all the time now.

"I'm OK, apart from making an idiot of myself at work."

"*You went to work?* But you don't need to! Your mum's left you very well provided for. Speaking of which…"

"Yeah?"

"You know how I've been thinking about setting up a window cleaning business?"

"Erm no. Have you?"

"I'm sure I've mentioned it. Anyway. Obviously, I'm going to need a water tank, a van and some other bits. So I was wondering…"

I know what's coming.

"About ten grand should cover it. I'll pay you back. Although you might just want to *give* it to me. A *gift*, rather than a *loan*, I mean. I came out of the marriage to your mother with the clothes I was standing in. She got the house, the furniture, everything." He hardly pauses for breath. His speech is probably rehearsed.

"She had *me* to look after at the time."

"Yeah. I know. But Jamie, it's not much to ask. Especially with the amount you're going to be getting your hands on. If your mother can build up a business like she did then I'm sure I can too. I just want to make something of my life. Make you proud of me son."

That's it. The clincher. I *do* want to be proud of him. I was proud of you Mum – you worked really hard. I guess if one positive thing has come out of your death, it's brought Dad and me back together. I hope you don't mind Mum but I'm going to say yes. You loved him once and I'm sure, deep down, you'd want me to help him. It might be the thing that puts me and him firmly back on track as well.

"Ok. I haven't got it yet though. Not till the life insurance comes through."

I can't help feeling a bit annoyed by the time I get off the phone. I think about our conversation for a while afterwards. I'd mentioned my meltdown at work to him, but he didn't even ask me about it, he just went straight onto money. Maybe you were right Mum. Maybe it is all about *him*.

Chapter Eight

"What's going on Jamie?"

"Eh? What?" I stare groggily at the clock. Six o'clock. "Is it night?"

"It's morning. Where are you?" Iain sounds well pissed off.

I'm as stiff as a board from where I've been crunched up on the sofa all night and my head feels as though it's been whacked with a cricket bat. I shouldn't have drunk all those ciders. I must have passed out. I had quite a few. "I'm at home. Where else would I be?"

"Have you been on Twitter?"

"When?"

"Last night. Today. I don't know. Some crank is tweeting from your mum's account."

"I know. I saw it a couple of days ago."

"Why didn't you say anything?"

"I don't know. Freaked me out, I suppose." I walk into the kitchen and fill a glass with water, trying to ignore the mug saying *MUM* on the draining board.

"Well I've only just seen the one from a couple of days ago. There's two that have been posted now. Are you sure you don't know anything about it?"

"No I don't! *Another one!* What? When?"

"If this is anything to do with -"

CHAPTER EIGHT

I cut him off and fire up my Twitter app. It takes ages to load up. It's the third tweet in my *in case you missed it* news feed.

@artistanna123 *All is returning to normal. How can this be? All has been taken from me. It should never have happened. I want my life back.* #**cuckoo** #**beforemytime**

I stare at it. *What's going on Mum?* The image of you when I came out of the shower last night re-enters my head. I've never believed in ghosts and even when I had a wobble about them as a kid, you said, *it's not the dead who hurt you, it's the living.*

I ring Iain back. "I've seen it."

"And you don't know anything about it?"

Prat. I should have known he would immediately blame me. "Of course I don't. First time I've seen it."

"Do you know the password for her Twitter account?"

Obviously, he doesn't believe me. "No. You'd be more likely to know than me. You were engaged to her."

"Well someone's messing about and I don't like it. And I won't rest until I get to the bottom of it. I'm coming over."

"Why?"

"Like I said, I want to get to the bottom of this. And I want to sort through a few things. There's a load of my stuff still there and I can take some bags of your mum's stuff to the charity shop whilst I'm at it."

"I don't want you to." My hand coils into a fist at my side. *Who the hell does he think he is, that he can just come across and bin all your things?* "I'll sort it. She was *my* mother."

"And she was my fiancée. Like I said. I've some bits and pieces over there too. I'll be over in a couple of hours." He ends the call before I have chance to argue any further. I grab a few of the charity donation bags that you've shoved in the letter rack. I've got a couple of hours. I'll sort your stuff, not *him*. Dick.

Your jewellery box is still laid on the bed from where Dad left it the other day. The room is stuffy. I open a window then sink onto your bed, unsure where to start. It's so *you* in here. The smell of talc, the hair in your brush and you haven't put the lid back on your face cream. I don't want to touch anything but if I don't, Iain will. *Pillock.* Misery becomes anger again. I want to punch something but instead I wrench open the first drawer of your dresser. It's full of knickers. I'm having nothing to do with that. I *will* leave that for Iain. The next drawer is full of neatly folded jumpers. I pull out the first one. It's the purply striped one that you always wore. I bury my face in it, the anger in me cooling. *It smells of you.* I chuck it onto the bed and yank the rest of the jumpers out. Maybe Auntie Liz will want them. I bag them up anyway. The more I do; the less time bloody Iain will have to be here.

I move to your wardrobe next. It's crammed, like Katherine said, when she was rifling through it. You never had enough hangers and used to pinch them from me. Everything is brightly coloured and patterned. A bit like you were. You literally wore yourself as an artist. That's it. *I'm* going to paint as well, Mum. I'm going to carry your work on. I'll make you proud of me.

My phone beeps on the bed. Iain. *Change of plan. There in half an hour.* Bloody hell. I'd better get on with it. I snatch things off hangers and shove them into the bags. Then clear the bottom of the cupboards of belts, shoes and handbags. Within ten minutes the wardrobe is empty and the bags are stuffed. I'm out of breath. Then I notice a big case on top of the wardrobe beneath the holiday suitcase.

I tug it down. Big fat tears plop over its contents as I rifle through them. You've told me about this case, but I've never been interested in it before. I pull out a blue stripy babygro, what might have been my first pair of shoes, baby socks and a silver hairbrush. There's a bangle with Jamie Phillip engraved on the inside and a bible. *Like, what was I ever going to do with a bible!* There's a scrapbook full of small boy drawings. *Me and my Mum*, declares one. *This is my house,* says another.

CHAPTER EIGHT

There are photos of me when small in various locations; holidays, theme parks, feeding the ducks. You gave me a good childhood. As I continue sifting through school reports, certificates, scout badges and my primary school shirt, I realise again how much I must have meant to you when I was younger. You've kept so much stuff from my life. As I cram everything back into the case, I feel even crappier. It's a feeling I have come to know well. It's following me around like a shadow.

I fasten it and grab your purply striped jumper and hairbrush from the top of one of the bags before taking them, along with the suitcase, to my room. I place it all on top of my wardrobe. I'll look at it again some other time when my brain's in a better place. I head for the bathroom and chuck all your bits and pieces into another bag. Dressing gown, toothbrush, razors, shampoo promising to cover all greys. Doing all this is like admitting that you're never coming back.

Sitting on the edge of the bath, I glance at myself in the mirror. My eyes, the same colour as yours, look like piss-holes in the snow. I need to start getting some proper kip and I must put some weight back on. Meghan will never fancy me if I let things slide any more. It lifts me a bit, thinking of her. I must get in touch. I need something to look forward to.

I'm dragged back into the moment by the doorbell. Iain's trying his key in the door when I get to it, but I've put mine in the other side so he can't use his. *Tough shit mate.* It's my house now – at least I hope it will be. Which reminds me, I've got the will paperwork to sort out. Iain marches past me as soon as I open the door, followed by our favourite person, Claudia. She doesn't even look at me as she strides into the lounge like she owns the place.

"I didn't know *she* was coming." I stand with my arms folded, staring at her.

"Jamie, there's no need to be so rude."

Perhaps there isn't but I don't want her in our house Mum. I carry on. "So what's she doing here? There's no need for her to be here."

"I don't have to explain to you why I've got my daughter with me."

"Yeah Jamie. Shut your face. Why do you have to be so rotten all the time?"

"I just don't see why you're in my house. It's not as though you'd ever want to pay me a social call. We don't have to put up with each other anymore."

"You're such a prick." She's in front of me, sticking her tits out with her hands on her hips. She thinks she's *it*. She's not a patch on Meghan. Looks or otherwise.

"Why can't you go and wait in your car?" I'm glad I no longer have to be civil to her. I'm unsure how we ever managed it.

Her venomous blue eyes lock with mine. Neither of us move. It's like pistols at dawn.

Iain stands next to her. "Jamie, I'm not letting you treat my daughter in this way."

"*Your daughter.*" I hope my voice is oozing as much sarcasm as I feel. "Exactly. And you need to remember *I'm* not your son, nor will I even be your *stepson* now. So you've no right coming into my house and telling me what to do." I step back from them both. "You've no leverage with me now that Mum's gone. We don't have to have anything to do with each other again, so get your stuff and piss off." The words tumble out of me, the hatred they drip with surprises me. I barely pause for breath.

"Don't be like this mate. Your mum wouldn't want us to fall out."

"We only got along for her sake." *It's true.* You were forever forcing me to apologise to him Mum. I suppose I was a bit sharp with him at times.

"That's not the case." Iain steps forward and puts his hand on my shoulder. "I know you're grieving but let me look out for you - it's what your mum would want – that's the bottom line."

CHAPTER EIGHT

I shrug his hand off my shoulder. "Don't tell me what my mum would want. We were alright till you came along."

"Bloody pathetic." Claudia flounces past us. "I'll be in the garden. I'll leave you to your false bonding session."

"Claudia. For God's sake." Iain calls after her. "You two are so jealous of each other. I can't understand it."

"It's her, not me. It always has been. She ought to grow up. Spoilt cow. I'm not the jealous one."

"Enough anyway." Iain's raises his voice. "This has to stop. Aren't we all going through enough? I'm not just here to collect some stuff. I wanted to check on you as well."

"Well as you can see, I'm fine. I'm a big boy. Why don't you get your stuff and then give me your key?"

"You're such a nasty little sod Jamie? I'll do no such thing."

"If this house is left to me, then you'll have to."

"Well, we'll find out in a day or two, won't we?"

"I was her son. You're, well, you weren't even married. Don't be getting your hopes up *Iain*."

"I haven't come here to fall out with you. Do you want to give me a hand with the tools?"

"No I do not. I'm off for a crap." I'm pleased to get out of their way and sit on the bog. I'll probably wait until they have gone before I emerge from here. I sit, glad of the peace, until I become aware of Claudia's whining tones from the garden.

"Yeah, we're here now."

Pause.

"Y'know. Same as ever."

A car goes by the front of the house, drowning her next sentence.

"He's OK. I wish he'd stop sniffing around Jamie though."

Pause.

"Getting some of his stuff. Clothes, tools and that."

Pause.

"Yeah, I know. I thought that too. He's no excuse to come back if his stuff's not here."

Bitch. She's not happy unless she's talking about someone. She's always hated her dad having anything to do with me.

"We don't know yet. The solicitor's going to write to everyone apparently."

Bloody hell. She's talking about your will Mum. *Who is she talking to? What right has she got?*

"You'd have thought so. They were engaged, weren't they?"

Pause.

"I agree. It was close though. Another three months and she'd have been my stepmother.

Pause. Cackle.

"Yeah. Wicked."

Pause.

"Nah. Don't be daft. She never did try to be my mum. And no one could take *your* place."

She is talking to Stacey. She left Iain for someone else ten years ago but has apparently regretted it ever since. Once when Claudia and I were at loggerheads over something or other, which we often were, she told me about how her mother had been laughing about your engagement, with a few of her friends. She'd apparently said that you always looked like you could do with a good wash. You were often covered in paint but even so, what a bitch! I'd wanted to punch Claudia that day. Why she was telling me about her poisonous mother, I had no idea at the time but now I know that she just loved being at the centre of drama and shit.

Without meaning to, I remain sat on the loo, listening to the one-sided conversation being conducted in our garden. *Knowledge is power,* as you always said.

CHAPTER EIGHT

"No. I don't think he got it back. He should have done though. That was Grandma's ring and it'll be worth a few quid."

Pause.

"Yeah, I know. I'd probably have to get it adjusted though. She was a right skinny cow."

Cackle. Pause.

"He honestly seems OK. A bit quiet at times."

Pause.

"Well if anyone can help him get over it, it's you."

Pause.

"Ugh! Far too much information. I don't want to know about your sex life. Past, present or future." She laughs again. "And yeah, once he's had his letter and all that, I will get something organised with him. I'll think of somewhere we can all go."

Pause. I'm fuming. In fact, I'm shaking. I can't believe what they're cooking up between them. To be fair though Mum, I'm not sure Iain's part of this 'conspiracy.'

"OK. At least we've a hope of getting you back together now."

Pause.

"Yeah, alright Mum, I'll keep you posted. I'm gonna stay with Dad tonight."

Pause.

"Yes, of course I will. Keep him busy. Keep his mind off Anna."

Pause.

"I know. It won't be long. See you tomorrow Mum."

Pulling up my joggers and rising from the toilet, I fling open the bathroom window so it bangs against the wall of the house. It's a miracle the glass doesn't smash. Claudia jumps as she looks up at me.

"I'm on to you," I say. "Don't mess with me. Or the memory of my mother."

"Are you threatening me, Jamie? I'll give my dad a shout. He's only out front, you know."

"I'm looking out for my mother," I tell her. "I heard everything you said. You're like a pair of witches."

"And I'm looking out for mine. You weren't supposed to be listening in to *my* private phone conversation anyway."

"You're in *my* bloody garden Claudia. I couldn't help but hear. If you want a private conversation, piss off somewhere else."

"What on earth are you two doing? Are things so bad that you've got to shout through windows?" Iain appears on the patio beneath the bathroom window, shaking his head.

"Have you got everything you want Iain?" I just want them to go. Before I lamp one of them.

"Just about. For now. I've just one or two things in the shed. I can come back for the rest."

It must be pretty horrendous for him, clearing out of the home he was going to live in with you Mum. I feel a trickle, and I mean just a trickle, of sympathy for him but I do want them gone.

"Just take it all now," I say quickly. "Then you and conniving Claudia don't have to come back again."

"Jamie. Stop being like this."

The guilt trip won't work on me. Mentioning you. "I'll wait here until you've both gone."

"I wanted to talk to you before I go about this *tweet* business."

I wondered if we'd get around to that. "Nothing to talk about. Someone's just messing around."

"But who? That's what I want to know."

"How should I know? I'm as fucked off with it as you are."

"There's no need for that sort of language. Not in front of my daughter."

I slam the bathroom window and sit on the ledge of the bath. I've heard enough of their bollocks.

Chapter Nine

I remember the first time I met Claudia. You and Iain made it into some big thing. Yeah, I was curious, granted, and wondered if I'd fancy her. I'd stalked her on Facebook first and thought she looked fit enough. But she seemed hard-faced with her posts about wearing a *bitch face* (whatever *that* is) or not giving a shit about what others think. Other girls I'm friends with are 'softer,' posting pictures of their dogs or little sisters and stuff. I looked at a couple of pictures of Claudia; one of her sticking two fingers up and the other of her 'trout-pouting' at the camera. I showed you as we were driving along to meet her and Iain that day.

"I know. I've seen them," you said. "She sent me a *friend request* so I had a quick look. All that stuff she posts will just be bravado. An age thing. I'm sure she'll be a nice girl. Hopefully we'll all get on."

You looked nervous though as we pulled into the leisure complex. We sat for a few moments. Then they pulled up on our right, beside us, meaning Claudia and you were side by side with just the glass of your car windows dividing you. She stared at us whilst you rummaged around in your bag.

We gathered at the back of our cars. "Anna, Jamie, this is my daughter Claudia. Claudia, meet Anna and Jamie."

"Lovely to meet you Claudia." You were talking in that daft phone voice thing you had. "I've been looking forward to meeting you."

"Yeah."

You looked taken aback but carried on wittering like you always do when you're nervous. She looked me up and down but didn't speak to me till we were in the Laser Quest queue.

"I can't believe they're forcing us to do this," she muttered amidst the kids screaming all around us. "Like we're five or something."

It was one of the few times we ever agreed on anything. "I know. I could have done without it too." She was pretty, yeah but even more hard-faced than she had looked in her photos. No way was she my type.

You probably noticed that she singled you out during the Laser Tag games. There were four teams of eight people. We agreed that me and Claudia would go on one team and you and Iain on the other. It was probably your idea Mum. Some weird 'bonding' thing or other. Claudia shot you repeatedly, so you were 'out' quickly every time. Your laser vest was lit up more times than a Christmas tree. If you noticed this, you never let on. Then she'd go after Iain. No one else. I saw him have a word with her once. Even in the darkness, I could see her scowl, then she went after you again.

That was my first time doing Laser Tag and I could live with it being the only one. It was agreed we'd go for something to eat while we were there.

"Nando's?" I've always loved a Nando's, especially if someone else is paying.

"I'm not going in there." Claudia pointed at Wagamama's. "That's where we'll go."

"I don't like Japanese food." It was true. Give me chicken or steak, not a load of slimy vegetables swimming around a bowl of perfumed liquid.

"Well you and your mum go to Nando's and I'll go with my dad."

"Claudia. That's not what today's about. We're all going for a meal

CHAPTER NINE

– at the same place if you don't mind." Iain looked at you. "I'm easy. We'll let Anna have the deciding vote. Where to love?"

"*Love?*" Claudia spat the word out.

You smiled at her. "We'll go to Wagamama's."

"Mum!"

"It's good to have a change."

I trailed in, behind you all, pissed off that you'd 'sided' with Claudia. But I understood. The place stunk like a chemist's counter and everyone was eating with chopsticks. I was going to ask for a knife and fork.

"Table for four," Iain announced to the waiter who then seated us. He sat first, then you sat, at a diagonal to him. Just as Claudia was about to sit next to him, he quickly moved, with a scrape of the wooden chair, to sit next to you.

"Dad!" Claudia slapped her menu onto the table. One or two of the other diners looked at us. "Why don't you want to sit next to me?"

"Cos I want to sit next to Anna." He smiled.

"Charming. Sit next to her then. See if I give a shit."

He laughed. "OK, OK." He stood up and moved back next to her.

It was like bloody musical chairs. I looked at you as I took the now empty chair next to you. If you were pissed off, you did a good job of hiding it. You were studying the menu.

"Right, who's having a starter?" Iain looked up from his menu. "Order whatever you want, all of you. This one's on me."

"You can't pay for *them* Dad." Claudia was scowling again. "It'll cost a fortune."

"Excuse me young lady. I'll do what I want with *my* money."

"Can I get you any drinks?" A waiter stood over us. He probably thought we were a family or something. In the end, we nearly were.

"Wine. Large." You pointed at me. "Just half a beer for him. He's driving."

I smile at the memory. At the time, I was irritated at having to drive. I didn't blame you though. Claudia was as prickly as a cactus. And became more so as time went on.

After what feels like an eternity, Iain calls up the stairs. "We're off Jamie. I'll see you soon."

I don't answer. I wait for the two car doors to bang and for them to bugger off. I shuffle back to your room and look out of the window to check that they've gone. Seeing your empty wardrobes and all your belongings dumped in charity bags reminds me that you're never coming back. I regret making the decision to bag up your stuff and for a moment I feel like putting it all back.

I notice the door to the cupboard where you've always kept photo albums hangs open and I'm worried Iain's taken them. I'm relieved to find they're mostly still there. It looks like one or two have been taken but hopefully they're ones that only contain photos of the two of you.

I know it's like picking the scab off a wound but I can't help myself. The first album is me as a baby and at different stages of childhood, wearing a variety of outfits, mixed in with just a few of you and Dad. I stare at one of you with me on your knee. We're both laughing and it's obvious from our laughter and ease that we were each other's world. The next album is a seaside holiday from when I was leaving primary school, crammed with pictures of either me with you, or me with Dad. From them, we look like a happy family.

I flick through to the last holiday the three of us had together. I'd have been about fourteen and it must have been me that took the picture of you and Dad. I can see the distance between you that I obviously didn't notice at the time. Both of you look knackered and aren't anywhere near each other, not like your earlier pictures. I wonder if you knew at that point you would be splitting up. All I remember are rows about who would be leaving, who would be staying and what belonged to

CHAPTER NINE

who. In the end, you slept on the sofa and gave Dad two months before you were going to get him out through the court. I thought you were a right cow at the time but now I know, you wanted to keep a roof over my head and you were the only one who was working. I remember being furious with him for taking the TV when he left.

Dad told me he was sleeping in his car after that which made me feel terrible. I used to lie in my comfy bed, trying not to think about him bedding down in the back of his Volvo. He lost a ton of weight, drank like a fish and would endlessly beg you to take him back. I hated you for refusing. I didn't understand it. I did miss him. There were times when me and him got on OK, like when we played computer games or watched Top Gear.

Then I didn't see him for a while. I was so busy blaming you that I didn't realise his sudden freedom had led to a string of on-line girlfriends to occupy him. They were far more important to him than spending time with his then-sulky teenage son. When he met Katherine, he came back to me a bit. Initially, he tried to rub your nose in his new-found happiness but if you were bothered, you never let on.

There's a picture of you and Iain just after your engagement, arm-in-arm in the garden. This is one of the happiest photos of you in all the albums. I know you probably thought more of him than anyone else – including me. I suppose I'd grown up and he was the one you were going to live with but still, it all pisses me off. I stare at the photo. You look younger than in one taken ten years earlier. I wonder what you would have done differently if you had known you were going to die a year after it had been taken. Would you have gone on holiday more? Worked less? I guess if you knew, you could have stopped it from happening.

Chapter Ten

The atmosphere in the waiting room is awful. I'm usually as tuned in to these things as that old radio we used to have in the kitchen, but this time, even I can feel it. Dad and Katherine are holding hands at the side of me. Dad's stroking the top of Katherine's hand with his thumb and it's making me want to puke. Iain and Claudia are at the other side of me. She is dangling a shoe from her foot, swinging it back and forth. It is irritating the shit out of me.

Auntie Liz and Uncle Si (I still feel a bit stupid calling them Auntie and Uncle at my age, but I can't help it) are sat across from me, a low hum of conversation occasionally passing between them. Cate's here and Dawn from the gallery. We're crammed in like commuters on an evening train and I wonder for the umpteenth time what business Claudia has here whilst we collect your ashes. She's fastened herself to Iain's side, telling everyone who'll listen how she's 'looking after him.' *I know her game.*

I unzip my hoody whilst looking about for evidence of air conditioning. The stench of lilies is back. It's as though it's haunting me, along with Claudia and those bloody tweets. I never knew I hated the smell of lilies quite so much. It makes my head hurt.

"Good morning," a voice sounds from the doorway behind us. "Are we all here for the same thing? Ms Anna Hardaker?"

CHAPTER TEN

Dad clears his throat. "We sure are." He gets to his feet before everyone else.

"I'll be right back," says the man at the desk. "I've got everything ready for you."

"I don't think this is your place Phil." Iain stands up to face him. They're about the same height, in fact, they're slightly similar in appearance. Stocky, fair-haired, same sort of dress sense. Notice I did not say *fashion* sense. If there's such a thing as a 'type,' Mum, you definitely had one.

"He's here to support his son," Katherine pipes up. "He's all Jamie's got now."

I'm surprised at her speaking out in front of this room full of people.

"That's not true." Auntie Liz calls out. "We're his family too."

"Jamie's a grown man, in case you hadn't noticed," Iain continues. "It's not like he needs chaperoning around now."

I notice Claudia staring at me, smirking. She's *chaperoned* everywhere. Talk about double standards from Iain. I jab a finger in her direction. "What are you doing here anyway. You're like an odour I can't shake."

"Behave." Uncle Si frowns across the room at me.

Claudia pouts. "I'm with my dad. Why are you always so nasty to us? You've got no right."

Ignoring her, I walk towards the reception desk, thinking of how irritated you must have been with her before you died. Everywhere I turn, she's there with her beak in. I wonder what she's after. I'm sure she wasn't always quite this bad.

Iain and I stand shoulder to shoulder as the undertaker returns to the reception area. He places a large black jar on the counter. I can't believe that you have been shrunk to something that could be contained in this way. My larger than life, lovely Mum, now a pile of ash. Why didn't I appreciate you when you were alive? I blink back tears, yet

63

again. Dad steps up behind me and puts an arm around my shoulders. Iain says nothing. I guess he's as much in shock as I am.

Iain and I stare at the urn until the voice of the undertaker startles me. "My deepest condolences to all of you." Then to Iain in a lower voice, he says, "I'll pop the final account in the post over the next couple of days."

"What final account?" I look at them both.

"The bill," Iain replies, drily. "Hopefully your mum left provision in her will. I guess we'll find out soon enough."

"And what if she hasn't?"

"We'll cross that bridge if we come to it. I can't think about that right now."

We reach for the urn at the same time but Iain lets me hold it.

There's a collective banging of car doors. We're in the car park at Cow and Calf rocks, halfway up Ilkley Moor.

"Do you still want to do this?" Iain turns to me, nodding down at the urn that I've got my arms wrapped around. It's the last time I'll have my arms around you Mum, really, I don't want to let you go but the thought of keeping your ashes at home gives me the creeps. I know some people do, but I couldn't.

Claudia's at Iain's side, as always, looking bored more than sad. There must be a word for people like her, getting off on other people's grief.

Dawn and Cate walk behind, while Auntie Liz and Uncle Si flank me. Uncle Si seems to have taken everything in his stride. Auntie Liz is in bits. You were close, the three of you but perhaps Uncle Si struggles to let his feelings show. If so, I think I probably take after him in that department. You used to say that you'd have them as friends if they weren't your brother and sister. I hope they'll stay *friends* with me after all this. I've liked being an only child but if I'd had brothers and sisters,

CHAPTER TEN

I wouldn't be feeling so alone now. We could all lean on each other. *Claudia's* the nearest thing I've ever had to a sibling – no thanks.

Dad and Katherine follow at a bit of a distance. I'm surprised they're coming up really. Katherine looks pissed off. I guess she's finding it hard, all this. She was jealous enough when you were alive and she's probably having to put up with Dad talking about you all the time. Maybe she's here to make sure we let you go or maybe, as she said, they are both here to support me. I hope so.

She's wheezing by the time we get to the top of the first ascent. Dad's always on at her to get some exercise and he's a bit rotten about it at times. The rest of us go up, no problem; a pack of gazelles.

"Where are we going to do it?" Iain glances around. There are people all over the place, enjoying the view across Ilkley. At this height, the day is clear and we can see for miles. You loved it here. I recall watching you when I was young, bent over your sketch pad, your hair fluttering in the breeze whilst I moaned at you that I wanted to go home.

"We should go a bit higher, where there's no one around." Auntie Liz sets off walking again. "My sister liked her peace and quiet."

Uncle Si quickens his pace to keep up with her. I notice the sun shining on the top of his head where his hair is thinning. You used to make fun of him for this.

"Are there any rules about this sort of thing," he asks. "You know – scattering someone's ashes?"

"Course there are." Dad's keeping pace with us now, having left a red-faced Katherine behind. I bet she'll give him some right shit for it, later. "You're supposed to only scatter human ashes in specific places."

"Who's to know?" Iain looks daggers at Dad. I can tell what's going through his mind. He doesn't really want Dad having anything to do with it. He needs to remember though that you and Dad were together for sixteen years, much longer than you were with *him*. He acts like he owned you. Prick. "Shall I take that?" Iain points at the urn. "It must be awkward, walking uphill and keeping hold of it – maybe we should take it in turns whilst we're walking."

"No thanks." I'm not letting you go Mum. Not until I have to.

"I don't mind taking a turn either," Cate says.

We're all puffing in the heat of the afternoon sun when we naturally come to pause on another flat area. Auntie Liz has got there first – five years your junior, she is slightly fitter than the rest of us. I look at her, sat on the ground, waiting for everyone else. From several feet away, she looks just like you Mum; the same athletic build and many similar mannerisms. Her dark hair is a couple of inches longer than yours was but your laughter always sounded the same. Though I reckon it will be a while before I hear Auntie Liz laugh again.

The area around us is deserted. "Here." Affirmatively, I place the urn on the ground, next to Auntie Liz. "But can we wait a few minutes first?" I sit and everyone else follows. After a few minutes, all the heavy breathing has died away. The only sounds to be heard are a faint breeze, a distant family enjoying themselves and the bleating of sheep.

"Shall we?" Iain's voice eventually cuts into the hush. "We need to be upwind." We walk to the edge. This is as good a spot as any. I lean over a rock and watch a stream cascade down the side of the hill. You've always enjoyed being beside water.

Uncle Si places his hand on my shoulder. "Time to let her go kiddo."

One by one, apart from Katherine, who declines, we all accept a handful of the ash and send it scattering down the hill. Iain empties the remainder out. It swirls in the breeze and he throws some petals after it that he's taken from his rucksack. "Lilies," he explains. "She was going to have them in her wedding bouquet." Then he produces a little solar garden light and spears it into the ground next to the rock. "She didn't like the dark." He wipes at the tears that are running down his cheeks. "I don't want her to be scared up here."

"She's dead Dad." Claudia's eyes are as dry as the rock we're all leaning over but nonetheless, she puts her arm around him.

Uncle Si pulls Auntie Liz closer so she can sob onto his shoulder. "What a waste. She had everything, absolutely *everything* to live for."

You've gone. You've really gone. Dad steps towards me. "Come on son. I'll buy you a pint."

"I don't want to leave her here." I look down to where the ashes and petals have settled. I hope *you're* settled too.

"I know son. But she's at peace now. We've let her go. And she'd want you to carry on." A sob catches in my throat. I turn away from you and follow him.

"You can come up here anytime you need to," Dawn reminds me. "And she'll always be in here." She touches my chest with one hand and dabs at her eyes with the other.

Down in the Cow and Calf pub beer garden, I can't see the spot where we've scattered you. Maybe now we've released you, the tweets will stop. They're still baffling me. I know you've gone, but still …

Iain slides a pint of cider in front of me.

"A toast," I say, surprising myself as I raise my glass. I don't normally do this sort of thing. "To my awesome Mum."

"To Anna," everyone choruses. Well, apart from Katherine and Claudia. You're dead but hatred will probably always snake through their veins. I almost feel sorry for them. It must be shit, hating a dead person so much. *They shouldn't be here.*

Katherine gets in the back when we return to the car. She never lets me sit in the front usually, so I can't understand it. I feel like an imposter. Dad slaps my arm, all father-like. "I'm proud of you lad. You handled that well. It's hard enough for everyone but it must be bloody awful for you."

I glance at him as he drives. It's weird. For years I've wanted this. I've needed to spend time with him but it's taken *this,* losing you, to bring us together. Or maybe he's just after a decent Father's Day present.

I'm reminded of a Father's Day when I was sixteen. Dad had met Katherine but not yet moved in with her. He still had his own place at the other side of Leeds. It was before I'd started driving so was a two bus each way job for me. Even though Dad had a car, he wouldn't have dreamed of collecting me, even when it was pissing it down. But I wanted to see him so I made the effort. Sometimes, I wondered why I bothered. Katherine wouldn't leave us alone and I always felt as though I was fighting her for his attention. I wanted to do dad-son things like watch football or go and see a film, but they just wanted to get drunk and go to bed early.

Much of the time, he didn't want me to go over at all. I'd ring and he'd make some random excuse or other. *I'm away. I've fallen out with Katherine. I'm working,* or get this one Mum, I never told you this at the time because you'd have either laughed or gone mad, *I'm waiting in for a delivery.* Eh?

But on that particular Father's Day, we'd agreed the day before that I'd go over. I'd saved some money for a present and card for him (much to your disgust after forgetting Mother's Day – sorry Mum!) As usual, I was on two buses in the rain but looking forward to seeing the look on his face at his present. It was a smart leather wallet, which he needed. His was falling to bits. I was starving when I got there and hoped we'd be having a takeaway since it was Saturday. However, his flat was locked up and there was no sign of his car. I tried ringing him. Switched off. Great. I peered through all the windows for signs of life. Nothing. I double checked my text from the day before. *I'll be back around mid-afternoon. See you then.* It was five o'clock. I looked under stones and plant pots to see if he'd left me a key. Throughout this time, I was getting wet through and there was nowhere to shelter. I tried him again. Nothing.

I had Katherine's number in my phone. Dad had borrowed hers to ring me once. (He'd smashed his in an argument they'd had – I didn't

CHAPTER TEN

tell you that either Mum.) Katherine's rang out. I sent Dad a text. *Where are you? I'm outside your flat.* Then waited.

If I stood really close to the building, I got the slightest bit of shelter from the overhead guttering and I could pick up a weak wi-fi signal from his flat. Enough to log into Netflix and start watching American Pie. I had to shelter the phone under my coat. After ten minutes, I decided to send Katherine a text. *Do you know where my dad is? I'm outside his flat.*

Twenty minutes later, she replied. *We're away for the weekend. Last minute thing.*

You're joking. He's arranged to see me.

He says sorry. Apparently, you shouldn't have set off without double checking with him today.

Can you get him to ring me?

He's drunk.

So what am I supposed to do?

I don't know Jamie. You're a big boy. Ring your mum or something.

Tell him I'll leave his Father's Day present behind the bin.

And then, as suggested, I rang you Mum. Whatever you might have thought about Dad, you didn't let on. You just came and got me. And I didn't tell you how upset I was either.

Chapter Eleven

I catch Katherine through the wing mirror. She's rummaging for something in her handbag, her face looking like a smacked arse.

He's gone for someone completely different to you, Mum. She's plump to your slim. Moody to your cheery (well, usually!) and she lives in jeans and trainers whereas you were always in skirts and heels. I suddenly think of Meghan. I'm leaving it a day or two more before I text her. Can't be too keen.

"We'll come in for a bit," Dad says as we pull up at the front of the house.

"I wanted to get home actually," Katherine moans as they walk behind me towards the front door. "We're not staying long."

Dad mutters something that I don't catch and I push the door open against a pile of post behind it.

"Careful," Dad says, staring at the letters as I scoop them up. "There might be something important."

I walk through to the lounge and sink onto the sofa. Katherine and Dad perch on the armchairs, facing me. The room *still* stinks of lilies, even though it's over a week since I threw them out.

I set down two more sympathy cards on the chair arm next to me. I'm sick to the back teeth of them. The next letter is the life insurance form. Then a bulky envelope. I slide out its contents. *The Last Will and Testament of Anna Louise Hardaker.* There's a solicitor letter and a form signed by Cate; I think. I start reading down the page, not really taking it in but looking for the gist of it. The first paragraph tells of the life insurance document. I've already found that obviously.

"I wonder if I've got a copy of this too." Dad plucks the letter from my hands. I open my mouth to protest at him taking *my* letter but then decide it's not worth it. He's not someone I can ever challenge. Katherine sits as still as a statue, watching him. I still don't say a word, although I wish I had the guts to. Dad clearly still believes you owe him something. Maybe you do.

"Bugger me sideways. She had more than I thought she had." Dad lets out a low whistle.

"Do you have to raise your voice like that?" Katherine glares at him and then glances around our lounge as if trying to separate herself from the proceedings, her eyes falling on the many framed photos that are all over the place. It must upset her even more. Our photos, I mean, from before *she* ever met Dad.

"She's got an ISA, a savings account and a few investments too," he adds, excitedly. "She's left the lot to you son. Bloody hell! You'll have to find out what's in them."

He folds one page behind the other and continues. "She's left some art and antiques to her brother and jewellery to her sister. She wants to give them both some money which is to come from the ISA. She must *really* have a fair whack stashed in there. Right, here we go, the house." He frowns. "I should have some of this. Even just a bit. I lived here with her for ten years. I paid bills and everything."

"Didn't she buy you out? I remember hearing Mum talking to Auntie Liz about it."

"Yes, but that's not the point. We worked for everything together to start with. I supported her back in the early days of her career. That must count for something?"

"You were divorced though." Katherine's voice is flat. "If she's not left you anything, you might not have a leg to stand on. I was speaking to someone about it."

"You've got sixty per cent of the house and Iain's got forty - she says you have to be left to live here for as long as you want to. *Why's she leaving all that to Iain?* He's got his own house. They weren't even married!"

"They nearly were." Katherine crosses her legs. "It might have been a totally different story if they had been. Married, I mean. Jamie might not have got anything then."

"She's done the same with the business and the van! Dad slams the page down. 60/40! He's done alright, hasn't he? They've only been together a few years. She would never have got to where she was if it wasn't for me and all the help I gave her."

I look away. He's not being fair at all. I can remember Dad going on at you for locking yourself away in the spare room and *faffing around* with your paint. He thought it was a complete waste of time. I'm pretty pissed off about what you've left Iain though. I agree with Dad on that one.

"So that's that." Dad looks at Katherine. "I'm still skint - m'lad'o here's OK and Iain's definitely quids in." He stands up. "I need another beer. You coming love – we'll get one on the way home?"

Katherine rises from the chair. Dad won't look at me. He's gone cold on me, like he normally does. I feel suddenly panicky. "I said I'd lend you that money Dad."

"*Lend* me it?" His voice has an edge and his eyes are marble as he turns to me. "We're family. Families help each other."

"OK. I'll *give* you it Dad. You can start your own business, like you said."

Katherine's watching us, eagerly. "Ten grand won't be enough love. Why don't you ask him for more? He can afford it."

"Twenty grand?" Dad still won't make eye contact with me.

CHAPTER ELEVEN

My eyes fall on a photograph of you and Iain next to the TV. I make a mental note to give it to him. I don't want to look at it anymore. "OK. I'll sort it when I get access to everything." My phone beeps on the chair arm next to me. It's Auntie Liz.

LOOK AT TWITTER!!!! Your mum's account! What's going on?

"Hang on Dad, something's going on." I press the Twitter app, my chest thudding. The breath catches in my throat as I read your latest tweet:

@artistanna123 *I am not coping. Not coping at all. Someone needs to be brought to justice. Someone needs to pay. They can't get away with it.* #**cuckoo** #**beforemytime**

"Are you in there? Look at him." Dad laughs. "Who's texting you? You're in another world. Crack a couple of beers open son." He seems to be wanting to stay around now.

"Erm, what?"

"We've been here for ten minutes and you've not even offered us a drink." He laughs again. The money it seems, has put him in a better mood. "Call yourself a host?"

"I've none in."

"Well nip to the shop then. Bloody hell. What's a person to do for a drink around here?"

I leave the house, hating myself for the fact that even at my age, dad says *jump,* and I say *how high?* The voices of Dad and Katherine picking over the contents of your will, echo in my ears as I close the door behind me. I'm grateful to get away and walk the short distance to the shop. On my way back, I decide I'm going to tell him about the tweets. If I don't and he finds out he's the last to know, he'll go apeshit.

"It's the fourth one." I pass the phone to Dad.

Energy seems to physically drain from him as I watch him scroll through the tweets. "What's she on about? Someone needs to pay.

Hang on a minute. She's dead! What on earth is going on here?"

"Let me see." Katherine takes the phone from him. "Oh my God." A few moments pass. "Look, it's obviously just someone messing around. Maybe Twitter has been hacked or something."

Dad's face is pinched white. "I want this stopping. You'll have to get on the phone to them. Katherine, find the number."

Katherine's pressing around on the screen. "Ah, there's a help centre, hmmm, it doesn't look like there's a phone number though."

"There must be," barks Dad. "I want this sorting before we leave."

"Ah-ha, *contact us.* There's an option to *report an impersonation.* Oh, but it's by text. It's impossible to speak to a human."

"Well, if this isn't *impersonation* then I don't know what is." Dad snatches the phone from Katherine and thrusts it in front of me. "She was *your* mother Jamie. It will have to be *you* who puts in the complaint. Technically, you're her next of kin."

"I will do, but I'll have to ring Auntie Liz back first. She's seen it too and wants to know what's going on. She'll be in bits."

"Never mind Auntie Liz." Dad raises his voice as he paces up and down the carpet. I hate it when he yells. Suddenly, I feel eight or nine again, torn between running away to my bedroom or hanging around to protect you.

"Oh really?" We all turn to the doorway which, right on cue, Auntie Liz has appeared in. "You didn't text me back Jamie."

"I know, um, I'm sorry. Dad's here and he's a bit upset about it all."

"Upset!" He's still on one. "If I find out who's behind this, I'll show you *upse*t."

"I don't know what's wrong with you," Katherine hisses. "It's not as if you were still together."

"It's, it's, oh, I'm not going to get into it." Dad seems to have calmed slightly at the arrival of Auntie Liz. He always *was* on his best behaviour in front of her. She's stepped in a few times in the past to stick up for

CHAPTER ELEVEN

you. She was one of the few people whose opinion seemed to matter to Dad.

"So, what's going on?" Auntie Liz walks across the room and sits on the chair arm beside me, her voice sounds surprisingly calm. "Who's posting these tweets from my sister's account? I've only just seen them."

"We don't know."

"Jamie's just about to report them. Aren't you son?"

"Don't you think it might make things worse?" I imagine the police and all that getting involved. I can't take any more Mum. I just want to get back to normal.

"No love." Auntie Liz puts her arm around me and it makes me want to cry because her voice sounds so much like yours. "Reporting it will get it to stop. Whoever is doing it will get blocked by Twitter. They might even get prosecuted."

Katherine adds. "It's probably just one of those trolls or something. There's tons of them around these days."

"I can't ring them. There isn't a way. I can only send a message."

"Do it." Dad's voice is quiet and even. "Now. Then it's done."

I click on the *report an impersonator* button, type in my email address then add,

*Someone is pretending to be my mother. She died on 16th April but posts are being tweeted from her account. Her Twitter name is **@artistanna123**. Please can you delete her account?*

I get an immediate message after I hit submit. *Thank you for contacting Twitter Support. A colleague will be in touch within five working days.*

"Done." I say to my onlookers. "We can't do any more for now."

Auntie Liz gives my shoulder a squeeze.

Chapter Twelve

I've decided that I'm going to do at least one useful thing every day Mum. I've got to pick myself up a bit. Today I'm going to text Meghan and I'm also going to fill in the life insurance form. My compassionate leave will only last for so long and I need to keep this house going until I decide what I'm going to do with it. I've always hated filling forms in. I get pig-sick of them at work.

This one doesn't look too bad. There are just a few boxes to tick. I run down the list of documentation – I've got it all, or at least, I know where it all is. The next page is all about assignees and beneficiaries, I'm not sure, I might have to Google it, but I'm going to fill it in as best I can. If they chuck it back, they chuck it back. I pause at the *cause of death* section, not knowing whether *fall from stairs* or *broken neck* should be written. In the end I write what it says on the death certificate, *cervical fracture.*

It says at the top of the form that each beneficiary needs to complete one. I'm not going to tell Iain. I'll let him work it out for himself. Now then, what the hell is an *assignee*? Shit, I'm going to have to have to ask Dad and *bloody hell!* It looks like I get more money for *accidental death.* I just need to dig out the name of the copper who was hanging around.

I close my eyes as the memory of that day swims in front of them, trying to blink away the image of your body being slid into a body bag and being carted, in full view of the street, down the drive. *Talk*

CHAPTER TWELVE

about making an exit, you would have said. Remembering it all hurts like hell. Your life should have been fifty years longer than it was. *I need to get out of here.* I snatch up the keys to your Mini and blink as the afternoon sun stings my eyes.

"How are you doing?" Betty calls from her front garden as I'm locking the door. I cross over the road to her. She's a comforting sight. She always wears a housecoat; I think that's what it's called anyway.

"Ah, you know, bad days and slightly better days. I just feel so guilty all the time."

"What on earth have *you* got to feel guilty about?" She rises from where she's weeding, or whatever.

"Still being here, whilst Mum -"

"I know." Her eyes are glassy as she looks up at me. "I'm no expert but I do know that guilt is a normal part of the grieving process. It *will* pass - honestly."

"I hope so. I can't stand feeling like *this* forever."

"Don't forget where I am Jamie. I had a lot of time for your mum and would like to look out for you. Just remember that you never need to be on your own."

"Thanks." I need to get away from her before I blub. I can feel the hot rods behind my eyes again.

I slide into the driver seat, glancing at the van parked beside me. *First Impressions Fine Art. I can't believe it's now forty per cent Iain's.* Sixty-bloody-forty like the other big stuff. I wonder if Katherine had a point when she mentioned how things might have changed after you were married. What *were* you planning Mum?

I decide to go to the gallery. Check on my so-called inheritance. I arrive without being able to remember the journey. Parked in one of the bays outside for several moments, I recall my younger years, waiting for you in this very spot whilst you dealt with whatever you had to sort out in there. All is as it was. The monochrome signage which you deliberated over for days. The lights in the window on the ever-changing displays. It looks like mainly your work in the front window. *Stages of Life (The Collection)* says the sign. Four paintings sit in a square. Mother and baby, a carefree childhood, a stressed adult and a deathbed scene. They're a sample from a collection you put together last year.

"They're selling like hotcakes." Dawn, your gallery manager, informs me when I walk in. "I did a double take when I saw your mum's Mini pull up outside. I really miss her." She sighs. "How are you doing? After the other day, I mean. It must have been so hard for you at Ilkley."

"So-so," I say. It's not a lie. Sometimes I feel OK. I pretend, at times, that it hasn't happened.

"I've noticed a strange couple of things on Twitter," Dawn continues, frowning. "Do you know anything? Sorry, that is, assuming you've even seen it, of course."

Something plummets within me. "I've seen it, yeah and I've reported it. I'm waiting for them to get back to me."

"She's acquired a fair few new followers since she, erm -."

"Died?"

"Yes. She'd often wondered how to get more people to follow her."

"A bit drastic though, wasn't it?" I laugh, despite my misery. "There must be an easier way to get more Twitter followers."

"Hmmmm." Dawn looks at me. "Are you sure you're OK?"

"I thought I'd call in and see how it's all going." I don't want to talk about Twitter. It's doing my head in.

"Ah yes, you own 60% now, don't you? Which makes you my new boss, doesn't it?"

"How do you know?"

"Iain told me. He was in earlier. He brought a bit of new stock from some of your mum's students."

CHAPTER TWELVE

I bristle at the thought of him being on the ball with stuff. Until today, I'd hardly given the business a second thought.

"He's been full of ideas," she continues. "Of how to take the business forwards. Of course, he wants to keep the originals of your mum's work, but we can generate a fair bit of income from selling prints and calendars of some of it. Then of course, there's all her students and other contacts."

"He's full of shit," I say and then realise how pathetic I sound. He's come up with more than I have. You gave this business everything you had Mum. I remember when you spent days toiling over a business plan, trying to get somebody, anybody, interested in what you were doing to get a bit of money together to get you started. And the state of this building when you signed the lease. Amidst the tinkling of the background music, I glance down to where my trainers sink into the carpet.

"It's alright, you know." Dawn rests her hand on my arm. "I'm going to keep this place going, just as your mum would have wanted it to be."

"Cool," I reply, looking back at her. "I'll help too, when my brain's back in gear, that is." My eyes fall onto one of your paintings straight in front of me. It's a woman and a little boy in silhouette, looking out to sea. It could be us but it could be anybody – that's how your work sells, others can see themselves in it. If I end up being half as good an artist as you were, I'll be happy.

"That one's really popular and there's the usual interest in the 'toxic marriage' painting," Dawn says. "Perhaps more so. I can't believe how many framed prints have been ordered. I guess it's the *divorce* time of year though. Couples are going on holiday and realising they can't stand each other anymore."

I walk closer to the picture, seeing it through fresh eyes. You've painted it in oil. It's such a dark painting. The back of a woman, (she could be you) droopy and slumped with a distant, shadowy man, shouting with his fists in the air. It's a busy picture with a broken and strewn domestic scene surrounding the two figures. There's an upturned chair, smashed crockery and the gloom of their surroundings bearing down on them. I realise how unhappy you must have been with Dad for that to have come out.

Obviously, I remember your arguments, but would just keep out of the way. I wanted to stay on the right side of Dad. I can see why he went mad when this picture of yours took off. It's been shown and re-printed all over the place. Anybody who knew you would have known it represented him.

"Clever lady, your Mum." I'm so engrossed in my thoughts that Dawn's soft voice startles me. "Just think of how many people this picture will have spoken to and helped, especially now, since it's used by that women's organisation."

"My dad didn't hit my mum," I say quickly. "I lived with them and I never saw him." I always defend him to people. He's far from perfect but he's my dad.

Dawn leads me by the arm away from the painting. "It's all in the past. But if this painting speaks to people like it is doing, that's very good for business. Anyway Jamie, I'll keep things going and you just let me know when you're feeling better and want to get more involved. Your mum would love you to. She'd be proud of you, you know."

I blink back tears as I make my escape to the car. You were the same Mum. When you were having problems with Dad and anyone was kind to you, it would make you cry and you'd have to get away. I've had enough of feeling like this. I must make it better. Before I start the car up, I pull out my phone.

Hi Meghan. How RU? Do you want to get together tonight? X

My hands are shaking as I hit the send button. Then, as quick as my decision to send it, her reply comes. I'm used to waiting hours before girls reply to me.

CHAPTER TWELVE

Yes. I'd like that. There's an Italian opened by the river?? x

Oh my God, she said yes! My chest is thumping as I Google the restaurant's website. A posh restaurant with even posher prices. I've nothing 'posh' to wear apart from my black funeral suit. Erm, no. I'll have to go and buy something. Normally the thought of a clothes shop leaves me cold but I've just been paid plus I've got a load of money on the way. I can afford it. For once in my life, I don't have to think twice.

8 o'clock? I'll pick you up. X

Cool x

I spend two hours trailing around the Trinity Centre. *Who'd have believed it? And without a second opinion.* I'm feeling almost normal as I return to the car with a ton of new gear ranging from trousers to shirts to jeans to shorts. I'm nervous though Mum. I wish you were here to calm me down. It seems very *real* – taking a girl, well a woman out for a meal to a restaurant. I could do with your advice right now. What sort of wine to order? I can't very well order a pint of cider. I don't know which fork or spoon to use or whether my serviette should be laid on my knee or tucked 'bib-like' down my shirt. We've been for loads of meals in chain-type pubs, but this is a proper restaurant. I've got to impress her Mum. She makes me believe as though I've got something to look forward to again – a reason to go on. I'm so chuffed she's agreed to go out with me. I hope she isn't just feeling sorry for me at losing you, or after the money I'm inheriting. She doesn't appear that sort of person but you never know, do you Mum? I don't think I'll ever trust anyone completely.

But anyway, we're going to this upmarket Italian bistro-type place, where they'll pull our chairs out for us, take our coats and let us taste the wine before we order it. I can almost hear your voice Mum, as I flick through my newly acquired wardrobe. *You're a grown-up now Jamie. Choose your own outfit. Have some faith in yourself.* And so I choose my new navy trousers with its matching jacket and white shirt.

I'm going to look the business. She won't be able to resist me.

"Get you," Jake laughs at me as I lock the door. He's under his car bonnet on the drive next door.

If I ever bring Meghan home, I'm keeping her out of *his* way. He's filled out a lot more than I ever did. In fact, he's built like a brick shithouse and all the lasses fancy him, even Claudia.

"I was going to ask if you fancied a few rounds on the X-Box later mate. Ouch."

I laugh as he catches his head on the bonnet lid. "Easy Jake. Nah. I'm off out."

"Who's the lucky lady then? It's not that blonde one, is it? What's her name?"

"Claudia? You must be joking!"

"Well if you're not interested, I-"

"I think she's seeing someone." I can't think of anything worse. Claudia over *here* all the time, hanging around next door. I don't think so. "No it's this other lass, Meghan."

"Nice to see you getting out mate. Where are you off?"

"That new Italian by the park."

Jake lets out a long whistle. "Do you know how much it costs in there? I hope she's going to make it worth your while." He winks at me.

"I'll let you have the gory details tomorrow."

"Well let me know when you fancy an X-Box night." Jake takes a sip from a mug he lifts from his garden wall. "I'll bring some beers."

"Sounds good," I say. And it does. I've been missing spending time with my mates. They've all gone quiet on me since you died. I reckon no one knows what to say to me.

Chapter Thirteen

Meghan's wearing a black dress and high heels when I collect her. My stomach's churning. I might have to have a drink to help my nerves and abandon my car at the restaurant. Well your car - I know you'd go mad at me leaving Martha Mini overnight but I could hardly have picked her up in my battered Clio.

"Sorry about the other night," she says. "When I had to go to that party."

"No worries." I smile at her. "I'm far happier taking you out. You look well fit, by the way." I don't want her in any doubt whether I fancy her or not, but make sure I keep my eyes firmly on her face, though it's difficult.

"Erm thanks. You're not so bad yourself. That suit must have cost a few quid. I like a man in a suit."

She really seems just as interested in me as I am in her. It's a brilliant feeling and for the first time in a few weeks, I've managed to push you to the back of my head Mum.

"So how've you been?" She asks after we have been shown to our table. "Are you on with all that will stuff now; you mentioned it the other day?"

That's the last thing I want to talk about. So I say, "Yeah but that's boring stuff. Forms, letters and phone calls. Let's have a good night."

I was right about the wine, the coats and the chairs. It's a bit different in here from the 'chains' I've been used to, where they bring your meal out before you've finished ordering it. There's a live pianist and some fabulous paintings. You'd have loved it here Mum.

"I'll have the oysters to start and the steak. And another glass of this wine please?"

She's gone for the most expensive option on the menu. But what the hell. "I'll have the same please. It feels like ages since I had a good night out."

"It must be hard for you." She reaches across the table. Her eyes and hair are about the same colour as mine. I've read somewhere that we're attracted to people who look like ourselves. Must be something to do with reproduction. *Ha! Stop it – get a grip Jamie!*

"Let's not talk about my mum. I want to feel 'normal' tonight. Well as normal as possible!" I grin at her. "Let's talk about you."

"Not much to tell really. Born in York. Studying law in Leeds. Working in a supermarket. Live with my mother still. You know about my dad …"

"So you want to be a solicitor?"

"A barrister, then a judge. More money than a solicitor." She's running her hand up and down the stem of her wine glass and I'm finding it hard to stay focused, imagining where else her hand could end up.

"Nothing wrong with aiming high." I sip my wine. I've never been much of a wine drinker. It tastes like vinegar. She chose it. I wish I'd got a cider.

"I'm thinking of the pay packet."

I laugh and briefly wonder again about whether she's got her sights set on helping me spend my inheritance. She is stunning and I can't believe she's seriously interested in *me.* She has said hello to me before but that's about it. I can hardly believe my luck when she agrees to come

CHAPTER THIRTEEN

back home with me at the end of the evening for a coffee. Obviously, I wouldn't have dared bring anyone back with me if you were still here Mum. Meghan's linked her arm through mine, all friendly. Maybe I'll try and kiss her when we get back. Shit – this stuff's a minefield! I don't want to scare her off. I've come on too strong with girls before and learned my lesson. But if she's coming back with me. It can only mean one thing, can't it?

And it did. She's only just gone. What a night. I had a couple more ciders and she drank some prosecco I found in the fridge. She was on about us going on holiday sometime soon. I couldn't help but make a move. No matter how much I'd promised myself that I wouldn't. I feel bloody amazing this morning. *Did you feel like this when you first met Dad?*

I tried to keep the conversation on her – I'm sick of the conversation being about you. I can't be known just as *the lad whose mum died.* I lie on the sofa and doze off for a couple of hours. When I wake, the first thing I do is check my phone to see if there's a message yet from Meghan. What's there pulls me back to reality.

Stacey Price has retweeted a tweet from Anna Hardaker.

What the hell! I open it.

@artistanna123 *It wasn't just one life snatched, but two. Questions need to be answered. Someone must ask them. Everyone must listen.* #cuckoo #beforemytime

On retweeting, Stacey has written, *this is sick. The woman is dead.* Then a couple of people have 'liked' her post. There are some sick people out there. None so warped as Stacey though. Apparently, she was always bad mouthing you – even though you'd only briefly met. Claudia used to take great delight when imparting the things her mother had supposedly said. A recent comment was about you being a *charity case*! Somehow, Claudia had come to learn about the couple of successful applications you'd made for grants as an artist for your business, and then told her mother. Claudia often claimed they didn't get along and yet she told her everything.

I click onto Stacey's landing page – I'm shocked by the fact that *she* follows you – nosy cow. I scroll down a bit. She doesn't really tweet anything *herself* – she's more of a re-tweeter. Celebrity crap mainly. I click through to her Facebook page. Same crap there. I can hardly stand to look at her profile picture – albeit she's older and thinner, but she's another version of Claudia, although with the look of a horse. It's the teeth. I'm trembling as I notice the cover photo on Stacey's.

A smiley family photograph of the three of them with the sea in the distance. It must be recent as Iain is wearing the shirt you bought him last Christmas. He smiles for the camera, looking as though he hasn't got a worry in the world. *And why would he have?* He has pocketed forty per cent of your business, our house and the life insurance. And will probably be spending it all on them two bitches when it comes through. I click on the comments. *Beautiful family pic ... Are you back together ... OMG ... Nice to see you all looking so happy.* They're making me want to hurl. You've not even been dead two months Mum. The bastards.

She's not set privacy for her Facebook account so I'm able to scroll down and look at her pictures. There's several of them at Filey where *we* used to go. They must have had a day there. The shirt you bought appears again and again in the pictures. You're not even cold yet and he's already shagging his ex-wife. And what does the tweet mean *'it wasn't just one life snatched – it was two?'* Who's two? I don't get it. Why is this still happening?

I click onto my emails but there's still no reply from Twitter. *Two lives snatched.* Yours, obviously. Whose is the second? It must mean mine. Or Iain's. But more importantly, how are the tweets getting there? I don't believe in ghosts – at least, I don't think I do. This is

CHAPTER THIRTEEN

seriously creepy. If you *are* a ghost Mum, I'll probably crap myself if I see you. Please go haunt Dad instead. Or Stacey. I reckon this is some joker, I can't think about this anymore. I drag my running gear from the pile of clothes on the kitchen table. A run will clear my head and I'll collect your car whilst I'm at it.

I'm a bit out of condition and by the time I arrive at your car, I've not even done 5K. When I get back home, I'm sweating like a pig so run upstairs for a shower.

Really, I don't want to wash the scent of Meghan away from last night, but after the few ciders I drank *and* not a great deal of shut eye, a shower might clear my head.

I'm undressing in the bathroom when I hear a key turn in the lock of the front door. It's Iain – I must get that key off him. He's talking on his phone as he walks in. I sit on the edge of the bath, glad I haven't turned the shower on yet and hoping he won't realise I'm in the house, since I left my car at the restaurant last night. If I see him, I'm likely to lamp him, after what I've just seen on Facebook.

"Yeah, I'm here now."

I hold my breath. I think he's sat at the bottom of the stairs. I can hear him clearly anyway. That's one place in the house I certainly can't sit as I can still picture *you*, dead, laid out across the hallway.

"Who knows?" Iain continues. "It's all bloody rubbish. I'm not getting involved in it. But if I find out it's Jamie, he'll be in for it."

Arsehole! He thinks it's me doing the tweets. I always knew he hated me. I'm just going to stay in here and listen. Knowledge is power. *Who's he talking to anyway?* Of course. *Her.*

"I'm not saying that, Stacey."

Pause.

"Look, I'll talk to you about it all later."

Pause.

"Don't you think I've got enough on at the moment?"
Pause.
"Yes of course I do. She comes first, obviously."
Pause.
"I'll bring it back with me."
Pause.
"Yeah, me too."

There's silence for a few moments, then a bit of pacing around and clattering before the front door bangs and I hear a key turning in the lock again. I rise from the edge of the bath with a numb bum and pull my t-shirt back on. I'm boiling from where the sun has been belting in.

I catch my reflection. My weight loss has made me look a bit more like you Mum. I watch my own expression turn from peeved to furious as I hear the engine of your Mini fire up and reverse out of the drive. I get to the window in time to see it disappear around the corner. I run downstairs and out into the street but am too late. Your van is still here. I race back inside – straight to the key hook thingy and find the spare for the Mini has been taken. I take the van key and drop it into my pocket. He's not coming back for that too.

With shaking fingers, I slide my phone from my pocket. *Why didn't I come down and confront him?* Hopefully, he's just borrowed your car and is planning to return it. Iain's phone goes straight to voicemail. Obviously, he's driving. A few minutes later my phone rings.

"You rang?"

"Why have you taken my mother's car?"

"Claudia needs it."

I struggle to get my words out. I've never felt so angry. "You've no right taking my mother's car without saying something to me first." If she thinks she's going to be swanning around in your Mini -.

"Look here Jamie. I was about to marry your mother. She was going to change her will, in fact, I thought she already had. You're lucky I'm not contesting it. If we'd have been married *everything* would have automatically come to me. It would have been years before you got *anything*."

"I don't give a toss about all that." I can't believe he's got a beef about what he got. *Money-grabbing waster.* "I want that car back here now!"

"Oh do you now? Well tough. You've got your own car. Claudia needs the Mini more than you do."

"My car's a right shit-heap! I was going to sell the Mini and get something decent."

"Your mum wouldn't want it sold. She would be glad that it's staying in the family and helping Claudia out."

"Claudia's not family. Mum didn't even *like* her."

"That's enough, you nasty piece of work. I know there were sometimes issues between them but they got on ok. You've done well enough out of your mother's death. And Claudia's only using the car until she gets something sorted out."

"You had no bloody business entering *my* house without my permission. Keep out in future."

"It's forty per cent my house lad. So if I want to come in, I will do."

I make a mental note to get the locks changed. *Who does he think he is?* My jaw is clenched so tight, it's making my head hurt.

"You're back with your ex anyway, aren't you? My mother would be distraught at the thought of that slag going anywhere near her hard-earned money."

"I'm not back with anyone! What are you on about? Get your facts straight Jamie."

He's lying. I know he is. "I saw all your happy family photos on Facebook, you lying arsehole. Didn't waste any time, did you? My mum's hardly cold."

"Listen *you.* Go and peddle your filth somewhere else. I'm not interested. I never *did* like you?"

"I know you didn't." I feel almost relieved Mum. At least I hadn't imagined that he didn't want me around. He just wanted you all to himself.

"Look mate, I'm sorry." His voice has suddenly changed. "I don't want this. Your mum would hate it if we fell out."

"My mum's not here anymore. Not that *you* need reminding. Your nasty little family's doing alright out of her."

"It doesn't have to be like this Jamie."

"Yes, it does." I press the end call button and stare at the space where your car was parked. I can't believe spoilt shitty Claudia is about to get her grasping hands on it. I've never felt hatred like this and a strength rises that I have only ever experienced a handful of times. The last time was when Dad was leaving with the TV.

"Bastard!" I shout as I punch a hole in the plaster of the hallway wall before turning my attention to the lounge door which I kick, karate-style, over and over again. "Bastards. Bastards. Bastards." I can't stop. With three swipes of my arm, ornaments and framed photos crash to the floor. All that remains is hurled at walls. I grab the doorstop and launch it at the mirror above the fireplace. The TV is the last thing to get it before I plunge to the floor, sobbing. You'd probably slap me silly if you could see what I've done. I'm sorry Mum. I guess I've got my father in me. I feel like I'm going mad. Then I look up and see Betty framed in the doorway.

"What on earth …?" She walks over and wraps her arms around me and rocks me as though I'm five years old.

"I'm sorry. I'm really sorry." I feel like I'll never stop crying.

"It's alright sweetheart. You let it all out." I cry harder at her kindness. I don't deserve it. *Why did you have to die Mum?*

"Come on. I'll help you get this mess sorted out and then you can tell me what's put you in this state."

CHAPTER THIRTEEN

"He's taken her car." I try to steady my breathing through my pathetic sobbing. "Mum's car."

"Who? Your Dad?"

"Iain. He's enjoying nearly half of what my mum worked so hard for, with his daughter and his ex-wife."

"His ex-wife?"

"Yes, they're back together."

"I don't believe Iain would be back with his ex wife. He loved your mum too much. He'll just be trying to spend time with Claudia. She is his daughter after all."

I've calmed with the appearance of Betty. Wearing her housecoat and her hair a strange shade of blue, she feels like the nearest thing I have to family at the moment. "There's a picture of them all on Facebook. Having a nice family day at the seaside."

"You know I don't hold with all that Facebook rubbish. All gossip and speculation. Life was far better without it."

I look around at what I've done. I hate Iain and Claudia but I hate myself even more. "Mum would kill me for this," I say. Betty hugs me and I weep onto her shoulder.

Chapter Fourteen

I've swept the broken pot and glass into the bin. I've sent Betty home and I'm waiting for Dad to get here. He's the first one I turn to these days when I'm feeling like shit. I'm glad he's coming. It's hard to believe that I felt so good this morning after Meghan had stayed. You're not here anymore so who else can I turn to other than Dad? Within half an hour, he's on the doorstep with Katherine. I thought he'd come on his own. She's like his shadow. I hate her for it.

"Bloody hell son, you've been on a mission," he says as he looks firstly at the bare shelves and then at the TV.

"You're going to need some filler." Katherine smooths her hand over the gash in the hallway wall. "What happened?"

Dad's face clouds over as I reveal my account of things. "You're right about the car. Iain's got a bloody cheek, taking it for his daughter. I never did understand what your mother saw in him. She should have stayed with me."

It's Katherine's face that darkens now. She glares at Dad but her silent fury seems lost on him. "I read the tweet," she says, her voice stilted. "And *I'm* following her now."

"Anna's dead." Dad's voice is monotone. *"How can you be following her?"*

"I know she's dead." Katherine walks into the lounge. "But something is clearly going on? What I want to know is what does the *two lives*

CHAPTER FOURTEEN

reference mean? Could she have been pregnant?"

"Don't be ridiculous." I say. "She was far too old to be pregnant."

"What was she, forty, forty-one?" Katherine frowns. "That's not *too old.*"

"Well she wasn't. Pregnant I mean. She'd have told me if she was." I've had enough of all this. I just want life to be normal again. "When she says *two lives,* she means *mine* as well as hers."

"You were her world Jamie." Dad's inspecting the door which I've kicked off its hinges. "And it's *my* job to watch out for you now." This is the thing with Dad. I never know whether he's going to ignore me or be all over me. He's confusing. At least *you* were consistent – well mostly. Things could be a bit tricky when Iain was about. It would probably have been a lot easier if you and Dad could have just stayed together.

I've not given Dad any money yet – it's all still going through. I have to believe it's *me* he wants to spend time with and not what I can help him with. I hope he can keep *watching out for me* 'after' the money and isn't just being nice to me until he gets what he wants.

"We used to be the *three musketeers.*" Dad steps back from the door and looks at me. "We were really happy once, me and your mum. I'm not letting that leech take half of what she worked for, to feather his own nest."

"Neither am I Dad. I'm watching him. Don't you worry."

"What is it they say? *Keep your friends close and your enemies closer.*" Katherine has a handful of blocks of plaster from the hallway. I don't think she's heard what Dad's just said about you once being happy together. I think she'd be having a meltdown if she had. Either that or she's ignoring it.

"These tweets though." Dad picks my mobile up from the floor and passes it to me. "They need to stop. They're going to cause trouble. Have Twitter got back to you yet?"

I press the Twitter icon and click through to your account again. There's been 'no recent activity' since Stacey's retweet of your tweet. God, I'm referring to it as *your* tweet. *What's going on?* Dad's right. You're dead. Some crank is doing this. And I won't rest until I get to the root of it.

"I've got a new message." I notice the icon in the corner of my screen and swiftly open it. I can hardly believe my eyes. "Twitter say they've investigated the activity on the account and there's nothing to suggest anything that requires further action. They've closed the complaint and declare the issue to be resolved."

Dad rushes to my side. "Resolved! That's crap. You told them she's dead, haven't you?"

"Maybe someone is logging in with her details," suggests Katherine.

"Nah. Mum kept everything really secure. She was paranoid about anything to do with technology." You were always checking things. *Dotting the 'I's' and crossing the 'T's'* you called it. I couldn't even forge your signature when I needed to get out of PE. "The thing that worries me," I say, hardly believing what's about to come out of my mouth, "is the tweets are kind of like how she would talk. It's all starting to scare me. There's been once or twice that I feel like I've sensed her here too. Things have moved or been turned on or I've just like *felt* her here. I sound daft, don't I?" I stare at my feet.

"It's bound to be getting to you." Dad rests his hand on my shoulder. "You've had a traumatic time of it lad. Come on, we'll get you out of here for a bit. Let's all go for a pint."

Dad's answer to everything, like you always said. But this time, I think he's right.

The Royal Oak is dead, save for a couple of the regulars propping the bar up. Dad used to bring me here after school, much to your disgust. I remember you eventually deciding to pay for me to go into 'after school club,' even though Dad wasn't working. The place hasn't changed one bit. It could be a Wednesday afternoon either now or fifteen years ago. The blokes at the bar are probably the same. Apart from their livers will be pickled by now.

"One of you will have to get them in – I came out without my wallet." Dad looks first at Katherine and then they both turn to me.

Yeah right, I think to myself. "Mum's money hasn't come through yet, you know. I've only got what's left of my wage."

"Surely you could take some money out of her business if you need to." Katherine's words annoy me. She's got five properties and a good business herself. She isn't short of money. But as you would say Mum, she's as tight as a duck's arse. She pays all their bills but gives Dad peanuts when he's skint. Which is most of the time. She slides a card from her purse and rolls her eyes. "What are you both having?"

"So when's the money coming?" Dad sets his pint down next to mine, his eager eyes boring into me, as Katherine returns from the bar.

"How should I know? I've not quite finished the life insurance form."

"What?" Dad wipes beer froth from his upper lip. "That should've been a priority."

"I've had other stuff on my mind."

"Like what?"

"It'll take at least six months for probate to go through." Katherine puts her wine glass on the table. "So you're both going to have to be patient."

"What's probate?"

"The actual administration of the will."

"Oh."

"I could really do with getting that van sorted Jamie. Get that form posted off please."

"Will do." It's depressing being in the pub on a Wednesday afternoon. I want to get out of here, yet I don't want to go home to our empty house. "Can I come to yours Dad? I don't want to be on my own tonight?" The thought of looking at the damage I have caused depresses me beyond measure.

"Course. Stop for a few days if you need. That's alright, isn't it love?"

Katherine screws her face up. "A few days! Jamie's not far away. We can see him every day – it's not as though he's a kid anymore. My parents are coming over tonight anyhow so we haven't got the room. Sorry."

"You're kidding. Why didn't you tell me?" Dad laughs but it's a tinny, almost fake laugh. "It might be *me* moving in with *you* Jamie."

"I'm not saying Jamie can't come. I'm just saying not tonight. It's-"

"It's OK, don't worry." She's *never* wanted me around.

"How about Friday night?" Her voice exudes a faint brightness. "At least then I've got some notice."

"*Notice?* What for? You don't need notice. Jamie's my son."

"No worries." I can't look at her. I've taken the hint. I don't know what to feel really. Pleased that Dad seemed to want me to stay or concerned that his fists are clenched under the table. Because of her and not me, presumably.

"Your round son," he says after a few moment's silence.

I look at Katherine but she remains where she is. Any bit of warmth I was starting to feel towards her has melted away again. "I'll pay, you go." I relish this momentary power as she accepts the note I slide towards her and heads to the bar again.

"Sorry son. It's difficult for all of us at the moment."

"You've started calling me *son* again." It feels good. You called me it all the time, didn't you Mum?

"You *are* my son." He ruffles my hair. "No matter how tall and lanky you get. Gosh, I remember when I could swing you above my head."

"Mum used to hate that."

"She thought I'd drop you. She always was a bit overprotective."

CHAPTER FOURTEEN

"Do you remember that holiday? I'd have been about ten. Water rafting and all that?"

"Oh yes. And jumping from that sea wall. If there was a risky activity to be done, we did it. I thought your mother might combust!" We both laugh. It feels good, for a moment, anyway.

"What's so funny?" Katherine approaches the table balancing three glasses.

"Just doing a spot of reminiscing."

"About your ex-wife?" She bangs the glasses in front of us. "Why don't I just go home and leave you to it?"

"Don't be like that love. I'm allowed to talk to my son about his mother. We *did* have some good times in the past, despite everything."

"So why did you split up then?" She takes a large swig of wine.

Your 'Toxic Marriage' painting suddenly appears in my mind. Dismally showing the darkness of marriage. "When did she do that sad relationship painting Dad?"

"Just before we split up. It was the final nail in the coffin really. She wouldn't listen."

"What painting?"

I open Facebook, tap into your profile and show Katherine your 'banner' page.

"Bloody hell." She nudges Dad. "That doesn't put your relationship in a good light, does it Phil?"

"I'm surprised you've not seen it before." I stretch my arm out to retrieve my phone but she's scrolling down your photos, a pinched look of hatred chiselling at her features. "Weren't you friends with her on Facebook?"

"Hardly," Katherine laughs, coldly. "The former-wife of my husband. Why would I befriend her on Facebook?"

"Not short of a run in or two, were you?" Dad takes a gulp of his pint.

"Neither were you." She smiles at him and I want to slap her.

The silence of the journey home is broken by the text message beep of my phone. It's Meghan. She really is my oasis in an otherwise very dark world. *Hi handsome, hope you've had a good day.* Hardly, I think to myself. *Thanks for an awesome time last night. Looking forward to next time. Perhaps we could make a weekend of it? M xx*

"Who is she then?" Katherine turns around in the passenger seat and nudges my knee.

"What do you mean? Who?"

"There's only a woman who could put an expression like that on your face. It's good to see."

I smile despite my former anger. I can't be pissed off anymore. If this is 'love,' then bring it on. Katherine seems grateful to change the subject from *you* Mum.

"Is this the Meghan bird you mentioned last week?" Dad glances up in his mirror.

"Yep. It seems to be going well. She seems like high maintenance though. Reckon she's going to cost me a few quid."

"Well don't let her take you for a mug. It always feels good to start with." He grins, the corners of his eyes crinkling.

"Do you remember when we first got together love?" Katherine touches his hand on the gearstick.

Dodgy ground. I bet you remember Mum, especially as you and Dad were still together.

Katherine sharply withdraws her hand when Dad doesn't acknowledge her question immediately. "I bet you can remember when you first got with *Anna* though." She practically spits your name out.

"Look love. I'm sorry. I know I'm a bit preoccupied, I'm waiting on this money stuff and yeah, if I'm honest, Anna's death has knocked me for six." He glances sideways at Katherine. "We had a kid together, for God's sake." He looks again at me in the mirror. His expression is hard to read. She must do his head in.

"Don't I know it?"

I'm not sure what she means by that so I let it go.

"Maybe I'm sick of hearing about *Saint Anna,*" she continues. "All your memories, how it's affecting you – you're supposed to be married to *me* now."

"Give it a rest Katherine." Dad's voice has that awful edge to it. "Have some respect. If not for me then for Jamie."

She doesn't answer and I'm grateful. I'll be glad to get out of the car. She's always been jealous of you Mum and I can't believe she still is, even though you're dead. She needs to get a grip.

"I want a text off you later," Dad says after a few moment's quiet.

"Why?"

"I want to know that you've posted that letter."

"What letter?"

"The life insurance form. Ring me if there's any bits you're not sure of."

"Here." Katherine passes me a little red card with one stamp stuck on it. "No excuse now."

"Thanks love." Dad puts his hand on her knee. From where I'm sat behind her, I notice the sides of her face relax into a smile.

"So can I come on Friday then?" They might not be *family of the year* but I need a change of scene. Meghan still lives at home so I can't go there. When some money comes through, I'll take her away. I'll –

"Yes. So long as you've posted that letter. You need to give the mortgage company a ring as well."

"And say what?"

"I tell you what. Fish out all the details and get over to mine for about three on Friday. I'll help you with it. That alright love?"

"Don't mind me," Katherine sniffs. "I'll still be at work anyway."

Even though I'm slightly cheered by Meghan's text, I still feel desolate when I walk towards our front door. I don't want to face all the mess I made earlier and I don't want to be in the empty house.

I linger on the doorstep, mentally composing my reply to Meghan. I won't send it for another hour or so. I don't want to seem too forward. You'd probably tell me off for playing games. I know it sounds weird but she reminds me of you in a way. You're about the same height and have the same dark hair.

I ignore the lounge and stride straight into the kitchen to make a brew. I jump as I see one of your paintings (the one of the Knaresborough viaduct where we always used to canoe) on the floor. There's washing powder all over the place and your cafetière is out. I never touch it – I only drink instant. I notice a pair of your flip-flops by the door and the fridge is ajar. I stand, fixed to the spot and realise I'm shaking.

Obviously, there will be an explanation. Probably Dad or Katherine from earlier today. *But they didn't go into the kitchen.* What's going on Mum? You always said, once you're dead, you're dead and your soul settles somewhere else. It's more likely Iain has been back.

I've already had two drinks but feel like I need another one. Especially whilst I sort this bloody paperwork out. I've definitely got Dad in me, needing a drink, I mean. I'll finish sorting the life insurance and post it. The rest of the stuff, the bills and all that, can wait. I know I should do it all, but I can't face it right now.

"You in there mate?"

I jump, then I'm glad to see Jake peering around the door clutching a six-pack of beers and an X-Box game.

"Do you feel like a bit of company? I've not seen you much since – "

"I know. Sorry bro. I haven't been much company."

"Hey, it's alright. You must be in bits. Can't imagine it myself."

I notice him glance around the kitchen. "What's been going on in here then? It looks like a bomb's dropped."

"I dunno. I didn't leave it like this. Before I went out, I mean."

"Really?" He peels two cans from the six-pack and hands one to me. "Has someone been in?"

He's looking at the dents I've made in the walls. "Doubt it."

"Reckon it's your mum, letting you know she's still watching you."

"I don't believe in all that shit. Do you?"

"Not sure. I'll come and stop with you one night. I'll tell you then." He grins at me but something in my expression must make his grin fade.

"You OK mate? I'm sorry. I didn't mean to joke about it."

"I guess so. It's just that stuff's been done that I didn't do. In here, I mean. I had a bit of a moment earlier but not this bad."

Jake takes the game out of the box and switches on my X-box. "I heard you shouting. That's kind of one of the reasons why I'm here. Your telly still works, doesn't it?" He rubs his hand over its dented edge.

"Yeah, I've checked it. Anyway, I'm alright. It's just that wanker who my mother was seeing. He's taken her car. I got pissed off."

"I can tell things aren't going well there." Jake says as he places the game disc in the machine. "I think the whole street must have heard you and Claudia having words the other day."

"I can't stand her."

"You don't say. She's bang tidy though. I wouldn't say no."

"Whatever. What are we playing anyhow?"

"FIFA?" He chucks me a control pad.

"Nice one."

And just for a couple of hours, Jake's company and a bit of FIFA makes me feel *slightly* normal. I push you, the tweets and all the rest of the crap to the corners of my mind and vow, once again, to get my sorry self back together.

Chapter Fifteen

The day starts like any other. Normal. Well as normal as anything has been since you died. I wake up far too early as I'm still not sleeping properly. The daily reminder that you're dead hits me with its usual impact. There's always a split second when I first wake up before it whacks me around the head or punches me in the stomach. I shower. Brush my teeth. Get dressed. Eat breakfast in the kitchen.

A couple of people say 'good morning' to me as I walk to post the life insurance documents. *Is it?* They don't know you've just died. The only thing that is *good* in my life is Meghan. I suppose I've got a couple of other decent things in my life. I'm not going to worry about money for a long time, if ever, and me and Dad have got more of a relationship now. I know I used to make out like I wasn't bothered about Dad when we talked Mum, but I can't pretend that I haven't craved more of his attention for years, well my whole life really. I'll do anything to keep him on side, even if it is going to cost me a bob or two.

When I get back home, I remember his instructions about the mortgage settlement and set about trying to find the paperwork. Reading between the lines, it seems this will be a piece of cake. Fill in the form and the mortgage gets paid off. I own sixty per cent of the house, Iain owns forty per cent. If we can agree about selling, one of us can buy the other out.

CHAPTER FIFTEEN

I'm not sure what I want to do yet Mum. Half of me wants to stay here, where we've been for years, close to our memories, but the other half of me wants to start again and lay the ghosts to rest. Maybe you'll follow me – I don't know. In fact, I do not know what is real and what I'm imagining any more. The things that got moved around last night are still niggling at me, even though it's likely there's a valid explanation. I was on one yesterday. Maybe it was even me who moved things. I sit here, clutching your mug, staring at one of the several dents I managed to put in the wall, wondering what the hell I'm going to do with my life. Then I remember my decision to give the art stuff a serious shot and this lifts me a little.

I head up to your work room and stare at one of the oil paintings you started before you died. It's a scene from Northumberland – somewhere you used to take me when I was a kid. You've kind of sketched the outline; the castle and the contours but you've only just started filling in the colour. I daren't touch it; I'll ruin it and I'd be gutted. Carefully, I lift it from the easel and put a blank canvas in its place. I'm going to have a go at a portrait. One of you, Mum. If I get it right, it might end up being worth a fortune. You always said that most artists aren't worth anything until after they are dead. What's the phrase you used? *Posthumous fame,* or something.

I need a photo to work from. I take my phone from my pocket and open Facebook. The comments and tributes have slowed now. People are getting on with their lives. There's an Anna Hardaker shaped hole in the world but no one feels it like I do. I've seen you nearly every day of my life, we lived together for years and knew each other inside out. I would probably have been thinking of getting my own place soon but imagine I'd still have seen a lot of you. Even with Iain around.

I'm aware of the notification banner at the top of my phone screen. I've set my account up to receive Twitter alerts when something happens on your account. I need to be the first to know if there's anything else posted. And there is. *Anna Hardaker has tweeted. Find out what she has to say.* It's a few minutes before I can get myself together enough to look. Then, with a thudding chest, I follow the link.

@artistanna123 *Jealousy can rob everyone of everything. It can tear families apart, like mine – I've paid the price. I should be in the final stages of planning my wedding, instead I'm rotting in hell. It's not fair.* #cuckoo #beforemytime

Just as I'm staring at the tweet, the ringing of my phone makes me jump. It's Uncle Si. At least it's not Iain.

"How's it going Uncle Si?" My voice is wobbly. These tweets are really messing with my mind Mum.

"Have you seen Twitter? Our Liz has just rung. It's the first I've heard of it."

"Yeah. I've just seen the latest one. I've already reported it to Twitter. They say they've investigated and there's nothing untoward."

"*Nothing untoward.* That's madness. She's dead for God's sake. Can you close the account?"

"I've already thought of that. I don't know her password."

"Can't it be reset?"

"It would have to go through to Mum's email to be verified."

"Can you get into that?"

"No. I've tried. You know what she was like. Never trusted anything on computers. She had everything locked up and password protected to the hilt."

"Won't Twitter close it?"

"No. Because it's active. Her password's still being used."

"I can't get my head around it. What's going on Jamie? Our Anna has been dead two months now. Who is doing this?"

"I don't know. But it's really freaking me out."

"The latest one's going on about jealousy. Who was jealous of her?"

"How should I know? Claudia probably. She'd be the main one. But

CHAPTER FIFTEEN

then there's Katherine, Dad's wife. And Stacey, Iain's ex-wife. All three of them have been well jealous of Mum."

"So you're saying maybe one of them are something to do with this."

"Who knows? I've no idea anymore – my head's battered."

"Well, if Twitter can't close the account without the password, we're going to have to get the police to sort it. They'll be able to get it closed down."

I swallow. Bloody police. I guess they'll be able to slap some sort of order on Twitter though. This is serious shit.

"Look, whatever is going on, it needs stopping. Bring your mobile so we can show them, and I'll meet you at Weetwood Station in half an hour."

Anger consumes me again as I leave the house and register the non-existence of your Mini. I jump into my Clio – I am going to sort this over the next week or so – I need a new set of wheels. I will see about taking some money out of the business, like Katherine suggested.

My heart is thumping as I make the turn twenty minutes later into the police station car park. Uncle Si's Golf is already here.

"You alright mate?" He gets out of his car as I pull up beside him, talking to me through my open window.

"Yeah, let's get this over with. I'm not quite sure what we're going to say. I'll let you do the talking."

The waiting room is stuffed. Everyone stares at us as we walk in. People sit on green plastic seats which are bolted to the floor. Apart from the whitewashed walls, all is green. And the stench of BO is threatening to snatch my breath away.

"Can I help you sir?" The desk sergeant, if that's what he's called, is looking at Uncle Si with a bored expression.

"We're here to, erm, ask for some help with a situation we've got." Uncle Si leans forward. "Can we speak privately somewhere?"

I glance around at the expectant waiting room, who have all evidently been sat where they are for a while and are waiting to hear something juicy.

"You'll have to wait until a room becomes free," the sergeant says, his voice passive. He asks for Uncle Si's name then calls "next."

There's nowhere to sit so I lean against the wall. Uncle Si gets the last available seat. I have another look on Twitter in case there's anything else to tell them. Every time I open it, it's unbearable looking at that thumbnail photograph of you.

Stacey, the absolute fruitcake, has again liked the latest tweet, but has not retweeted it this time. Maybe the 'jealousy' accusation has hit home. Someone else **@asyeasel** has put a series of **??????** in the comments.

I click onto my messages and the latest one from Meghan perks me up. *Hey sexy. What are you up to tonight? My mum's away* ... My already anxious pulse suddenly doubles in speed. *Blimey* – I'll end up having a heart attack if I'm not careful.

I send her a smiley face back then *What have you got in mind?*

Quick as a flash, she sends me a wink and *8pm*.

"A girl, I take it?" Uncle Si looks at me from where he's sat.

"Erm, yeah, Meghan. She's about the only decent thing I've got going on at the moment. It takes my mind off -"

"I know. I'm glad. And your mum would be too. You deserve a bit of happiness lad."

The momentary smile fades from my face as I remember why we're here. This is my life now. Every time I'm happy for a moment, thoughts of you snatch it away.

"Simon Robertson?" The voice of the desk sergeant cuts into my thoughts. "If you'd both like to come this way please." We squeeze past his pot belly and wet armpits into a tiny, airless room. He gestures for us to sit and looks glad of a seat himself as he positions himself opposite us. "So how can I help you?" This room's worse than the waiting room.

CHAPTER FIFTEEN

It's even greener. *Everywhere.* "I'm Sergeant Pete Reynolds by the way."

"Simon Robertson." He shakes the sergeant's hand like they're doing business or something. "This is my nephew, Jamie Hardaker. We're here about my sister, Jamie's mum. Show him the tweets Jamie." He nods towards my mobile, placed before me on the table, still lit up from the last text I sent to Meghan. "What we're about to show you are four tweets from my sister's Twitter account from over the last couple of weeks."

"Your sister's account?" The sergeant takes my phone as I slide it towards him and he begins scrolling.

"Yes. Anna Hardaker. She's, erm, she was Jamie's mother. She died two months ago -."

"But these tweets are recent. This one's been posted today." He points at the screen as he holds it aloft.

"I know. That's why we're here. We need it investigating." Uncle Si squeezes my arm.

Sergeant Reynolds stares at the screen then resumes his scrolling for a few moments. "So if your sister's dead, where are these messages coming from?"

"That's what we don't know." Uncle Si clasps his hands together on the table. "If you ask me, they're layered with something – they seem to have a double meaning. We have to find out who's behind them, and obviously why they're posting them."

"Wait a minute." Sergeant Reynolds places the phone on the table, his brow furrowing. "Are we talking ghosts here?"

"No of course not," I say quickly. *God's sake. The whole thing must sound off its head.*

"Have you reported this to Twitter? Surely it's down to *them* to close the account if your mother, and sister, has passed away." He looks at each of us in turn as he says *mother* and *sister*.

"They won't. We've tried that. You know how hard it is to speak to a real human being on these sites. And one who speaks English for that matter. They say they've carried out an investigation and found *'no untoward activity,'* whatever that means." I asked Uncle Si to do the talking but I seem to be doing much of it myself. "We don't know my mum's password to do anything ourselves. They won't do anything whilst the account is still active and being logged into."

"We were hoping that by coming to you," Uncle Si adds, "there might be something in the law whereby the police or the courts can impose something on Twitter to force closure of my sister's account." He leans forward. "The thing with these social media companies is it's all so impersonal and they don't treat things on an individual basis. It's all a ticking boxes thing."

"I just want it to stop," I say.

"Hmmm." Reynolds or whatever-his-name-is stretches his arms above his head and cracks his knuckles. The sound makes me want to hurl. "But you've absolutely no idea where these posts might be coming from? Have you asked around? Your family and friends? It does seem, on the face of it, to be some kind of hoax."

"Maybe. We don't know what to do though. The tweets just keep on coming." Uncle Si puts his hand on my arm. "That's why we've come here."

"I'm not sure it's a police matter." He shakes his head and looks at us, apology written across his face.

I jump to my feet. "Come on. I said this would be a waste of time. I'm out of here."

"No, you were right to come with your concerns." The sergeant stands up opposite me. "I just haven't heard anything like this before and I'm not sure what we can do about it. It doesn't appear like an actual *crime* is being committed."

"Impersonating a dead person?" Uncle Si remains seated. "Is that not a crime? Surely it's a fraud or deception? I can't believe you're

CHAPTER FIFTEEN

unable to deal with it. Or don't want to perhaps?" Uncle Si's face is pinched and white with fury. It's rare to see.

"It all depends." He writes something in his notebook but snaps it shut before I can decipher what he's written, upside down. "Look. I'll get some advice on this. If I turn anything up that might help you, I'll be in touch."

Uncle Si pulls out his wallet and then a business card, which he slides across the table. "That's my number, and thanks. I appreciate this. I'm sorry if I seem a bit stressed."

"I understand. If we *can* help, we will."

Uncle Si gets to his feet, his voice more composed. "I'm sure you can appreciate how hard things are for us right now."

I step towards the door. "I just want my mother to rest in peace," I say, hoping to add weight to our 'cause.'

"Her memory is being sullied by this rubbish that's being bandied about on the internet." Uncle Si shakes his hand again. "Please do what you can to help us get to the bottom of it."

"Leave it with me." The sergeant holds the door open. I pass by him, making brief eye contact and giving him a parting nod. I feel like an idiot. All these people in the waiting room will be reporting burglaries, car thefts and fights and what are we doing? Reporting tweets from a dead person. We must sound barmy.

"I'll let you know if I hear anything." Uncle Si slaps my shoulder as we exchange the gloom of the police station for the afternoon sunshine. "Oh, by the way, did you get your copy of the will?"

"Yep," I say, wondering what's coming next. Will he agree with what you've left him? With what you left for Iain?

"I have to say; I was a bit surprised by it all. I know Auntie Liz and I have our own lives, money and all that, but we all grew up together. And we were close. I can't understand it. She and Iain weren't even married. He does seem to have done pretty well out of it."

"I know." It feels good to have Uncle Si on side. "He came and took Mum's car the other day."

"He what?"

"He said it was for Claudia. Hers has had it, so he says."

"Claudia didn't even like your mother. Anna was always in bits about it. What would she want with her car? Nah, this isn't on!"

"It looks the part, doesn't it? And it's worth a few quid."

"But she can't just *take* it."

"*She* hasn't. It was Iain. Mum left forty per cent of nearly everything to him." I look at Uncle Si who is shaking his head. "You ought to look at his ex-wife's Facebook page as well."

"His ex-wife's page. Why?"

"Iain's plastered all over it. They've been having lots of *quality* family time – going to the seaside and stuff after Mum has died. It's pissing me right off."

"Bloody hell – I'm not surprised. They're not back together, are they?"

"I don't know. He says not but I don't think I believe him."

"Well if I find out they are." Uncle Si looks as though he's clenching his jaw. He'll stick up for you Mum – he always has. For the first time in a while, I don't feel quite so alone. I probably need to turn to him a bit more. I reckon he gives more of a shit than Dad ever will.

"Look Jamie, keep in touch. If and when I hear back from the police, like I say, I'll let you know, and in the meantime, make sure you keep a record of *everything*, especially anything on the internet. Conversations with Iain and his *clan* – that sort of thing."

Chapter Sixteen

As I get into my car, I sit for a moment. I can't make sense of any of it. I don't trust Iain. For all his smoothness, there's a nasty piece of work lurking in there too. Maybe I should have told Uncle Si about the massive row I heard you having with him not long before you died. He's not the saint he makes himself out to be.

I'd been alerted to something going on when I heard you crying. You'd been out together and I'm not sure you realised that I was upstairs when you came in.

"She won't be happy till she's split us up."

"Leave it Anna. I'm sick of you always going on about it."

"You're a coward Iain."

"She's my daughter."

"Don't I know it?"

"I have to put up with *your* son though!"

"He doesn't speak to you like you're something he's trodden in."

"No, but I have to sit back and listen to him talking to you like that though."

"I'm not getting into this with you."

"But it's acceptable for you to slag my daughter off."

"I'm sick of her spouting off about me. To anyone who'll listen. I've got to be honest with you Iain. I've had enough of her. And of you too.

We're supposed to be getting married. I'm marrying you not *her*. And certainly not your *ex-wife*."

"At least they're not narcissists like fucking Jamie. It's all about him, him, him. When's he going to pay me that money back he owes me? And when's he going to be a big boy and go and get his own place?"

I sat, seething. Part of me wanted to go down and lamp him, but the other bit of me decided to stay put at the top of the stairs and find out what he really thought of me.

"Iain. We were fine before you came along. You don't get to barge into *my* home and start throwing your weight around. I had enough of that with Phil."

"Phil." Iain shouted. "I wondered when we'd get around to him. *Saint Phil.* On Jamie's tallest pedestal. And you're always on about him too. Bet you wish you were still shagging him."

"Iain! What the hell's got into you?"

"Look I'm sorry. I just can't cope with all the shit. I'm sick of rowing about bloody kids. I just want us to share our lives, our money, everything."

"What's money got to do with anything?"

"Look, I don't know. We'll talk about it tomorrow. I want everything joining together. If we're marrying."

"*If* we're marrying. What do you mean *if?*"

I heard glasses been taken from the cupboard and the clanging of bottle tops being removed.

"Anna. I'll go back to what we were originally discussing. Before the subject of either of our kids came up. If we're marrying, we do it properly. That means insurance, wills, pensions, property *everything*."

"I need to think about this. To get some advice."

"Don't you trust me?"

"I'm not sure I trust anyone. And after what you've said to me this evening, I think you should go home."

CHAPTER SIXTEEN

"I'm over the limit. Leave it till the morning. For God's sake."

"I'll call you a taxi." I shout as I descend the stairs. The comment he made about you shagging Dad wouldn't leave me so I decided to get involved.

"Who asked *you* to stick your beak in? Do one Jamie." Iain slammed his bottle down on the kitchen counter.

You started unloading the dishwasher. "I didn't realise you were in Jamie." You pretended to be busy doing something Mum, hiding your face behind your hair like you always did when you were crying.

"Why are you shouting at my mother?"

"We're a couple Jamie. Couples have arguments. Usually privately. It's none of your business."

"You make it my business when I can hear you." I looked at him squarely in the eye, prepared for the same shit Dad would have given me if I had ever interfered.

"You shouldn't be here. Aren't you old enough to have your own place by now?"

"I'll get my own place when I'm good and ready. Not when you force me out."

"We'll see."

The next morning, he was all meek and mild with me, apologising for being drunk and blaming pre-wedding nerves. I accepted his apology but it made me realise that he was as much a dick as his daughter. And it made me more wary.

If you can hear me Mum, I say, as I slip my shitty Clio into second gear, please sort all this lot out. It's all so messy and I can't cope with it.

I'm five minutes early heading up Meghan's drive with a bottle of Prosecco and a bunch of flowers – Asda specials. At least I've remembered to take the price off.

"Oooh, you've brought me roses – that's dead nice of you. No one's ever done that."

It's the first time I've bought flowers for someone too. Apart from you, Mum. I used to get them for you Mum, once a year. I remember every Mother's Day, feeling like a ponce clutching flowers, taking the back-way home. You loved them though. They might as well have been a bunch of diamonds.

"I've cooked for us," Meghan grins. Her hair is pinned up, showing off the shape of her neck which I immediately want to sink my teeth into or something. She's wearing a red dress that I just want to rip off. *And she's mine! Kind of.* At least it feels that way. Better not get too ahead of myself.

"Did I say we've got the house to ourselves?" She kisses me, in full view of all her neighbours.

"You might have mentioned it." I resist the urge to grab her arse. "Come on, let's get inside." We stand in the hallway, snogging for a few minutes. No one has ever made me feel like she does. I battle to control myself.

"Laters baby," she breathes into my ear. "I'm sure you won't want burnt chicken."

"I'm not sure I care." I reluctantly lift my hands from her hips and take in the surroundings of her home. It's like ours Mum. She's also an only child to a now-single mum. There are photos all over the place and a homely feel. Obviously, she's still got her mum. I feel that knife of sadness stabs me again but then I notice pictures of her with a man. "Is that your dad?" I pick one of them up. Meghan's younger, with pigtails and freckles.

"Yeah." She looks over my shoulder.

It's not the greatest thing to have in common but at least we understand each other.

"So does your Mum know you're having me over?" I follow her into the kitchen and watch as she opens the prosecco.

"Yeah. I've told her. She said we're to behave ourselves." She winks at me.

"As I'm sure we will." I grab her from behind, pressing myself against her as she pours fizz into the glasses.

She turns quickly, stepping back to pass me a glass. "Easy tiger, we've not had the first course yet."

"Do you know," I clink my glass into hers. "You keep me going. You really are the tranquillity in my barmy world."

"That's the first time anyone has referred to me as *tranquil*," she laughs. "Erm, thanks. Your world must be *batshit* crazy."

You don't know the half of it, I think. For a moment, I want to tell her all about the tweets but I know how weird it all sounds. And I don't want her feeling sorry for me either. If we keep seeing each other, which I really hope we will, then she'll find out what is going on soon enough. I want to enjoy her company and forget what's happening. Be normal for a change.

I sit at the kitchen table, watching her as she clatters plates about.

"Do you want any help?"

"No, you sit and chill." She drains some veg through a colander. "You can take me out next time."

I'm chuffed that she mentions a next time. Life feels *slightly* better. I keep pinching myself I've got Meghan in it, I'm on Dad's radar, Iain and Claudia are not as much in my face, I've got family and I'm not stuck in a dead-end job. I've got sixty per cent of a house and a business. I've got money on the way, I've got choices. But what I haven't got is you Mum. No matter what blessings I try to count and wherever I look, I can't get away from that.

Chapter Seventeen

It's mid-morning when I get home. Meghan's mum is due back at lunchtime so we agreed I should make myself scarce. It wouldn't do for her to find me still in her daughter's bed. *What a night!* I feel like ten men this morning. Meghan is bloody amazing even if she is a bit too interested in where I might be able to take her and what I might be able to buy her. If it keeps nights like these coming, I don't mind her latching on to half a promise of what I might do for her.

I realise I must have left the back door unlocked and the freezer door wide open last night. No doubt you'd have had a few words to say to me about this Mum. I've also managed to leave the hot tap running in the upstairs bathroom and the TV on in my bedroom. *Eh, that's strange - not like me at all.* I click it off with the remote.

An overwhelming feeling of sadness steals over me as I run back downstairs, taking the steps two at a time. I snatch up my ringing phone from the kitchen table, thankful for distraction from the craziness I've walked into.

"Dad?" I'm glad it's him. "I need to get out of this house. Can I come over *now*, rather than waiting until later?"

"Sorry son. Katherine and I have had words. You're going to have to give me time to talk her round."

"What? *You're joking.* What's up with her now?"

"The usual. A bit of jealousy and stuff."

"Over Mum?" I feel hatred rising in me like a serpent.
"I can't go into it now. Give me a few hours and I'll ring you back."
"A few hours?"
"Might be sooner. Just try and understand, eh?"
"But I can come over later, yeah?"
"Should be OK son."

I press the end call button without saying goodbye. *Same old, same old.* You tried not to slag him off Mum but he has always, *always,* let me down. I think it's all starting to hit me now. Yeah, I've got Meghan in my life but everything else feels screwed. If only time could be rewound by two months. I'd much rather be skint and working in my boring job than be feeling like this. You'd still be here. *Fucking Dad. Fucking Katherine.* I need to find something to occupy myself before I go insane. I feel like punching a wall again. I don't want to be here on my own all night.

I've never known anyone who picks a fight like Dad. He was the same when *you* were married to him. *The amount of times I had to keep out of the way!* Some days, he'd be in a dark mood before he even went out, so we'd expect him back in a far worse one. You and I would look at each other as we heard his key in the door. We'd have been doing something normal like watching TV, but his coming home would change the mood completely. I'd bolt upstairs, anxious to keep out of his way. Sometimes I'd listen from the landing. I remember the row that you said *was the last straw.*

"What the fuck have you been saying about me?" He was shouting at the top of his voice. I could hardly look Jake next door in the eye anymore. God knows what next door, the other side, must have thought of what went on here.

"I've no idea what you're talking about." Though you were obviously trying to keep your voice steady, I could hear the tears in it.

"Your so-called *friend. That fucking Cate.* Totally ignored me, she did. Walked straight past me like I was something she'd stood in."

"Where were you?"

"In the supermarket. Ignorant cow."

"Maybe she didn't see you." You were always trying to pacify him Mum.

"Yes she did. She just can't stand me. Like *all your friends. And family. Cos you keep going around slagging me off.*"

"You're being paranoid Phil. I haven't said anything to anyone."

His voice rose some more. *Stop it Dad!* I thought to myself, sat on the top stair, gazing down into the darkness of the hallway. Through the window at the top of the front door, I could see the house lit up next door to Betty. I bet the family there never rowed like this. I'd lost count of how many times I'd sat here, in this place, listening to the two of you fight. Partly because I wanted to know what was going on and partly to make sure Dad didn't go too far and hit you. He wasn't normally directly violent towards you, as far as I could tell, but he was no stranger to smashing things in the house. Sometimes you'd row about me – he thought you were too soft on me. Those were the rows that pissed me off the most!

"You're a mental bitch," he was still ranting. "And not happy unless you're talking about me, are you? Does it make you feel better about yourself, slagging me off?"

"I'll have a word with Cate," you muttered. I could barely hear you. "I'll check whether she actually saw you. I'm sure she didn't."

"So you're calling me a liar now? Of course she saw me. You wonder why my confidence is so low. Why I drink so much? Probably because my wife is always running me down to boost her own ego!"

"You drink so much because you're an alky." It was your turn to shout Mum. Whilst I was partly glad that you were sticking up for yourself, I knew that it would make Dad even angrier.

"What did you call me?"

CHAPTER SEVENTEEN

"You heard."

"If I drink a lot it's because *you* drive me to it. You ought to look in a mirror before you call me names. At least I'm not mental and frigid. Not a good combination."

"Phil. I don't have to listen to this."

"It's about fucking time you did. Saint fucking Anna and her crappy little business. Who do you think you are?"

"Leave me alone Phil. Go out and calm down."

"Give me some money then. I'm sick of *you* having all the money. I shouldn't have to ask for it like a little boy."

"Perhaps you should think about earning your own."

"I've spent the last five years chasing after you. All the support I've given you! You owe me."

"*Owe you*? What on earth for?"

"I've been the brains behind *everything*. You could never have started a business on your own. You're as thick as pigshit."

You laughed at that. "Whatever you say. Go somewhere else Phil. Please. I've had enough of you."

"I'm going, don't you worry."

"That's right. Go and get some beer down you. Phil's answer to everything."

"I only drink because I'm married to *you*."

"Of course. I sit astride your chest and pour it down your throat."

"Sit astride. That's a laugh. You wouldn't know how to *sit astride* anything. You ought to see a doctor. It can't be normal for a woman your age being so frigid."

"Will you two shut up!" There's only so long I could have sat at the top of the stairs, listening to that shit.

"Jamie." You'd looked shocked Mum. "I thought you'd gone out. Your shoes had gone."

Dad didn't even look at me. He just grabbed his coat from the back of the kitchen chair and stormed out. He banged the door so hard, the house shook.

You and I looked at each other. It was relief mixed with *here we go again.*

"Get a few things together Jamie," you'd said. "I want to be out of here before he comes back."

I didn't argue. I knew the drill. We had a variety of boltholes for when Dad was on one. "Where are we going this time?"

"Cate's, I think. I'll just drop her a text."

Your voice was shaking but he hadn't made you cry. I think you were hardening to him by then. It wasn't long after that when you told him you wanted a divorce.

The other thing you sometimes did to cope with Dad's shite, when it wasn't quite to that scale, would be to head up to your studio, which is what I decide to do now.

I look at the blank canvas I assembled yesterday and recall the bloody tweet that stopped me in my tracks. I'm going to paint your portrait from memory – I'm not touching my phone this time. I need to do this.

I decide to stick with watercolour. You've taught me more about watercolours than oils. As I choose a pencil from the rack to sketch the outline, I get a sudden urge to look into the course you once suggested to me that's offered at Art College. I'll Google it later. I've a long way to go before I'm anywhere near *your* standard but I've got to start somewhere. Somehow, I will make it and in doing so, I will get that grasping waster Iain, along with his family, out of your business, once and for all.

Half an hour later, I'm well chuffed with the outline I've captured. Glancing at the side wall, I notice a photo of me and you, taken a few years ago. OK, you've gotten a little older since, but I can copy the contours and the shading. I feel safe and fairly content in this room – the one in which you spent many hours, stuck into your work. I'm feeling strong and with focus. In the last half hour, I have pointed myself in the direction I must go.

I've nearly finished the picture when I hear my phone ringing downstairs again. It's stopped by the time I reach it. *Dad.* He said he'd ring me when I could go, so I decide just to get my stuff together and go round, without ringing him back. I don't want a night on my own, here – no way. I throw a few things into a bag and within minutes, I'm locking up the house.

"Yoo-hoo," Betty calls as she crosses the street towards me. "How are you getting on? Are you managing to eat enough? I've got a couple more dishes in the freezer for you. I always try and cook a bit extra."

"Thanks. That's good of you. I can't stop. I'm just off to my dad's."

Her smile fades. "I'd better let you go then. Let me know if you need anything."

"Thanks Betty."

My phone rings again whilst I'm driving, then I receive a text alert. I glance at it at the lights. *Sorry mate. Katherine's really on one – can we make it tomorrow?*

I'm gutted. He's let me down again. *Nah! I'm not having it this time!* I tuck my phone into my bag and decide to pretend that I haven't seen the message. Within ten minutes, I'm pulling up outside his house. Through the window, I can see them sitting together on the sofa. Either he's lying about a so-called row or Katherine has calmed down because I'm supposedly not coming. I am uninvited and unwanted. You never made me feel like this Mum. If he thinks he can lie to me, fob me off and then take money off me –

"Jamie!" He swings the door open and steps out into the porch. He's wearing scruffy joggers and needs a shave. "Didn't you get my message?"

"Erm, what message?"

Katherine's behind him. "It's alright. Come in. Take no notice of your dad." She looks unkempt too in gym pants that her midriff is spilling over, wild hair and no make-up. She's forcing a smile. "We've had a few words but we're fine now."

"I've got some beers in the fridge." Dad opens the door wider, inviting my entry. "Come in son."

"What were you arguing about?" I whisper as I follow him along the hallway, into the kitchen. There's dirty dishes and empty packets everywhere and more alcohol than food in the fridge. It's unusual. Katherine is normally clean and tidy.

"Since when is our marriage any of your business Jamie?" *Shit!* I thought Katherine had gone back into their lounge. I didn't realise she was behind me. "We've had a lot of extra stress in the last couple of months."

"My fault, I suppose." I push past her. *Witch*. "So sorry that my mother died."

"Jamie! She didn't mean it like that."

I storm back along the hallway and slam the living room door as hard as their thick living room carpet will allow me to. I throw myself onto the sofa, feeling like a teenager again. Though two walls divide us, I can hear them start to go again at each other in the kitchen and wonder if I should just bugger off and leave them to it. But I decide that if I hang around, hopefully Katherine will piss off somewhere in a rage and let me spend some time with Dad. At first, I try to catch snippets of their crap.

"He's my son."

"I'm absolutely sick of hearing about her."

"Nothing's changed. She's just dead."

"It all wants dealing with."

"You know the situation."

CHAPTER SEVENTEEN

"Saint bloody Anna."

Eventually I crank up the TV to drown them out. I again toy with the idea of just going home or to the pub but instead decide to text Meghan. A little text conversation will cheer me up. *Hey sexy. Thanks again for last night. How's your day been? X*

I sit rock-like for nearly half an hour before Dad and Katherine appear.

"Sorry son." Dad passes me another bottle of beer and takes a large swig of his own. Katherine sits in an armchair next to the window, placing an overflowing glass of wine onto the windowsill next to her and the bottle on the floor. She presses buttons on the remote control, rendering any sort of conversation impossible as the surround sound booms at us from every angle. I try to watch TV but can't concentrate. Instead I stare at the photos, all around the lounge, of her sons at different stages of their lives. I wonder why there's none up of me. It's like only her sons count and Dad's son can't exist. I'm close to mentioning it but will probably get kicked out if I do.

I recline my side of the sofa back and reach for my phone. There's no reply from Meghan yet. She must be in the bath or something. I wish she would reply. It would make me feel better.

"Steady on love," Dad shouts above the theme tune for Coronation Street or whatever similar crap Katherine is engrossed in. "You'll be hammered if you carry on like that." She's refilling her glass, having downed the last one in record time. Dad grins at me and takes a massive swig of his beer.

I'm thinking that I probably would have been better off staying at home and finishing my painting. I could have asked Meghan over again, but I then don't want to seem desperate. Although it would have been good to wake up with her on my birthday tomorrow, especially the first one without you Mum.

You'll know when you meet the one, you used to say to me. *One day you'll fall for someone, leave home and live your own life, which is why I must live mine too.* This was your stock reply whenever I used to moan about Iain butting into our lives.

Perhaps if you'd never met Iain, you'd still be here now. You may not have had to climb up on the banister to paint the ceiling. I don't know why you didn't get someone in. You could afford it. But you always said *why pay someone for something you can do yourself?* As well as that, you said you enjoyed decorating. Dad's words return to me again from your wake, *it wouldn't have happened if she'd still been with me.*

Chapter Eighteen

I keep thinking that Iain must have meant a lot to you, to leave him forty per cent of nearly everything you had. As Uncle Si has mentioned, you weren't even married yet. I'd have most likely been up shit-creek if you'd got as far as your wedding before you died.

"I'm off for a walk." Katherine rises from her chair and whisks her handbag from the coffee table. "I need to clear my head."

"It's a bit late love." Dad glances at the clock on the mantlepiece then towards the window where dusk can be seen descending beyond the net curtain. "Look, I'll come with you."

"Nah you're alright, thanks. You stay with your son." She lingers over a few more sips of wine. It's as though she's playing for time, hoping Dad will insist on coming with her and protect her from the big, bad, wide world beyond these four walls.

He does. "I'm not having you walking around the streets alone at this time of night."

I feel like applauding her as she slides her arms into a cardigan and without even looking at me, strides from the room. She's got her result.

"I won't be long." Dad stands up and starts towards the door. "There's more beer in the fridge."

I'm not sure what I've done that offends her. I glance again at my phone. Still nothing. I wander into the kitchen in my bare feet and help myself to another bottle of beer and a pork pie. I could tidy up –

that might get me into the good books, but stuff it – why should I?

There's hardly any evidence of Dad within this house, apart from a few gadgets. It doesn't have a welcoming feel like ours used to, well, especially before you met Iain. He changed everything and you let him. Apart from the decorating, he got stuck into all the repairs, the garden and thought he could order me around as well. *Well he's going to be my husband,* you would say. *This will be his home too.* Like how could I ever forget?

I settle back onto the sofa, wondering why on earth I bothered coming here to escape a night of loneliness at home. The TV is still booming away but I'm not watching it and there's only so much Facebook you can look at. I'm dying to talk to someone. They're gone ages and have clearly had a fair bit more to drink when they return. Katherine's eyes are red as she glances at me before going upstairs.

Dad comes into the lounge and stands behind where I'm sat. He rests his hand on my shoulder. "I'd better go up too Jamie. I'm sorry about tonight. I'll make it up to you. Bloody women, eh?"

I say nothing. *I can't believe he's going to ignore that I'm here and just go to bed with her!*

"You could at least answer me Jamie. I feel bad enough as it is. I did try and warn you, didn't I? About the mood she's in. I rang to let you know things weren't too good."

"Why? What's going on?"

"Oh, you know. All sorts of stuff. She's probably going through *the change* or something. It'll be fine."

"Whatever. I guess I'll see you in the morning."

"Night son."

He's not even mentioned my birthday tomorrow. Probably forgotten, as usual. He's always gone to bed early. You on the other hand Mum, used to stay up late, painting and stuff. Dad often used to moan about it. He'd accuse you of staying up to text other men. *Don't judge me by*

CHAPTER EIGHTEEN

your own standards is what you would have said to that.

I never felt lonely when you were around – you just did my head in at times, nagging me about my room or the amount of time I spent on my X-Box. What I'd give to feel like that again. I've hardly touched my X-box since you died. I need to get Jake round more. I've got to start getting back to normal.

I sit for a while, waiting for Dad to use the bathroom so I can go up. I listen for the thud of his bedroom door before venturing up to the guest room and stripping down to my boxers. I've not stayed here much and I hope I don't encounter Katherine on the landing through the night. *Embarrassing, or what?*

I open the window as far as it will go which does little to alleviate the heat in the room. Chucking the duvet on the floor, I lie back, pondering over Meghan's non-reply. I hope she hasn't gone off me. I feel anxiety knot in my stomach. She's the only good thing I've got going on. I'm going to have to sort my shit out. I sometimes think I'm sliding into a bit of depression. Hopefully she'll see that it's my birthday through Facebook in the morning and get in touch with me.

I can hear Katherine's tearful voice from across the landing and the low tones of Dad trying to pacify her – at least that's what it sounds like. I can't make out what they're saying but she sounds proper upset. This can't be down to me, or to you Mum. Either he's done something bad or she's just pissed. I listen to this for nearly an hour – I can't tell you how much I feel like shouting *shut the fuck up* but obviously I don't. The whole situation is too fragile – they'd just boot me out. Parents are supposed to love their 'kids' no matter what, but Dad never has.

Someone goes into the bathroom and fills two glasses of water before the bedroom door clicks. There's a few more minutes of conversation before all is quiet. I get up for a piss and fill the plastic bottle from my rucksack with water. It's thirsty work, this not being able to sleep business. I lie here, thinking about what I'm going to do. I'm twenty-five today and must get my life sorted out.

I decide I'm going to join a gym and build myself up – that'll impress Meghan if nothing else. I'm going to start Art College in September and get more involved in the art gallery. No way am I going back to that poxy insurance company, especially after making a show of myself.

I must have dozed off for a bit because heat, bright sunlight and irritating bloody birds wake me again. I stare at the wallpapered ceiling, feeling utterly fed up at my insomnia. There's barely any distant traffic noise so I know it's still early. I will sleep to rescue me for a little bit longer. I should have just got wasted last night.

I grab my phone, mainly to feed the faint hope that Meghan might have texted through the night and to check the time. 5:35. Noooo! I click the Twitter icon which is showing a notification. I've not checked it for over a day. Shit. Shit. Shit. You've tweeted.

Have you heard me? *You've tweeted!* I'm talking like you're still alive. This is seriously messed up. Stacey's re-tweeted, as usual, adding 'eh' and a row of question marks.

@artistanna123 *No one is listening. I should have been having my scan this week. No one cares.* #cuckoo #beforemytime

I jump out of bed and tug on my clothes. *Scan!* Shit. What sort of scan? There might have been something wrong with you, or maybe … There must be someone else who knows about this. *Iain.* He *must* know. I'm going to go and confront him. I creep down the stairs, thankful they don't creak like ours and tiptoe around the kitchen as I make myself a coffee. I've got a fair drive from here and I'm so tired all the time that I don't want to risk falling asleep at the wheel. I sit in the garden for a few moments, sipping from my mug, whilst hearing the silence, broken every so often by the stupid birds. I'm a bit calmer for the moment but am painfully aware that it won't last. I try to breathe more deeply – I want to feel less shit.

CHAPTER EIGHTEEN

I click the front door behind me and embark on the drive that shouldn't take me longer than an hour at this time of day. Despite the clear roads, it seems to take an age to get there and my head is mashed. I take a bend too fast and end up braking on the wrong side of the road. Then I overshoot a junction, having not noticed a *give* way sign. I need to get a grip but I can't think straight. What is this crap Mum? *I should be having my scan this week.* The whole thing is getting more and more weird.

Chapter Nineteen

It's just after seven-thirty when I pull up outside Iain's house, thankful that Claudia's (erm YOUR) car isn't outside. I recognise another car parked here though. It's the same grey Golf as Sarah's. *What would she be doing here?* All the curtains are shut.

The first time we came here, was after that wedding you'd been invited to as Iain's 'plus one.' You'd not been together long. Dad had let me down with something he was supposed to be doing with me. You'd taken pity on me and asked Iain to turn his invitation into a 'plus two.'

It was just the night do we were going to, but you'd spent *all day* getting ready. You'd been to the hairdressers, had your nails done and bought new stuff to wear. Then you'd forced me to shower even when I'd already had one that morning. You even sent me back to my room when jeans and t-shirt weren't good enough. I felt like I was five again, being made to change into a shirt and trousers. I didn't really want to go with you, if the truth be known. I could think of many better ways to spend a Saturday night, but you weren't listening.

I mean, come on Mum, you didn't even know who was getting married and you were making all this fuss. The only person you were going to know at the wedding would be Iain.

So we drove here, to his house and I remember being sat here, in this very spot waiting whilst you went inside for him. You were bloody

CHAPTER NINETEEN

ages. We would be sleeping here, which I wasn't happy about either, but you wanted a drink. I hoped I wasn't going to get shoved onto a sofa.

I got moved into the back seat as soon as Iain surfaced. That pissed me off too. The two of you had only been together five minutes, but already, he seemed more important than me. I watched as we passed through the streets. It seemed like a not too bad area – about as boring as where we lived.

"My ex-wife Stacey is going to be there, I'm afraid. I didn't know she was going."

You went quiet then. *This could be interesting,* I thought to myself.

I was glad you'd made me put on shirt and trousers when we walked in. It was one of those big poncey places with chandeliers and all that. A bride who looked like a Barbie doll was standing beside her new husband. They both shook hands with me as Iain introduced us. It was bloody strange meeting someone for the first time at their wedding. Still, I'd get a few ciders and a good feed. There might even be some fit lasses around.

I turned towards a cackling sound coming from the right-hand side of the bar. The owner of the laugh needed no introduction. There, wearing a beige dress that looked like sausage meat stuffed inside its own skin was the person that must be Stacey, an older version of Claudia but with short hair and smaller tits. Claudia stood beside her and neither of them were taking their eyes off us. Stacey nudged another lady who stood near them and they all cackled again like a coven of witches.

It took an age to get served. The queue for the bar was three deep all the way across. Every time I looked, Stacey was staring at us. I couldn't understand why Claudia didn't come over to say hello. To her dad, at least. I smiled but she didn't smile back. You busied yourself, pretending to rummage around in your bag.

"Wine. Large," you said when Iain finally made it to the bar. I resisted the urge to order two ciders at once.

Finally, we 'guests' were herded into a huge room with a buffet and a DJ. I felt more comfortable now we were able to put some distance between us and that stupid woman who wouldn't stop giving me and you the dead eye. Iain introduced us to more people. They all talked funny and I remember thinking I'd rather be *anywhere else* than here. The fittest lass in the room was Claudia. And the music was dire.

She didn't come over once, throughout the whole evening. *Ignorant cow*, I had thought. After all, we'd been to laser quest and dinner, and we were all Facebook friends. She didn't even speak to Iain. You said it was probably out of loyalty to her mother or something. At one point, you went off to the loo and I watched as Stacey followed you. I wondered if she was waiting to get you on your own to have a go at you.

You told me she'd made sure she'd got behind you in the loo queue and *'bumped'* into you a couple of times but didn't actually talk to you. You thought she was trying to intimidate you in some way but you could handle her. *You were used to bullies.*

It wasn't a late night but it was bloody long enough. You didn't even dance. In fact by eleven o clock you looked fed up. Iain was busy talking to people he knew. Not many people talked to us – they were all probably wondering who we were! Finally, you asked him for his house keys so we could get a taxi. He came with us though. I think it would have given Stacey and Claudia something to really cackle about if he hadn't.

Iain's street is quiet this morning. He must be sleeping peacefully, unlike me these days. You're dead Mum. *How can he sleep?*

I sit in the car a moment longer, wondering what he'll say when he

CHAPTER NINETEEN

sees me. He's going to get a rude awakening. I push the gate open into his back yard which is now filled with pots of flowers and hanging baskets. He never bothered with all this crap before. He was planning to move in with you Mum, and sit in *your* garden with *your* hanging baskets. Claudia's obviously been busy – or Stacey. I try the back door. Locked. I hammer on it. It's a few minutes before I see a shadow moving behind the frosted glass.

"Alright. Alright. Just let me find the key." Finally he flings the door open. "Jamie! I thought it was the bloody police. What the hell are *you* doing here at this time of day? It's only seven o'clock!"

"When Mum died, you said I'd *always* be welcome." I push past him and flick his kettle on.

"Make yourself at home Jamie, *why don't you.*" He closes the kitchen door behind him, his voice dripping with sarcasm.

"Well you always have in *my* house."

"What do you want?"

I turn and face him. His hair's on end, his face is sleep-lined and he's wearing baggy boxers. *What did you ever see in him Mum?* You could have done far better. "Have you been on Twitter?"

"Not for a day or so. Why?" His eyes are boring into me, then reality must dawn. "Oh no, not again. Where's my phone?"

I point to the microwave - his phone is on top of it. I watch him frown as he reads the tweet.

"Even your ex, if *ex* is the right word now, is putting her oar in." I watch as he places his phone on the kitchen counter.

"She *is* my ex, Jamie, but, yeah, I'll have a word with her about that – these tweets have got nothing to do with her."

"So, what's this about a scan?" I'm facing him. Our eyes lock. "Was mum ill?"

"It doesn't matter now."

"It does to me." I don't move. "Is someone here Iain? You seem a bit on edge."

"No, not at all. Just me."

"So. My mum?"

"Ok. Ok. She'd have been three months gone when she -"

"She was pregnant? And you knew?"

"Of course I knew. We were going to get married."

"So why didn't you tell me?"

"There didn't seem to be any point. Not after-"

"Did you want it?"

"Jamie. I've had my time as a father. I didn't want any more. But things happen. We would have dealt with it."

"It?"

"He? She? Whatever. We'll never know."

"What do you mean *dealt* with it? Would you have made her *get rid* or something?"

"Of course not. What do you take me for?"

"So, you were happy about it then?"

"No, not at all. But we'd have sorted it, like I said."

"How come no one else knew?"

"It was too early. Things can go wrong. Your mum was in her forties."

"I know how old my bloody mother was!"

Iain's giving nothing away. I get a sense that there's more to this.

"Does Claudia know? Did she know?"

"No."

"Well, if she didn't *then*, she will *now*. She's following my mother on Twitter, which is almost funny when you think of how they got along with one another."

"I can't think of a thing that's *almost funny*." Iain steps across the kitchen and fills two mugs with coffee. "Here." He passes me one.

"Thanks. She'd have gone apeshit. Claudia, I mean. She couldn't bear sharing *you* with my mum, let alone a wailing brat."

CHAPTER NINETEEN

"Don't speak about her like that please. Anyway, it's hardly relevant now, is it?"

Princess Claudia, you used to call her, when she was getting on your nerves Mum. It's true. Because she's 'pretty,' everyone panders to her and when she doesn't get her own way or isn't the centre of the world, she sulks and creates. You often said that her dislike towards you was nothing personal. You just took her dad's attention away from her. She'd have never shared him with a new baby. The whole thing is off its head. *I can't believe you went and got pregnant.*

This is the calmest, Iain and I have been for a while. I expected him to kick off with me turning up at this time of day. He's twitchy, if anything. Sometimes I feel almost sorry for him.

"So, did the doctors and all that know she was pregnant when she died? They must have done tests and stuff."

"What are you two on about?" The back door bangs into the cupboard.

It's so sudden that I slop my coffee. Claudia marches in.

"You're not talking about Anna, are you? *Pregnant?*"

"Yes," Iain's voice is calm. I'd have thought he'd be more rattled having to explain this to Claudia. "She was three months pregnant. We hadn't told anyone."

"*Why not?* Don't you think I had a right to know?"

"We were going to?"

"Why haven't you told me since?"

"There was no point causing more grief. Everyone has had enough. But something has gone onto Twitter, so you'd have found out about it anyway."

Claudia's quiet for a few moments. Maybe she's thinking of something consoling to say to her dad. Then she comes out with, "Just as well she died if you ask me."

I stare at her. "What did you say?" I turn to her and our faces are nearly touching in the tiny kitchen. I smell toothpaste on her breath. "Go on. What did you fucking say, you evil little-?"

"Jamie." Iain's voice has a warning edge. "Leave it."

"That's your so-called fiancée she's talking about. Are you going to allow her to get away with it?" I can't believe it Mum. I know she was jealous of you but to hear her like this, after you've died, turns my stomach. I realise my fists are clenched at my sides. If she was a bloke, I'd punch her lights out.

"I'll speak to her when you've gone, don't worry."

"And that's it. It's no wonder she's like she is. She's spent her whole life getting away with stuff. You're a nasty bitch Claudia. And my mother thought so too."

"I really don't care what she thought." There's a ghost of a smirk playing on her lips. "*Karma* is what it all is. Which is why I'm still here and why she's, well, not."

I've had enough. I lunge towards my half-drunk cup of coffee and hurl it into her face.

She screams and jumps back. "You bastard! Dad!"

I snatch up my car keys and stride out into the yard.

"You get back here," Iain shouts after me. I can't believe he could be thinking of having a go at me after how Claudia's just behaved.

I grab the rock reserved for propping the gate open and poise it over the windscreen of the Mini. Forgive me Mum for what I am about to do but she deserves it. The windscreen cracks and splinters in all directions. I sprint towards my car with the sound of the Mini's car alarm howling in my ears. As I drive down the street and look in my mirror, I notice Iain running after me. For the first few miles, I'm checking my mirrors, fully expecting to see the prick driving after me but he doesn't. Probably too busy trying to placate Claudia.

Chapter Twenty

It's a few miles before my breathing restores itself to a regular rhythm. As I drive through the next village, I notice my second-least-favourite-person. Yes, it's Stacey, Mum. She's outside a newsagents talking to a couple of women. Without any thought, I pull up at the side of the road opposite them.

"I want a word with you," I shout to her, across the road, whilst getting out of my car. She says something to the people she's with, then crosses the road towards me. She's chubbier than I remember and her hair is long and straggly. She's no match for you Mum, no matter how designer her clothes are.

"This had better be good." Her nasty voice is like Claudia's. "Showing me up in front of my friends."

"I'm surprised you've got any," I say. "But I'm not here to slag you off. I'm here to tell you to leave my mother's memory alone."

"What on earth are you on about?" She stands in front of me and folds her arms. She looks at me with more venom than I've ever experienced from anyone before.

"The retweets and your gossiping about my mother." I fold my arms too and face her, squarely. "It stops now, do you get it?"

"And are *you* going to make me." She laughs a nasty cackle which shows me exactly where Claudia gets her ways from. "I only retweet stuff I'm interested in, and your *mother*," she says the word *mother* like it's a dirty word, "supposedly tweeting from beyond the grave is pretty interesting, don't you think?"

"It's got nothing to do with you."

"I'm Claudia's mother."

"Yes, I can see that. But it's still none of your business. And you can't hold a candle to *my* mother."

"She broke my marriage up."

"That's bollocks. You'd already split up when Iain met her."

"If it wasn't for *her*, Iain and I would have got back together years ago. Now she's out of the -"

"Did you know she was pregnant?"

"I've seen that twaddle on Twitter. Iain was going to get the -"

"Three months. It would have been born in October."

"Well it won't be now, will it?" She laughs again.

A mist of fury drapes itself over me. I push her backwards, as hard as I can, into the path of an oncoming car. It slams on, missing her by an inch. Her friends hurtle over to us.

"He tried to kill me," she gasps, her cheeks wobbling. "Someone call the police."

I'm like a rabid dog as her two friends and a couple of other people try to keep hold of me whilst a passer-by rings the police. "You should hear what she's been saying about my mother," I sob, the fight draining from me as I stare into the face of one of my captors. "My mum's dead and she's throwing a party about it."

My fight is rekindled as a cop van pulls up a few minutes later, sirens echoing and lights blazing. Suddenly there are about six pairs of hands pinning me to the pavement. I'm flailing under them like a beached fish. They're hurting me.

"Just a couple of seconds later and I'd have been dead," Stacey's shrieking. "Ask my friends. He wants locking up. You *are* going to arrest him, aren't you?"

CHAPTER TWENTY

After a few moments, I'm allowed to peel my face from the tarmac and look into the eyes of all the gathered onlookers.

"Come on. Up you get." I feel the weight of a hand on my arm and am hauled up by a cop. There's another one right behind him. I still can't believe they've turned up in a van. Mum, if you could see me now, you would kill me. Although maybe, you would understand why I pushed her. You might have done the same thing.

The stupid bitch is still carrying on. "I want him locked up. I'm lucky not to be injured, or worse."

"I saw him." A female voice says. "He *did* push her in front of a car. She's lucky it slammed on. It was close."

"She was slagging my mother off!" I've got fat tears rolling down my cheeks. For you Mum, but also for the predicament I'm in. They must all think I'm a right wuss. Everything's worse today because Meghan hasn't rung either. "She died two months ago," I continue. "And *she* won't stop slagging her off."

The officer relaxes his grip. He looks at one of his colleagues. "Into the van lad. We'll have a chat. The rest of you, apart from PC Shepherd, you might as well get on a new job. I'll keep you in the loop." He steers me towards the back of the van which isn't as I expected. It's dark and partitioned into four. In each 'cell,' there isn't enough room to swing a rat, let alone anything else.

The crowd has dispersed when they let me go. Amazingly, they're not going to do anything Mum. It will just go *'on record.'* They didn't even arrest me. They gave me a number to get some counselling and said that if there is a next time, they *will* arrest me. There won't be a next time though. I'm going to block the slag on all social media. Then I never have to see her again. I think the police felt sorry for me, to be honest. I told them about the tweets. They double checked this and said they're still being worked on. When they asked for my date of birth, they also realised that it's my birthday today so that maybe added to the sympathy vote.

As I drive away, I feel shaky and sick. My phone's ringing. I pull over. It's Dad. *Great. Just what I need.*

"Where the hell are you?" He sounds puzzled but his voice has an angry edge too. "What time did you leave the house? I never heard you go."

"This morning. First thing."

"Why didn't you let us know? Or leave a note, at least."

"I dunno. I had something to sort out."

"Like what?"

"Have you seen Twitter?"

"No. Has there been another one?"

"'Fraid so."

"So where did you go?"

"To see Iain."

"Why?"

"To talk to him."

"What about?"

"Bloody hell Dad! It's like being on the *Twenty Questions* show. Mum was pregnant. Before she died."

Silence. "She can't have been! I'd have thought she'd have been too old."

"Well she was. Pregnant I mean, not old."

"Did Iain know?"

"Yep. Course he did."

"Did he know, erm before?"

"She died? Yep."

"Do you have any other word in your repertoire other than *yep*?"

"Nope." This conversation would be funny if it wasn't so tragic. I reckon you'd have liked to have had a girl Mum. If I'd been younger,

CHAPTER TWENTY

I'd have probably liked a sister. I've always been a bit envious of mates who had brothers and sisters. I'd have taken her out perhaps, in her buggy, say to the park or something, people would have thought she was my daughter, instead of my sister.

Then there's the part of me that wouldn't have wanted to share you, having had you to myself all my life. I wouldn't have wanted a bawling kid around. It was bad enough having to accept Iain, and as it's turned out, that's cost me forty per cent of my inheritance. If there had been another kid, I *really* would have got jack shit.

I can't stop thinking about this inheritance situation. Dad must be a mind reader because he says. "Have you checked your bank yet today? That life insurance will probably go in this week."

I can't believe that he's not a bit angrier about the fact that there's another tweet – he's gone ballistic before. He doesn't seem bothered about you having been pregnant *and* he's forgotten it's my birthday too.

"No I haven't. I'll let you know, don't worry."

"Twenty grand, remember. You should still have my bank details."

"I've got to go Dad." I really can't be bothered talking to him. "And thanks for remembering my birthday."

"Birthday? Is it today? Oh shit. I -"

I cut him off. I wanted to tell him what happened this morning but he wouldn't care. All he cares about is money and his fucked-up wife. I probably won't see them for dust after I send his money. You'd never have forgotten my birthday Mum. Never. I notice a few Facebook notifications showing but there's still no text message from Meghan. I chuck my phone onto the passenger seat and resume my journey.

At home, I try to force down some toast and tea but feel like I want to puke. I sit down to check out the Facebook notifications. About ten people have wished me a happy birthday. There's one from Auntie Liz, *your mum would be so proud of you. See you later for dinner. Happy*

Birthday.

I click through to Stacey's page, planning to block her but I also want to see if she's posted about this morning before I hit the block button. She's obviously that thick that she hasn't sorted her settings so that only 'friends' can see what she posts.

She's feeling 'stressed' according to her status. *Had a miracle escape this morning,* she's written. *The son of Iain's ex hates me so much that he pushed me in the path of an oncoming car.* There's a string of omg's and are you ok's? One has said, *I hope they throw the book at him.*

I add to the responses: *Stacey, you thick bitch. Anna was not Iain's 'ex.' She died two months ago. They were engaged and she was pregnant so how can she be his 'ex?'*

I click through to your page, wanting to find photos you've posted in previous years on my birthday. I miss you so much Mum. Especially today. I find one from a couple of years ago, when you've posted a selfie of me, you and Iain in Nando's. There's a picture from the year before, not long after we'd first met Claudia, before we went to that wedding when she totally ignored us. She took it, all hair and trout pout, then tagged us all in it. You'd become Facebook friends with her a little while before.

Anna Hardaker and Claudia Price are friends, announces an automatic post. *Looking forward to meeting you Claudia* (smiley face) you had typed under it and you'd added an excited GIF. Stacey must have loved that. Her daughter befriending *you.* Claudia never replied but she'd *liked* what you'd put. All must have seemed fine then.

I try to check back to Stacey's page to see if anything else has been said on the situation and realise she has blocked *me*. She must have worked out how to do it. Hopefully she's done the same on Twitter. I'll check later. I wander through to the hallway and have a cursory glance at the doormat. *Nothing.* The postman should have been by now. Today is a far cry from how it used to be. The mantlepiece would

CHAPTER TWENTY

be full of cards and you'd go all out with balloons, cake, presents, although it had started to tail off a bit in my twenties. Maybe because I'm supposed to have 'grown up,' or maybe because Iain had taken over a load of your attention. I occasionally caught his snide comments towards you for not 'letting me go.' Perhaps you would have forgotten my birthday, like Dad, if you *had* stayed alive and had another baby.

I lie on the sofa, remembering my 21st, just before you met Iain. You got on well with my then girlfriend, Izzy, and the three of us had gone bowling and for a meal. By the next birthday you *had* met Iain but you didn't see him on my birthday. I didn't have a girlfriend at the time so you cooked us a steak and we watched a film. *Fast and Furious*, it was. Not really your thing but you said you quite liked Paul Walker. He's dead too. I fire up YouTube for that song *'See you Again.'* I've hardly been listening to music or watching TV since you died. More fat tears slide down the sides of my head and pool onto the leather sofa. Some birthday this is turning out to be.

I never realised at the time after Dad had gone, but you and I were central to one another's lives. Then knobhead Iain came along and made little secret of his opinion that I should have left home long before. He just wanted me out of the way. I can't think any more. I'm knackered. I close my eyes.

I jump as my phone beeps. I must have fallen asleep. In my groggy state, I try to focus on the time display. 4:35. For a moment I wonder whether it's afternoon or morning. I remember then that I hardly slept last night and feel grateful for the couple of hours respite I have had. With a heavy chest, I remember that nearly being arrested and sleeping all day are not ways in which a twenty-fifth birthday should be spent.

Gutted. It's not Meghan that has texted. I'm *not* going to text her though. It's against the rules – no more than one text should be sent without a reply. It's Dad. *Have you checked your account yet?* I'm not answering him. I can't be arsed. *Selfish pillock.* I fire off a group text to

Auntie Liz and Uncle Si instead. *What time can we meet. I can be ready in an hour. I need to get out of here. Usual place?*

By half past six, I'm sat in the Tap and Spile with them. Part of me is grateful for their company – the other part of me feels like a div. Sat here with my uncle and auntie when I should be out with Meghan or my mates. I feel like they're all avoiding me. Twats. Maybe they don't know what to say. I remember when Ben Hamilton's dad died back in year ten. He kept bursting into tears and everyone avoided him like he had warts or something. I remember not knowing what to say to him too, beyond *sorry to hear about your dad,* which kind of didn't cut it.

Jake next door has a girlfriend now and spends most of his time with her. Same with Tom. I've not heard from Harry or Adam since the funeral and a couple of my other mates have drifted off too. I'll have to get back on X-Box – see who's on. Life has changed so much. I need to make some decisions. Starting with what I should do about Meghan. *Surely she will know from Facebook that it is my birthday?*

Everything is getting to me Mum; I can't ever have another day like today. I've got to get my head out of my arse and get my brain onto other stuff. Today is my twenty-fifth birthday. You're gone. I can't change anything. I'm going to start doing normal things again, you know, X-Box, like I said, Game of Thrones, running and all that. As well as the gym and art college, I'm also going to take some of your business on. *Fuck Meghan!* It's time I focused on me.

"Penny for them." Auntie Liz smiles at me.

"I was just thinking that I might apply to art college."

Their reactions say it all. Uncle Si slaps the table "You go Jamie. Our Anna would be right proud of you."

"You've got her talent. I remember the pictures you drew when you were little." Auntie Liz sips her wine. "And if you end up completely taking over her business…"

CHAPTER TWENTY

"With Iain though." My cheer vanishes as quickly as it arrived. "I'll never get rid of him, will I?"

"I always got on with him." Auntie Liz's tone is gentle. "You did too, didn't you Si?"

"Yeah." He points at his phone. "But I wonder when Anna was going to tell us about being pregnant. And I wonder even more why Iain hasn't told us since."

Auntie Liz looks like she might cry. "I know. I thought she told me everything. I was her only sister."

"Then there's this *will* business."

"What do you mean?" Auntie Liz looks at him. "I'm not really fussed at not being left much but I have to say, I'm a bit shocked by what she left for Iain. Forty per cent of *everything* is quite a lot."

"At the moment, I'm mostly concerned about this tweeting," Uncle Si adds. "I won't rest till we get to the bottom of it."

They both look at me and I feel defensive. Like when you've done nothing wrong but a policeman is looking at you. Or when you're a kid and the whole class gets kept in until one person who has done something, owns up to it. I shrug my shoulders. "It's doing my box in too. Have the police been back in touch yet?"

"Yeah." Uncle Si picks his pint up. "I was coming to that. They're not going to do anything. It's not a police matter apparently as no crime has been committed. They sound like they don't know what to do with it, to be honest."

"Surely it's some sort of fraud?" Auntie Liz's voice rises a notch. "Someone is pretending to be my dead sister."

"People do it all the time on social media. Think about it. There's Sylvia Plath, Ernest Hemingway, Michael Jackson, Elvis." Uncle Si corresponds his list with his fingers as he points to one finger in turn.

"That's different. They were famous. Mum can hardly be compared with Elvis."

"Your mum was on her way to being famous as well. Especially after that *Toxic Marriage* painting."

"Don't mention that." I laugh, although really, nothing is particularly funny. "Dad wanted to sue Mum, at the time, for defamation of character. He said everyone would know it was about him."

Auntie Liz laughs now. "I think he went as far as to see a solicitor. She had a lucky escape from *him*."

Uncle Si frowns. "I don't think the word *lucky* can be used in the same sentence as Anna's name."

We all sit silently, the evening sun casting its glow amidst conversation and tinkling glasses, all seemingly lost in our own thoughts. I'm grateful for their company, I couldn't have stood being stuck at home on my own all night. Birthday or not.

"I nearly got arrested today."

"What?" Auntie Liz's voice is so loud that some of the surrounding tables glance towards us. "Why?"

"Bitch ex-wife of Iain," I say, as if that explains everything. They're both watching me expectantly. "She's been all over this Twitter thing and on Facebook too; she's making out like she is back with Iain and I just happened to see her at the side of the road with her friends."

"What happened?" It's gone quiet. It's as though others in the pub garden are listening, although they probably aren't.

"I wanted her to know Mum was pregnant. She's making out like Mum meant nothing to Iain and was just an inconvenience standing in her way. I'm also pissed off because I think that's part of the reason she's sniffing around Iain - for Mum's money."

"She is a cow." Auntie Liz glances at her watch. "She was awful to your mum a couple of times. I suppose that's how it goes with an ex-wife situation. I'm lucky that George and I have only ever been married to each other. Even if he is always working away."

"Well Stacey was just as awful about Mum this morning. It's a shame she didn't get run over when I pushed her onto the road."

"You did *what?* Auntie Liz's voice is a screech again.

"Oh Jamie." Uncle Si gets to his feet. "We'll talk about this more over dinner. You're going to have to rein this in. Come on. We'd better go inside."

As we're waiting for our plates to be cleared, I wonder why they keep looking towards the door. Then I realise. Your brother and sister, so keen on giving me some kind of decent birthday, have pulled out all the stops to ensure a better end to what has been, up to the point of seeing them, the shittiest birthday imaginable. Dad forgot it. I've had a run in with Iain and Claudia, then nearly been arrested. But now I watch as a waiter strides towards us, cake in hand, singing Happy Birthday. My face burns as the rest of the restaurant joins in.

"Why five candles?" I stare at them until their flames cast blind patches in front of my eyes. Then my phone vibrates in my pocket. Maybe you're pulling some strings wherever you are Mum. It's Meghan. At last. *Sorry for not being in touch. I've had some sort of stomach bug. Anyway, I'm outside your house. Will you be long or should I just leave your card here?*

I fumble about in my pockets. I don't think Auntie Liz and Uncle Si were particularly happy at me leaving so suddenly. I had to see Meghan though. *Where's the bloody back door key?* I pull out a perfectly folded pair of twenty-pound notes, a pack of chewing gum, some fluff, no key and a condom. *Yes, a condom.* My face burns again.

"Sorry, but we won't be using *that* this evening!" She stares at it, her eyes larger than normal within her pasty face. "I've only left the house today cos it's your birthday."

"We'll have to go around to the front door." I'm just glad she's here. Action or no action. And she *must* think something of me too.

Chapter Twenty One

I rub my eyes and blink a couple of times when I check my bank balance. It's often the first thing I do on a morning, after years of being skint and usually overdrawn. It's to reassure myself that direct debits haven't gone out at bad times. I've spent most of my adult life so far, just living month to month. You were always subbing me until pay day. *Bloody hell Mum!* You've really looked after me! My balance says £120,459. One hundred and twenty grand! Get in!

It's a shame Meghan didn't stay last night. I could have taken her somewhere nice today. She didn't say a right lot. I pressed her on it, obviously worrying that she's going off me, but she blamed it on feeling ill and tired. She was in her mum's car and said she had to get it back to her. I was well disappointed, but hey-ho. That's life.

I'm twenty-five now. This is where it all starts. The first day of the rest of my life as they say. A text from Dad is showing as a banner at the top of my phone screen. *Have you checked your bank balance? Can you transfer that money yet? Sorry about yesterday, by the way. It was all the shit with Katherine that made me forget your birthday. I'll make it up to you.*

I click the transfer option in my banking app. Phillip Hardaker. Fifteen grand. Not twenty. He's a shit dad and he forgot my birthday. It's all madness anyway and I doubt he will ever pay it back. I click send, knowing he will hassle me until I do the transfer. I suppose he did leave here ten years ago with just his stuff and the telly. I'd been outside on my skateboard as he carried it out.

"Where's your dad taking your telly?" Jake had asked. I was somewhere between humiliated and gutted.

He *still* believes you owe him something though. I wonder how long the money will last him. I'm certain he will be back for more. I type back *it's in your account. I've transferred it.*

Within minutes, my phone rings. "It's not in mate." Dad sounds breathless, excited. "Have you sent it across?"

"It might have to clear with it being so much money. Keep checking." I've got so much money in my account that what I've given Dad doesn't feel like that much in the grand scheme of things. But it's life changing, or at least, it could be. He's always been able to manipulate me, and *you* for that matter. I could never say no to him.

"I hope it will be enough," Dad says. *I must be psychic.* I bet you could have warned me about this Mum. That he might keep coming back for more. "You know how much vans cost these days."

"No. I don't."

"I'm going to make a go of this son. You could come and work for me. One van today, ten by next year. We could end up with a fleet of window cleaners."

I listen as he describes his plans. He's only ever interested in his own life. One day he might ask about *my life*, but I doubt it. He doesn't care. I'm going to get my art college application done then get working on a few examples of things I can take to the interview. According to the website, I've got to put a portfolio together.

I've got that partially completed portrait of you. I go across the landing to have a look at it. Your eyes look sadder than when I created the picture and there's a blob of water on your cheek. *Weird.* It looks like a tear. I feel cold inside. How can it be? I glance at the smiling, framed photograph I referred to. *Seriously weird.* I think I'll do a landscape next time. A lake or something. As I chuck my phone onto the desk, it lights up.

In case you missed it, Twitter has notified me.

@artistanna123 *Greed. It's all I have come to know from people. One of the seven deadly sins. It was deadly for me.* #**cuckoo** #**beforemytime**

I want to launch my phone against a wall. The greed thing is too coincidental with the payment of the life insurance. I don't get it. *What's going on?* I tug on shorts and a t-shirt. I need to get out of here. I need to run. I wave at Betty as she calls out to me. I can't stop. I don't want to talk. I need to make sense of this bloody Twitter madness. Her voice is still in my ears as I get to the end of the street. I watch the pavement travel beneath me and hear my breath whooshing in my ears.

You'd give anything to feel this alive Mum, so I will do it for both of us. I'll step into your artist's shoes. I know it will take a while, but I'll take over from where you left off. My breath and blood are pumping and my arms propel me along. I don't feel the burn today – I'm too fired by adrenaline. Thoughts whirl around my head as I continue to run. I don't even notice I'm running.

Greed. It must have something to do with Dad. He's the only person who's really wanted something. But he and Katherine haven't been getting on. Could it be *her* behind the tweets. *It can't be you Mum.* Like if it was, we would be talking *ghosts.*

By the time I'm home, I've done ten kilometres according to my tracker. I'll have to live for two now, well three – I keep forgetting about the baby. As I step into the shower, I wonder what it would have been like to have had a little brother or sister twenty-five years my junior. Nah. It's unthinkable. I'm not a fan of babies anyway and would have had to watch you and Iain fawning all over it and playing at *happy families*. I would have been out on my ear.

CHAPTER TWENTY ONE

I've been thinking about Iain's response when I confronted him. He didn't seem too concerned by the subject of *the baby* when it came up. He was really matter of fact. I suppose he's had lots of time to get used to the idea.

Speak of the devil. I grab my phone.

"What's this latest greed thing?" He asks. "On bloody Twitter?"

"How am I supposed to know." I turn the shower off. It's drowning him out. If only.

"Things have been bad enough for us all. I need to know who is behind this crap. I've had enough of it."

"Twitter don't want to know." I rub the towel up and down my legs. "The police don't want to know -"

"I've been thinking - there must be a way of analysing IP addresses from where the tweets are coming from," he says. "I'll get on to it. I've been Googling it and it seems that only the police and the courts can force Twitter to act on something like this."

I'm no computer expert but it doesn't seem all that hopeful. "Have you had your money?" I change the subject. I don't want to think about the tweets anymore.

"Yep. It goes without saying that I'd give anything to have your mother back instead though. Baby or no baby."

I ignore the baby comment. "Well at least you've got Stacey." It's half question, half accusation.

His voice hardens. "No, I have *not* got *Stacey*. It's all in her head. And whilst we're on the subject, stay away from her, do you hear me? I couldn't believe it when I was told about all that shit that went on yesterday."

"Bit protective of her, aren't you?"

"It's for everyone's sake mate," he sighs. "I know she's got a mouth on her but she's still the mother of my daughter. And I don't need this crap."

"Well tell her to keep away from this stuff on Twitter then. If she hadn't have got involved, I would never have gone near her."

"I agree with you. But I think everyone, including Stacey, is intrigued by what's going on, if *intrigue* is the right word. And a little scared."

"It's got fuck all to do with her." He's always sticking up for Claudia and Stacey. It pisses me right off. Was he like that if *you* ever complained about anything Mum?

"Cut the language Jamie. It's not *just* Stacey. I don't want *you* getting into trouble either. Stacey said she will insist on pressing charges if you go near her again. Plus she knows people. No one is going to take kindly to a young lad being physically threatening to a woman."

"I don't need your concern, or your advice, cheers. I can look after myself."

He sighs. "I know you can, but you've been through enough Jamie, I don't want to see you make anything worse for yourself."

"Have you seen how many followers Mum's got now?" I laugh, despite myself. "She'd be well chuffed."

"To be honest, I'm not even sure how Twitter really works. I've never had that much to do with it. Anyway, I'm going to sort the IP address thing out and things will get easier. But remember, the last thing I want is for us to be enemies."

He keeps trying to be my friend. *Weirdo.* "Well bring my mother's car back then and butt out of the gallery." He doesn't reply straight away so I continue. "Claudia's got no right to that car and you don't know the first thing about art." It's true Mum. His eyes used to glaze over when you talked to him about anything to do with the art world. I remember you even had to explain the 'toxic marriage' painting to him – what it was about and what it meant.

"No, on both counts. Claudia's using the car for now and I'm retaining my stake in the business. I was about to be married to your mother."

CHAPTER TWENTY ONE

"Yeah, but you didn't want a baby with her, did you. How would Princess *Claudia* have coped?" I force her name out, making no attempt to disguise the hatred in my voice.

"Look it's all irrelevant now. I'm going to the gallery soon. What are you doing today?"

"Erm. I was planning to go too." I remember that saying of yours again Mum. *Keep your friends close and your enemies closer.* I don't trust him. I also think he knows more than he's letting on.

The portrait of you looks even sadder when I return to your study. I decide I *will* include it in my art portfolio as it is, without finishing it. It shows my ability to capture a person's likeness and emotion. They'll understand why I couldn't take it all the way to completion. I clip a new sheet of paper onto the easel and pluck a pencil from the pot.

I section the page, then I begin capturing the scene from Lakeside Café, where we used to go for hot chocolate and cake after walking around Roundhay Park. I'm cold, despite the late morning sun that streams through the open window. I recall Waterloo Lake, at the park, which has claimed several lives and know that I've got to paint it. I strain to see it, in my mind's eye. I hover my pencil, but instead of being able to bring the picturesque lake to mind, I see sunlight-infused, lifeless bodies drifting on the water's surface and then you, teetering as you balance on the banister, then broken-necked at the bottom of the stairs, your hair fluttering in the draft from under the door. Then I hear a noise which sounds like you … *sobbing!* By the time I've yanked the door open, it's stopped. It's either my mind playing tricks or something from outside. Whatever it is, I'm out of here. I'll go and work at the gallery.

Iain's in your office when I get there; I can see him through the vertical blinds. I feel calmer the instant I walk into the gallery, it's the smell, the music, everything, well apart from Iain. Despite his presence, I'm still glad I've come.

The Toxic Marriage painting still hangs in pole position, now surrounded by replica postcards, notebooks, coasters and prints.

"I'm going to put a calendar together of her best work." Dawn's sudden words startle me. "I think it will sell well given the circumstances, you can help me choose which of her paintings we should use, if you like. Maybe *Toxic Marriage* should be the front cover since that's the one that seems to attract the most attention."

"Yeah," I say, my gaze flitting back to Iain, who's leaning back in your chair, deep in a telephone conversation. He's probably on the phone to Stacey whilst pretending to be some hot shot businessman. "He's made himself at home, hasn't he?"

"It's fine. We've all got to work together and I'm certain your mum would want him to get involved." She takes hold of my arm. "Come on, let me show you a bit of the new gallery stuff. Some of your mum's students have put together an exhibition to commemorate her. You're going to love it." Dawn pushes her glasses up, so they rest below her greying bun. "I was thinking of having an open evening to show it all off."

It's impossible not to be inspired by this work Mum. I'm going to be as good as this, once I get to art college. There's a painting showing the pupil-teacher dynamic, one of you, in front of a canvas, where you were always at your happiest, another of a scene of the garden where you held an artist's retreat last year and one that could be a male response to Toxic Marriage.

I then decide that no matter who it may piss off, I'm going to do an 'offspring response' to Toxic Marriage. Who knows, it may end up being displayed beside yours. Then I realise display decisions can be mine. I own sixty per cent of this place. If I want to display a painting, I probably can.

"Not bad, eh?" Dawn peels off her cardigan to reveal her skinny, freckled shoulders. "I've got all sorts of ideas. When Iain's finished in the office, perhaps we could all have a chat?"

"Yeah, OK. Can I use the studio for a bit?" Maybe I should be telling her I'm using it, rather that asking. I'm supposed to be *her boss* now! But she knows what she's doing and I'm not going to interfere, not yet. Though really, I could go and kick Iain out of your office, right now, if I wanted.

Dawn's excited when I tell her of my plans for art college and says you would have been too. "And I'll do whatever I can to help you," she adds.

I feel guilty then for having any grand ideas about 'lording it' over this place.

"Ah, Iain's finished." She strides across the gallery and taps on the door. "Can Jamie and I come in for a chat?" She opens the door and I change the *come in* sign to the *in a meeting* sign on the door.

"Who said you could do that?" Iain gets to his feet.

"I don't need permission."

Iain's eyes narrow but he lets it go. I'm fuming because he doesn't move from behind your desk. We pull up chairs like we're being interviewed or something. He and Dawn discuss plans to have a *formal* business meeting to go through the accounts. I can't stand it anymore.

"Why are you sat there? I own twenty per cent more than you?"

"Hey Jamie." Dawn touches my arm, the fabric of her dress rustling. Her fingers are bony. "It doesn't matter. It's only a chair."

I want to wrench his sad arse out of your chair Mum. He was only in your life for four years. What if you'd had the kid with him? Married him? *What then?*

Iain stands, walks around the desk and pulls me up by the scruff of my shirt. "You sit there then, you spoilt little shit, there is no need for this."

"If we're going to work together," Dawn looks from me to him. "You two are going to have to bury your differences. I'm not going to be your referee every time you're here."

Silence. It's the baby thing Mum. It's made everything worse.

"Did you know my mum was pregnant Dawn?"

"Yes, she was here when she took the test." She replies without hesitation.

"So you were the first to know? And I was the last?"

"Dawn, can you give us a minute please?" Iain cracks his knuckles. First on one hand, then the other.

"Sure."

Iain follows her to the door and twists the blinds so they close after her. "Jamie. There's no point in you going on about this ... *baby*." He spits out the final word like a piece of gristle. "It's upsetting everyone, me especially."

"Upsetting who? Princess Claudia, you mean?"

"Stop calling her that, for God's sake. Grow up! Yes, she's upset about it. Just like I was."

"Were you? I thought you must have planned it. Get my mother right where you wanted her."

"You must be joking! It's the last thing I wanted!" Iain looks older than he did. There are flecks of grey on his unshaven chin and the space around his eyes is lined. "Look, it's been bad enough losing your mum. I don't want to be reminded about the baby and I don't want to be at loggerheads with you."

He's a trier Mum. I'm not sure why he's always trying to keep me on side. Maybe because we are still stuck with each other. Well, until I can buy him out anyway. Maybe he's just after more money. Like Dad.

Being in your studio at the gallery for a couple of hours eventually chills me out. I begin my response to *Toxic Marriage*. Dad will probably kill me but I know it could be a money spinner. I'll also use it for my

CHAPTER TWENTY ONE

college portfolio. I decide to have a go at doing this one in oils, like your original, but I've got to sketch out the proportions first. It needs anger, darkness and a staircase.

I recall how often I sat at the top of the stairs, as a kid, scared, listening. The stairs. As I start to sketch them, I remember how this was your final perspective. *What did you see as you fell? What were you thinking? Did you know you were going to die?*

Phone again. Dad. No prizes for guessing what'll be up with him.

"We agreed twenty grand Jamie. What are you playing at?"

"Hello to you as well Dad."

"Don't get bloody smart with me. Where's the other five grand?"

All my bravado slides away. Everything I had stored up in my head to say to him. *You've never been there for me Dad. You didn't even get me a birthday card. You were a shit to Mum. Ya-di-ya-di-ta.* The familiar sense of feeling small creeps over me. "Sorry. I must have pressed the wrong button. My head is all over the place. I'll send the other five now." I hate myself for the hold he has over me. It's a combination of fearing him and wanting to please him. You just accepted me as I am Mum.

"I'll keep checking." He doesn't even say goodbye.

Next Iain bursts into the studio and slams his phone onto my canvas, still just a collection of pencil strokes. "I've had enough of this! I want to know which sicko is behind it." He's close to shouting. I've never really heard him shout. In fact, I remember you saying that it was one of the things that drew you to him; that he never shouted; that he was always calm and considered, that he -"

"Read it!" His voice is even louder.

I glance down.

@artistanna123 It *wasn't an accident. The death of my baby and me. Our lives were taken. Why is nobody doing anything?* #cuckoo #gonetoosoon

"I'm going to have to go to the police with this." Iain slips the phone into the pocket of his jeans. "The tone of the Tweets has changed."

"My uncle and I have already been." I feel considerably calm, given the circumstances. "They wouldn't listen. They weren't interested."

"They will be when I speak to them. This is the first time she's suggested that it wasn't an accident." Iain sinks onto a stool beneath a half-finished nightscape.

"What do you mean, *she*?"

"Your mum."

"It's not *her* tweeting. You just said *she's* suggested. She's dead. You don't believe in all that *beyond the grave* crap, do you?" I must admit, I'm starting to wonder.

"Nah. I guess not. But someone is behind all this and it needs investigating."

"Good luck with that then. The police were seriously not bothered when we went." It was probably our fault – we could have been a bit more insistent, I guess.

"Why didn't you say you'd been to the police anyway?"

"You never asked." I want to say that I'll never tell him anything – he's nothing to me now but he looks so tired and miserable that I haven't got the heart. I still think he's a dick though.

Iain stretches his arms above his head and cracks his knuckles. He speaks with a renewed energy. "Jamie. You don't think your dad's involved in some way, do you?"

"With what?"

"This tweeting business. He's always had a large axe to grind with your mum, and -"

"Not his style," I cut in. "If he had something to say, he wouldn't be saying it on Twitter. I don't think he even knows what a *hashtag* is."

"What about his wife? She's not exactly a paid-up member of the *Anna fan club*, is she?"

CHAPTER TWENTY ONE

Who does he think he is? Blaming my family, first Dad, then Katherine. Not that I really see *her* as family. "You should look more in your own neck of the woods if you're looking for shit stirrers who hate my mother."

"What do you mean?"

I laugh. "Like you really need to ask!"

"Are you talking about Stacey?"

"And Princess Claudia."

"I've asked you to stop calling her that." The wooden stool clatters to the floor as he stands up.

I notice that he hasn't ironed his shirt. It's hanging off him too. *Poor Iain*, I think. Perhaps it's all getting to him.

Chapter Twenty Two

I'm sitting in your studio watching life go by through the window. Dawn is doing a great job of keeping this place going. You chose well when you gave her the job of manager, Mum. Now I've got all this money in the bank, I'm thinking of having a holiday – maybe Meghan will want to come with me. I haven't been away for three years, not since that attempt at the one in Northumberland. Honest Mum, I did try to make the best of it. Though what possessed you and Iain to think we'd enjoy a holiday in such a dead and boring place, I don't know. I managed to keep quiet about it whereas Claudia spent the whole week complaining.

"All my friends have gone abroad," she was wailing before we'd even set off, whilst we were strapping bikes onto cars. Do you remember Mum, how glad we were that we were in two cars, so at least we got some peace from her on the journey?

We all, apart from Claudia, carried everything in when we arrived at the crappy chalet. She immediately bagged the second bedroom, whilst I got the fold-out sofa bed in the lounge. She slammed her bedroom door behind her and pretty much stayed in there for the rest of the day, apart from when we all went for a meal and she sat there with a face like a smacked arse, still complaining that at the age of twenty, she deserved to be taken somewhere better than Northumberland.

"I'm off to the supermarket," you announced the next morning. "We

CHAPTER TWENTY TWO

need to stock up for the week. Any requests?"

"I'll come with you," Claudia replied, smiling.

I was amazed. *Was she going to help you?* "I'll come too."

She was weird in the car on the way to the supermarket, quizzing you about Dad, do you remember? *So why did you break up? When did you break up? How long were you together?* I felt like telling her to keep her neb out but you answered without going into too much detail. As we drove around, looking for a space, she was recounting in great detail about her own parents' break up and how much it had affected her and how no one ever thought about her and on and on till I jumped out of the car. "I'll get a trolley. I'll see you in there."

You soon gave up trying to stop us putting what we wanted into the trolley. We had a moment of feeling like a team, me and Claudia, as we overruled you and chucked everything in from Vodka to ice-cream. She took the piss more than I did. I stopped after a bit when I saw how full the trolley was getting.

You grimaced at the checkout, not only with the final total but also with being left to pack it all up. I needed the toilet.

I agreed to go on a bike ride that afternoon. Two miles in though, Claudia started shrieking that her ankle hurt and Iain ended up having to take her back to the chalet leaving me and you to do the bike ride on our own. For the rest of the holiday, Iain spent most of the time running up Claudia's arse, constantly asking if she was alright and trying to make her laugh. By day five, I overheard you and him having words. You were threatening to go home early and telling him you were sick of his miserable daughter and of his ex-wife ringing. He was saying that he had a past and if you didn't like it, you knew what you could do. You looked like you'd been crying when you emerged an hour later.

That evening, me and Claudia ended up falling out as well. It was supposedly our turn to cook but I couldn't be arsed. I was making a balls up of everything I touched, granted, but I saw red when she called me a *thick bastard.* She deserved to end up wearing the Yorkshire Pudding mix, if you ask me. Iain didn't agree though.

In the end, we went home a day early. It was pissing it down and no one was speaking to anyone. "Next time Mum," I had said on the journey back, "leave me at home!"

"It was a bit awful, wasn't it?" You looked stressed and sad. I remember thinking that you and Iain would probably split up after that.

I notice a Twitter notification at the top of my screen. *Has anyone seen this shite?* Stacey has retweeted and commented on your last tweet. *She's causing as much trouble dead as she did when she was alive.*

In the twenty minutes since Stacey has re-tweeted, she's had a barrage of comments from your now two hundred and sixty-three strong following.

Someone has put that *the whole thing needs investigating.* I reply to this one. *We're onto it. My stepdad and me.*

Claudia tweets. *He's not your stepdad.*

I write, *why don't you and your mother disappear and let my mother's memory rest. Neither of you should be 'followers' of her.*

She's dead dear, Claudia replies. *How can we be following her?*

Fighting the urge to throw my phone against the fresh, white walls of the studio, I mutter my goodbyes to Dawn and head out into the sunshine towards my battered Clio. I get in and text Iain. *Tell your daughter to back off. And good luck with the police – you'll need it.*

Then I text Meghan. I'm going to be more of a man about it and stop waiting for her to get in touch with me. *Hey babe,* I type, then delete it because it sounds cheesy. *Hey gorgeous* (all women like being called that.) *Hope you're feeling better. Let me know when you're free.* That will do. I fire it off and feel instantly better. I point my car in the direction

CHAPTER TWENTY TWO

of home and then decide that I can't face going home yet. I need to get rid of this energy Mum. I'm going to try that gym, the one *you* were a member of. In fact, I'm going to join it. The time I went with you, I was only into the weights and the rowers. This time I'll appreciate the pool and the jacuzzi. Plus, there's tons of fit birds around there to take my mind off Meghan if she doesn't text me back.

I end up being at Virgin Active for nearly five hours. By the time I've done the paperwork, been shown around and have been in all the different areas, I'm starving. I order a wrap and a smoothie, grab a newspaper and sit in the *adult only* area. I'm bright red and sweaty from the steam room. I like that I've joined one of your favourite places Mum. I wonder if you used to plan out your paintings whilst you were swimming up and down the pool like I just have.

My phone beeps so I snatch it from my pocket. It's Iain. *I've made a formal complaint to the police,* says his text. *Not sure what they're gonna do but I'll keep you posted.*

I click through to Twitter, to your page and scroll up and down the eight tweets that have been posted since you died. The whole thing is off its head. There's been nothing new added since that awful one this afternoon. Iain can be persuasive when he wants to be, in a measured but repetitive way. It's irritated the shite out of me over the last couple of years. He's probably done this at the police station, repeating *she's dead* or something over and over. The officer, or whoever, will have thrown their hands in the air and said *alright, alright, we'll deal with it!*

He's no doubt also taken his *actions have consequences* approach and threatened them with something if they don't act. Another annoying position of his that I could never beat. I was having a huge row with you over some chore or other that I hadn't done a couple of years ago, and you wouldn't do something I needed in return. I can't remember what it was, it was that pathetic, but Iain kept repeating *actions have consequences.* I just wanted to lamp him.

It's nearly ten when I pull into our driveway. It's not dark yet but we had the longest day a couple of weeks ago, so the nights are going the other way again. I have more than a twinge of sadness as I contemplate daylight reducing all the way to winter. I'm dreading winter without you and can't imagine pulling the curtains across at 4pm, shutting myself alone in the house for the entire night. A feeling of gloom opens in the pit of my stomach as I stare at the darkened windows of our home. It's as though there's a hole of loneliness inside me, a void that threatens to turn itself inside out and devour me within it.

Despite it being the end of June, the house feels cold. Maybe I could get a dog! I would have company and 'someone' to say hello to whenever I come back. It could come running with me. I've always wanted a dog, but you'd never allow it. *You can't look after yourself* was your argument. *And it will be me who ends up feeding and walking it.* And then there'd be the age-old stock statement of *when you get your own place, you can do what you like.* You said you didn't want the hassle, the dog hair or the smell.

The house currently smells of your perfume, combined with the sickly air freshener which must be nearly running out. And lilies, always lilies. I wouldn't usually know a rose from a daisy, but the smell of lilies will never leave me. I wander from room to room, from the hallway to the lounge, then to the kitchen and I'm struck by how grey and empty home now feels. No longer full of colour and music. I know I'm going to have to make some decisions soon. Either I will make the place mine, I won't *paint you out* Mum, but you know what I mean, or I'll 'up sticks' and start again. Somewhere where I'm not known as *the lad whose mum's dead.*

I look out at the back garden which is in as much need of a tidy up as the house, but I can't be arsed. I shiver, violently. What was that saying you used to use? Oh yeah, *someone has walked over my grave.* I grip the sink and sigh. God Mum, it's all messed up. I've never felt so on my

CHAPTER TWENTY TWO

own. Feeling the familiar rush of heat behind my eyes, I splash them with water then reach into the cupboard at the side of me for a glass. As I open the door, I gasp as one falls out, splintering into a million pieces at my feet. I flick the main light on and grab the dustpan and brush. *For God's sake.* As I'm sweeping the shards of glass, I realise my heel's bleeding. In my peripheral vision, something moves alongside me, so I glance up. Nothing. It must be the shadow of a car passing the uncurtained lounge window.

After I've cleared the glass, I close the blinds and grab a beer. It's about all I've got in the fridge – you'd go mad Mum. It's no wonder I've lost so much weight. I've always been like that though, haven't I? I lose my appetite when I'm stressed and miserable. Do you remember when I was doing my A-levels? You were going mental with me.

I settle onto the sofa, grateful for the 'company' the TV offers. Some people live like this all the time. *God, I'm so depressed.* I check my phone for the millionth time. I wish I could stop. Still nothing. I click through to Facebook to see if Meghan's been on there and stare at the smiling selfie of her with her supposed ex, Connor. Two hours ago, he's tagged her in Leeds Centre, feeling 'loved,' and he's typed, *this girl.* They must be back together. She was here the other night. Maybe she's just not had the courtesy to tell me. Nah. She wouldn't do that. She knows you've died. They can't be back together. She's a decent lass, she wouldn't not tell me, surely? I stare at the picture again, into eyes that have looked into mine in the throes of - sorry Mum. I'm gutted. Absolutely gutted.

I can't sleep. I lie here, staring into the night, hearing the house creak and tick. There's the occasional whoosh of traffic in the distance. I must have dropped off at some point because suddenly I jump. Something has woken me and I don't know what. A bang. I don't know if it's real or if I have dreamt it. I feel around and find my phone on the floor. 2:55. I'm so fed up with not sleeping and am considering getting some pills or something. *Mum, why can't I sleep?* I feel like I'm drowning in misery and am only given respite when I sleep. I lie for a bit longer until I can't stand it anymore. I tug on a pair of jeans and a t-shirt and head down the stairs. I need to know what's going on. If she's back with him, I'll get over it. Or kill myself. Only joking Mum. But I need to know.

The car rattles more than usual and the fan belt shrieks as I set off down the street. *Bloody car!* It'll have woken the whole street up. It used to be impossible to sneak in and out at all hours, when you were here. You, with your bedroom at the front of the house, would hear my car a mile off, and you told me that you didn't settle properly if I wasn't in my bed. Now no one gives a shit. If you were here now, you'd probably be telling me to get a grip.

I need to know what's going on with Meghan and Connor. There's no doubt she's gone cold on me and I can sense in my gut that it's all over. I wonder how much more I can take. All I need now is for art college to reject me then I can be justified in jumping off a cliff.

It's becoming normal, this driving whilst everyone else is sleeping. The roads are deserted and every traffic light is green. I'm outside Meghan's darkened house within minutes. Her bedroom window is uncurtained in the darkness. Her mother's VW Golf isn't on the drive. *Maybe they're away together.* Nah, the other window is open and the closed curtains flap through it in the breeze. Meghan's shagging Connor's brains out somewhere.

I know where he lives. Connor, I mean. Easy to stalk people nowadays. The knot in my belly tightens as I swing my car around in the road and embark on the next leg of my journey which may put my mind at rest but probably won't. "Please. Please. Please," I whisper in the darkness as I turn the final corner. I pull up a couple of doors away, two or three car lengths behind the VW Golf with its pink air freshener suspended from the mirror.

CHAPTER TWENTY TWO

Bitch. Bastard. I thump the steering wheel so hard that the horn sounds. I'm not sure whether the curtain twitches in one of the upstairs windows. I feel like marching up to the door and dragging her out of there. Make her see the life she's giving up with me. I thought she cared about me. I thought we were going places. I thought – *well to hell with what I thought!* She's in there with him. I tug my glove box open and fumble around until I find a pen and an old receipt. It's dated 11 April, five days before you died Mum. It's for bread, milk and wine. Ironically it says *you were served by Meghan.* I write on the back of it *Thanks. What an idiot I've been. J*

I sneak to her car and tuck it under one of the wipers, hardly breathing until I'm back in the 'cocoon' of my car again. I wish you were at home Mum. You'd tell me that it's all her loss and that someone else will snap me up soon. I feel like shit. Hopefully she will as well, when she finds that note.

Chapter Twenty Three

In contrast with last night's gloom, I wake, fully clothed, on the sofa with the sun belting through the window. I check my phone to see if Meghan has found that note and decided to grovel. Nothing. I've slept till after ten, for which I'm grateful. It's the first of July. Monday. A new week. A new month. Time to get on with it. I'll go to the gym again today. With the money I've got in the bank, I shouldn't have any problems attracting another woman.

I notice an email from art college. They want to interview me on the 8th. *One week away.* I've got to take evidence of a variety of my work. So far, I've got 'my take' on the *Toxic Marriage* scene started, the partially finished portrait of you, and that's it.

I decide to go for a walk and to think over what else I'm going to do. It's good to get out of the house. The walls close in on you after a while, don't they Mum? You often used to take off somewhere to work on your art. I keep walking. I realise I can follow you but with a different slant. I can use your name to get me 'into' places, but I have to be unique. My chest bursts with pride for the legacy you've left and the artistic ability you've passed onto me, which I didn't realise I had. But now that I have, I'm sure as hell I'm going to use it.

I feel excited suddenly. Despite the rejection from Meghan, I really do have a future. I've plenty of money and a career path I've never

CHAPTER TWENTY THREE

had before. No more crappy insurance company for me. Then the bubbling joy is whisked away in the wind as quickly as it arrived. *You're dead.* None of this would be happening if you were here. *Will it always be like this?* Will I always feel smothered by a blanket of guilt and misery whenever I feel glad about something? I try to bring my attention back to the college interview and the kind of artist I will be. *A piss artist!* I laugh at myself, despite how rubbish I'm feeling.

There's a grey van blocking our drive when I get back. That sort of thing used to annoy you Mum, even if you weren't going out anywhere. It was *your* house and people shouldn't be parking outside it! I can make out the outline of the old British Telecom logo but the van has been stripped of that, leaving it empty for a sign writer to advertise another business on it. Dad steps out grinning, with a can of Carling in one hand and a cigarette in the other. If either of us were to draw him Mum, the cig and can combo would absolutely sum him up.

"What do you reckon?" He lifts the can to his lips to take a long drink, then wipes his mouth on the back of his hand before taking a similarly long drag on his cigarette. "Proper workhorse, don't you think?" Smoke escapes through his mouth and nose as he speaks. "I'm happy as Larry with my belated divorce settlement."

"What do you mean – *settlement?* You asked to lend the money, didn't you?"

"I thought you'd agreed to *give* it to me. You can spare it, can't you? You're minted now."

"That's not the point. I -." I trail off as Dad goes to the back door of the van and tugs out a large suitcase.

"I've had a big bust up with *her.* It's all this pathetic insecurity. I can't stand it anymore." He presses his key and the van locks. "Anyway, it dawned on me that I don't have to dance to her tune. Not when I can have a home here again."

"Here?" My voice is a squeak. I was not expecting this Mum. If you can hear or see this from wherever you are, you will be having kittens. "We'll have a great time son. It'll be like the old days. Have you still got your X-Box?" He drops his cigarette and drives it into the pavement with his heel.

I think of your bedroom, which you used to share with him, now untouched apart from all your clothes that still sit in bags. I don't want him to sleep in there. "Where will you sleep?"

"In my old room of course. You can give me a hand getting the rest of your mum's stuff bagged up. For the first time in a long time, no woman is going to give me shit."

I follow him to the front door then he turns around.

"You'll have to get me a key cut."

I unlock the door and wait for him to go in, turning his suitcase sideways on as he does. Although I'm six foot one, I feel feeble behind his confident stature. I always have done. As I turn to close the door, I wave at Betty who is watching from her porch. She shakes her head.

"Make us a butty lad. I'm starving."

"I've nowt in Dad. I've been buying sandwiches when I'm out and getting takeaways or pub meals."

"I expect you can afford to now," Dad laughs. "You can treat me to a steak and a beer later instead then." He plonks his suitcase at the foot of the stairs.

"I think I've got a pizza in the freezer."

"That'll do for now."

It's like the old days with Dad ordering me around. I'm a grown man of twenty-five and my father is moving in with me. I should be pleased, but I'm not. You'd go bananas. By the time I've unwrapped the pizza and shoved it in the oven, Dad's sat in your armchair, feet on the coffee table, telly on and another cigarette dangling from his mouth. I watch as he cracks open another can of Carling.

"Mum doesn't let anyone smoke in here." I'm aware of how pathetic

CHAPTER TWENTY THREE

I sound. To be honest, I can't stand the smell of smoke either but I daren't say that to him. Suddenly I'm a little boy again, hiding behind your skirts.

Dad snorts. "Just as well your mother's not here anymore to get on at me then." His smile fades. "Sorry Jamie. That was insensitive. Here, have a beer."

I accept the can he peels from a four-pack and open it immediately. Yes, I need a beer. I wasn't wrong when I called myself a 'piss artist' earlier. I don't think I'll be stopping at one beer either. My phone beeps. *Friend or foe,* I think to myself. Nothing good ever happens when I look at my phone. Could it be Meghan? Something inside me sinks. I've hardly thought about her for an hour or two. No. It's Claudia.

You bastard, shrieks the text. I can picture her, all nails, lipstick and tits. One or two of my mates couldn't understand why I didn't want to get off with her, but to use one of your best-used sayings Mum, beauty is only skin deep. I read on.

You ever go near my mother again and I'll make sure you pay for it. I've just found out what you've done.

Is that a threat Claudia?

It's a fucking promise.

I grin. *"Now, now. That's not language a 'lady' should use.* I press send and then add another. *But you're hardly a lady, are you?*

Fuck off.

Within a few minutes I've drained my can. "Any chance of another Dad?" Bloody hell. I never used to drink at home when you were alive Mum. Now I'm turning into a right alky.

Dad plucks another can. "I'll be sending you to the shop for some more soon," he chuckles. He's cheery for someone who's packed a case and walked out on his wife.

"*Send me to the shop?* I'm not ten anymore! You'll be telling me I can

171

have a packet of sweets for going next." My grin fades as my phone beeps again.

Stay away from my dad too. There's no need for you to keep in touch with him now.

That riles me. Who does she think she is? *You're a jealous cow, aren't you? I'll keep in touch with whoever I like.*

Jealous of what? You? Hardly.

I'd love never to see him again and I'd especially love never to see you again, but he's fleeced a share of my mother's home and business.

She's straight back. *He should have got more. They were going to be married.*

Nothing to do with you. When are you bringing my mother's car back?
I'm not.

You hated her guts but you'll drive around in her car. Two faced cow.
Yep.

"Who are you texting?" Dad plucks his own phone from his pocket. "You've got a face like a smashed crab."

"Claudia. Stupid bitch."

"Well if you don't like her, don't be texting with her."

"She keeps texting me. I'm just responding. Look, another one."

Just think. You and me could have had to share a brother or sister. That would have been awful.

Well, thank God that won't be happening. I feel bad as soon as I hit send. Sorry Mum. Obviously, I'd endure anything to have you back.

You're bad news Jamie. I just want you to stay away from my family. You're a weirdo and you make my skin crawl.

I decide to follow Dad's advice. What's the point of answering her? The doorbell goes. Dad and I look at each other.

"Well, aren't you going to get it." He's only been here five minutes and he's ordering me about like he owns the place.

"Is your dad here?" Katherine barges past me as I open the door. *Can*

CHAPTER TWENTY THREE

today get any worse?

"Come in," I say to her retreating form as she enters the lounge, towering over where Dad is sat – hands on hips.

"What are you playing at," she screeches. "You can't just fill a suitcase and clear off. We're supposed to be married."

"I've had enough of you," Dad frowns. "All we ever do is row about Anna and Jamie. She's bloody dead and you're more jealous than ever."

"Why would you be jealous about my dead mother?" My voice is strangely even. Katherine can't lick your boots Mum, dead or alive, and she knows that.

"She might as well still be alive." Katherine's voice is a nasty whine, not dissimilar to Claudia's. "Your father's always going on about the past." She turns to Dad. "You've changed. You're either slagging her off or you're acting like you're still in love with her. It's Anna, Anna, Anna, all the time and I can't take it anymore." Her voice trails off like she's running out of breath. A tear runs down her cheek. I hate to see women crying. I almost feel like comforting her because she's a woman and she's, well, *crying*. I remind myself of who she is and why she's crying.

"You don't have to *take* anything anymore, as you put it." Dad rises from his seat and passes her as though she's invisible. "I'm staying here now. Go home Katherine." Then in a nonchalant voice which must infuriate her further, he says, "how's that pizza doing son?"

I check on its half-cooked state before returning to the lounge to see what's going on. Dad's picked up his suitcase and is climbing the stairs. Katherine is literally launching herself after him. "Phil! Please! We can sort this out."

"Maybe I don't want to. I need some peace and to spend some time with my son."

The warmth that begins to spread through me at these words is rapidly chilled when she says, "you can't stand him half the time."

How could she say that in front of me? It makes me feel sick to think of Dad slagging me off behind my back too. I've spent my whole life chasing him. They're at the top of the stairs now, shouting into each other's faces. All I can see is *you,* balancing on the banister. My phone's ringing. I head back to the lounge, grateful for the distraction. It's Iain. Probably wanting to have a go at me about the 'text row' with his precious princess.

"I wanted to let you know that the police have been back in touch."

"Oh yeah?" I bet they've said the same thing to him as they said to Uncle Si.

"They're going to ask Twitter to trace the IP addresses on your mum's tweets."

"So they'll find the exact place where the tweets are being done?"

"Yes."

"Can they really do that?" I should have known *Iain* would get somewhere with it.

"Apparently, yes. It's information that Twitter doesn't give out, for obvious reasons, but they've got to when there's a court order or a police investigation."

"A police investigation?" Bloody hell. This shit is real Mum.

"Yes. I told you I made a *formal* complaint, rather than just messing around like you and your uncle did. I think the tweet about things not being accidental has piqued their interest as well."

"We weren't *messing about.* We want it stopping as much as you do. How long before we'll get to know about this IP address thing?"

"As soon as they know. The detective said to leave it with them and they'll be back in touch ASAP. What's all that shouting?"

"Dad and Katherine. He's moving back in. He's had enough of Katherine. But she's turned up here. She's saying he's obsessed with Mum but it sounds more like she is – it's all fun and games at this house." I feel like a bit of a traitor but maybe I *should* let Iain step in.

CHAPTER TWENTY THREE

"Moving back in!" Iain echoes. "No chance. That's half my house now!"

"Forty per cent."

"Whatever. Your mother would be fuming if she knew."

"I know. It's not going particularly well."

"I'm coming round. By the sound of them, we need to get 'em out before they wreck the place."

He's gone before I can talk him out of it. Although I'm secretly glad he's coming. I certainly can't deal with it. Meanwhile they're still screaming at each other. Their neighbours must love them. I remember him shouting at *you* like this Mum. You never really shouted back, even when he was following you around the house, you mainly just made sure you kept out of his way when he was in this frame of mind. Dad's cigarette has burnt itself out in the ashtray leaving a long trail of ash. It stinks. I help myself to another of his cans. He probably won't notice.

"I'll tell him the truth!" I've never heard Katherine shout so loud.

"Well tell him then. You'd do that wouldn't you?" I don't know what they're going on about and don't really care. I've had enough. They go on and on and on. I take my newly acquired beer into the garden. It's honestly like the good old days, listening to world war three rage around me. Except you managed to get rid of him Mum. I hope I can. I don't want him here either.

He went to stay with his parents for a while, not so long after you broke up. I don't know why he can't go there now. You had got on well with Gran and Grandad once but suddenly they stopped speaking to you, then me. I've often asked Dad to take me to see them but he refuses, making excuses all the time. You reckoned that he had told them a pile of crap about why you'd split up. Someone's lying somewhere. I've not even had a birthday card from them since you separated. One of my first thoughts after you died was that Gran and

Grandad might want to see me again, but they didn't. Dad still sees them, but they've had nothing to do with me. Weirdos. I don't get it. I've thought about contacting them but will be too pissed off if they still don't want to know me.

My phone lights up in front of me on the bistro table.

Claudia Price has started following you. She was telling me she hates me an hour ago. Then I realise that there's another tweet on your account.

@artistanna123 *I didn't fall. I was pushed. Is anybody listening? Why should others be enjoying life when they've taken mine?* **#cuckoo #beforemytime**

Chapter Twenty Four

Dad and Katherine are still going at it, when Iain arrives. I can't make out a lot of what's being said although there's a lot of bangs and crashes. He was sometimes 'handy' when he was married to you, but I thought he'd moved on from that.

"What the hell is going on?" It's the second time recently that I've heard Iain shout. His calm manner was, you said, one of the things you loved about him. "Oi, get down here," he shouts up the stairs.

"So what's happening?" He says to me, slightly more evenly as he sits in an armchair, crossing one leg over the other. I have to say; he *does* have the upper hand in this one. You'd be amused if you could see the shame on Dad and Katherine's faces, Mum, as they file into the room. Dad grabs his can and sits opposite the spot from which he rose. Iain points the remote at the TV. The room falls silent.

"I was watching that." We all look at Dad who might as well be sticking his pet lip out. I want to laugh. He points at Iain as he speaks. "You don't get to come in here and start calling the shots."

"This house was my fiancée's." Iain's voice is low. "I was going to be living here. Anna might just have been able to stomach you here if you were offering some support to Jamie, but she'd be literally whirling in her grave if she knew you were upstairs, in *her* room, bawling and carrying on with your girlfriend."

"Wife!" Katherine corrects.

Dad turns his pointing finger towards himself. "This used to be *my* house. And for the record, Iain." He leans forward in his armchair. "I'm going to be staying here, with my son, in *my* old room, which yes, I used to share with Anna too."

"Phil. Please. You're being stupid." Katherine tucks her hair behind her ear and stares at the floor.

"Over my dead body are you staying here mate." Iain stands up, towering over us all.

"Rather an unfortunate turn of phrase *mate*," Dad sneers.

"You are *not* staying here. Whether you like it or not, Anna left a proportion of this house to me, so I have a say in it."

"Doesn't Jamie get to decide?" All eyes turn to me at Dad's words.

"Shit. The pizza!" The smell of burning has wafted into the room. I rush to retrieve its blackened remains from the oven.

"Jamie. Come here. You need to hear this."

I slink back into the lounge, surprising myself by doing what Iain tells me to. *What now.* It's strange seeing Katherine's oversized form slumped in your armchair. She absolutely doesn't belong here. I stare at her, despising her more than ever.

"There's been another tweet," Iain begins, pausing as Dad and Katherine reach for their phones.

"The one about being pushed. I've already seen it."

"Who is doing this?" Dad looks up from his phone. "I've had enough of it all. You might think I'm a knobhead Iain, but I really don't want this shit being played out on social media."

"I'm on it." Iain sits down on the sofa, beside me. "I've made a formal complaint to the police – I need to let them know about this latest tweet as well now."

"What have they said?"

Mum, you wouldn't believe it! Dad and Iain are having a civil conversation. Especially considering that moments ago they were

CHAPTER TWENTY FOUR

squaring up to each other.

"They're going to drill down the IP address where the tweets are coming from." Iain waves his phone around as he speaks. "They're needing to put some kind of court order on Twitter to do this."

"I can't understand why they didn't just do that when I went to them with my uncle." I'm a bit irritated by it, to be honest. Iain getting things done. If it's not the art gallery, it's this police thing. I'm sick of feeling useless.

"You probably just weren't forceful enough." Iain runs his fingers through his receding hairline. "It comes with age." He looks knackered.

"*You* went to the police as well?" I think Dad's talking to me though he's not actually looking at me. Do you remember this Mum? He never looks at people straight in the eye if he's angry with them.

"Yeah. I went last week with Uncle Si. They didn't listen though."

"Why didn't you tell me?"

"I dunno. I forgot. There's been that much going on."

"I've a right to know what's happening." Dad slides a cigarette pack from his top pocket and takes one out. "In future, you keep me informed. Do you hear?"

"Who do you think you are?" Iain's voice rises again, though not to the same extent as before. "The big *I am*! Have you not noticed that Jamie's twenty-five now?"

I'm not sure if Iain's sticking up for me or just having a pop at Dad. I can't imagine him defending me and I'll never trust him. He's not been too bad since you died but I know he never really liked me around and mostly just put up with me. You were always falling out about me. I heard that telephone conversation you had with him earlier this year.

"What do you want me to do Iain?" You had said. "I have to put up with your bloody daughter and she's a lot more testing than Jamie."

Pause.

"I've just had enough of it all. It's not supposed to be like this. All the bad feeling and the bickering and …"

Pause.

"That's not true. He wouldn't have done that."

Pause.

"She's just jealous of him, and me, for that matter. She needs help."

Pause.

"I'll say what I want. You do. But I'm supposed to just put up and shut up."

Pause.

"Shouting and swearing won't get us anywhere, you know. Get a grip."

Pause.

"I thought you were different. I don't know how we've got any kind of future with all this around us."

Pause.

"I'm tired of rowing. I've lived like this before."

Pause.

"Well if you feel like that, then -"

And that was it. I heard you slamming things around for a while, so I put some music on to drown it all out. You can't beat a bit of Eminem to distract from family shit. Half of what he wrote was hitting out at his mother. An hour or so later, as I was on my way down for some food, I heard your phone ringing. I paused at the top, then sat on my usual *listen to arguments* step.

"What now Iain? I can't take any more crap."

Pause.

"No, I'm not prepared to do that. You can't ask me to do that."

Pause.

"Claudia's a damn sight worse, not to mention your dreadful ex-wife, and you're issuing *me* with ultimatums."

Pause.

CHAPTER TWENTY FOUR

"I don't need a week to think about it. I'm telling you now."
Pause.
"*You need a break!* From what? Me?"
Pause.
"I agree. It's not looking good. But if you need time away from me, maybe we should make it permanent."

From where I sat on the stairs, I could hear Iain's raised voice echoing through the quiet of the house, though obviously I couldn't make out what he was saying. He didn't like me and vice versa, Claudia didn't like you and vice versa. Me and Claudia couldn't stand each other. Add Dad and Stacey into all that and it was no wonder it was all messed up really.

"Bastard!" You eventually yelled, hurling your phone at the sofa.
I came down then. "You OK Mum?"
"No, I'm not. Leave me alone!"
"Don't bloody take it out on me. Just cos you got with an arsehole."
"Go to your room. It's got nothing to do with you."
"I think we both know that's not true, don't we?"

You *did* stay apart for a week. I found out from Claudia afterwards that he'd been accusing me of pinching money from his wallet. She was more of a money-grasping, deceitful cow than me. It was probably her. I kept out of his way after that. I didn't like how he looked at me. You and him seemed to snipe at each other all the time too. It was awful to see you unhappy again. Like you'd been with Dad. From the bit of time I spent with him, I could see *he* wasn't happy with Katherine either. And still isn't.

"I'm going home." Katherine gets to her feet and shoots daggers at Dad. "You can do what you like. I've had enough of the whole thing. I'll leave you to it."

I wait for Dad's reaction, but he stays where he is, slumped in the armchair with his unlit cigarette. I wonder if he's wary of lighting it in the house in front of Iain. Katherine doesn't look at any of us as she slings her handbag over her shoulder and stamps out of the room. She pauses in the hallway for a moment and then the front door bangs. I used to do that when I was about ten.

"Don't you think you should go after your *wife*?" Iain looks at his watch. "I'd better be going soon as well. I need to get to the police station. The officer I want to speak to is not on shift for much longer."

"I'll come with you." Really, I want to get away from Dad. I've spent my whole life running after him and now I want him to bugger off.

"No need," Iain stands up. "I need to get back to Claudia straight after the station, so I'll give you a bell if there's any developments."

"I might have known." Claudia. No one would believe she's in her twenties. She's a dick.

Dad cracks another Carling.

"That's it Phil. The answer to everything is always at the bottom of a beer."

"Get lost Iain." Dad's eyes are marble hard. "Mind your own business, have you got that?"

I'm looking at the tweet again and at the photo of you beside it. "What do you think the hashtag cuckoo thing means? I get the *before my time* bit but not the *cuckoo* thing. Doesn't it mean someone is crazy or something?"

"It can do." Iain pulls his car keys from his pocket. "Although, if it's taken literally, there's that *cuckoo in the nest* saying. Something about cuckoos laying their eggs in the nests of other birds. Or chucking other birds out of nests they want to live in."

"Oh." I'm not sure what this might mean. It's something to think about though.

"The police are on it anyway Jamie." Iain jangles his keys. "And like I said, I'll keep you informed." He pulls his phone from his jeans and strides towards the kitchen. "Oh, what does she want now? Hello

CHAPTER TWENTY FOUR

Stacey. What's up?"

I feel the hair stand up on the back of my neck. *Stacey*. Still, I'm glad that he doesn't seem to want to speak to her. Though that might be because he's in front of us two.

Iain closes the door behind him and is speaking in a really low voice. The telly is still off so I catch bits and pieces of their conversation. I hear your name mentioned, Mum, but it seems that they're mainly talking about Claudia. Poor little Princess Claudia! She's struggling apparently. She's quiet. Iain will do something nice with her. He will talk to her. *Spoilt little cow.* I can't look at him when he returns to the room.

"Right, I'm off then. I'll let you know what the police say." The door bangs again. It's like Piccadilly Circus in here today, to use another one of your sayings Mum.

"So, we're going to find out who's tweeting, are we?" Dad's starting to slur. He's had four beers now and obviously I don't know what he drank before he got here. Looking at the state of him, he probably shouldn't have been driving.

I can't be arsed with Dad today. He'll either spend the evening slagging Katherine off, or Iain, or you. Although, to be honest, he's eased off a lot, compared to what he used to be like. Before you died, he'd take great delight in recounting his version of events from when you were married. He'd never tire of telling me all the things he'd done for you and what 'pure evil' you were. It must have hurt you that I'd listen to it, but I had him on a bit of a pedestal then. He kept me at arm's length which made me go after him more. Eventually you asked me not to tell you what he was saying – you didn't need to know. It was all crap anyway. I wish I'd stuck up for you when he used to slag you off. But I couldn't. I knew *you* loved me no matter what, whereas *he* would swat me away like a fly.

I look at him now, eyes fixed to the TV screen again, can of beer firmly in hand. He hasn't shaved and desperately needs his hair cutting. You'd be mortified if you could see him. He looks as though he never moved out. He's got *you* a bit on a pedestal now by the sounds of it.

I pick up my phone and type *cuckoo* into Google. *Bird. TV programme.* Yep. Yep. I add *meaning* to my Google search. *Lays eggs in nests of other birds.* Perhaps this has something to do with you being pregnant. Could *beforemytime* be something to do with a cuckoo clock? I don't know. I've never been any good at cryptic clues. Straight down the line, that's me.

I scroll down. *A mad person. Unwelcome intruder in a place or situation.* I immediately think of Claudia. There's a picture of a newly hatched cuckoo fledgling, pushing the other birds out of a nest. I then think of Katherine and how she would like to push me into the next century, given half a chance. However, the overriding image in my mind is Stacey's terrified face when I pushed her backwards into the road. Suddenly I'm overwhelmed by a desire to capture this cuckoo thing. "I'm off upstairs to Mum's studio. I want to paint."

"Eh, what?" Dad doesn't look up from the TV. "Paint? *You! Why?*"

"I'm having a go. I've applied to art college."

"I guess it's better than that shite insurance job. Just. I still reckon you should work for me. *P.J. Hardaker and Son. It's got a bit of a ring to it, don't you think?* You could even put some more money in - become a *shareholder.* You're never going to make a living from *painting.* I can't imagine you'll ever be as good as your mother was."

He's off his rocker Mum. *A shareholder!* He really does my head in. One minute he tells me how much you ruined his life and what you owe him, and the next minute, he's saying that I'll never be as good as you. He makes my head spin. Since you died, my eyes have been well and truly opened to him.

I love the smell of your studio. Paint and paper. It reminds me of my school art classroom. I sketch out what's in my head before I start.

CHAPTER TWENTY FOUR

There's a knack to creating a bird. It starts as a conjoined oval and circle and is built up from there. Before I know it, I've created in watercolour, the image of a cuckoo flying away after leaving its egg in another family's nest.

I look at my wet painting, feeling sad, knowing that the young cuckoo will never see its mother. It makes me think of you. And then I think of Meghan. I feel lonely and empty again tonight. Even though Dad's here, there's a shadowy space inside me that I want to fill with something. Something that feels as though it will never be available to me again.

Dad's fallen asleep when I go back down. He grunts when I shake him and finally, after much persuasion, shifts himself onto the sofa, where I drape a blanket over him. I'm glad about this as I didn't want him sleeping in your bed. It shouldn't matter. But it does.

Chapter Twenty Five

Bollocks. Bollocks. Bollocks. Every time I come to Leeds I get lost in this stupid one-way system. I think I've gone around it three times now, willing you, Mum, to wave your magic wand from wherever you are and produce the College of Art, complete with a parking spot, in front of me. Instead I finally abandon the car in a multi-storey and fire up the Google maps walking route to get there. Fifteen minutes. Shit. I'm already ten minutes late. It's only now, that I'm late, that I realise how much I want a place on this course. I really hope I haven't blown it.

Ring them, instructs an urgent voice from the depths of my mind. I'm sure the voice is yours. *Erm, why didn't I think of that?* I'm a div sometimes.

"I'm really sorry," I pant as I burst into the reception area. "I'm Jamie Hardaker. I rang a few minutes ago." The fifteen-minute walk has only taken me seven. I'm more out of breath than normal, I haven't been running like I used to, so am a bit out of condition. I'm going to have to get back into it.

In contrast to me, the receptionist has a calm and efficient air and she has a look of 'perfect' about her, making me feel even more all over the place. "Take a seat," she points to a sofa with one hand and presses a button on her desk with the other. "Jamie Hardaker is here,"

CHAPTER TWENTY FIVE

she announces. "Yes, the one who rang." She looks like Meghan and I try not to stare at her. I wish I could get Meghan out of my head. She probably doesn't give me a passing thought.

I'm glad of a sit down for a few moments to get myself together whilst I wait for the interviewer. I'm nervous. He's not just a *Mr*, he's a *professor*. Dad's gone back to Katherine, thank God, so I've had a quiet few days to work on my portfolio. I'm pleased with my work although I'm still fighting not to slip further into my black hole. It's probably normal. You've died. Things didn't work out with Meghan. I can't shake this awful sense of dread. It refuses to relax its grip on me.

"Jamie. Good to meet you. Glad you made it." A softly spoken man with John Lennon-style glasses and a long, pointy beard offers his hand. "Professor Edward Blackstock. Call me Ed."

"Good to meet you too." I shake his hand. "Did you get my message? I'm sorry to be late. I got held up at my mother's art gallery." I'll get that one in, I think to myself. Plus, it sounds better than *I got lost in the one-way system.*

Professor Blackstock, erm, Ed strokes his beard. "And your mother is …?"

I stare at his weird blue-fringed shoes. "Anna Hardaker."

"Oh my goodness! You're her son?"

"Yes." I feel excitement rising in me like champagne bubbles. We're impressing him Mum.

"She's, erm, well, she's-"

"Dead." At least I might get offered a college place out of sympathy.

"Yes. I'm sorry for your loss. Such a waste. Well let's see if you've inherited her wonderful talent. Shall we?" He gestures towards a door off the reception area. "After you."

I watch as Ed flicks through my work. His expression is difficult to read. "Yes." He finally looks up. "This work shows great promise."

"It does?" This is all that matters to me at this moment. I must get a place. I respond to the questions about what inspires me. You, obviously, landscapes, relationships and I reel off some other artists, Monet, Turner, Van Gogh – the classics. He asks me about the art business I've inherited and about my favourite works of art. I admit I've got a lot to learn and other than GCSE Art, it's only recently, since you died, that this urge to be an artist has flared up in me.

"You've applied very late." He frowns as he runs his finger down a list. "We've only been able to interview you because one person has withdrawn." Then after a maddening moment of silence, he stretches his arm towards me. "Congratulations Jamie. I'm delighted to welcome you to the Extended Diploma in Art and Design."

"Brilliant!" I clasp my sweating hand around his. *I've done it Mum. I'm in.* It flashes into my mind that you had to die for this to open for me. I kick the thought away. I can't think like this anymore.

"If you'd like to take this to admissions," he hands me a slip of paper, "they will get the ball rolling and give you the course preparation details." I scoop my portfolio up, feeling lighter than I have for a long time. I'll have to let work know that I'm not going back. I'm still covered by a sick note for stress and depression and on full pay so they probably won't be happy.

I'm crackling with unspent energy as I leave the college an hour later. I run back to the car, well as much as running is possible with trousers, shoes and a large, bulky file. I'm pleased my gym stuff is still in the car.

I walk into the gym feeling like the business. Rather than my usual scuttling about, I catch myself in the mirror with my head held high and chest puffed out. Five minutes into my cross-trainer session, I notice someone checking me out. I smile at her and she responds to me. She also has a look of Meghan. I definitely have *a type*. Petite girls, long, dark, straight hair. Pretty.

So I'm now sitting in the steam room next to the Meghan lookalike racking my brains for something to say. "Hot in here, isn't it?" *Blimey Jamie! Is that the best you can do?*

She giggles. It's a pleasant, tinkly sound that sends a tremor up my spine. "That's the idea."

"I just meant hotter than normal." I want to add *like you*, but instead say, "how long have you been a member here?"

"Oh a while – you?"

I'm trying not to look at her perfect tits bulging out of her white bikini top. I keep my gaze fixed firmly on her eyes. I can't make out what colour they are in the steam room but I'm sure they'll be brown.

"Just a couple of weeks."

"Do you like it?"

"Yeah – it's cool."

"But not in here."

She's stroking the top of her thigh. I wonder if she realises how much she's getting to me. I'm melting in here but I need to find out if she's got a boyfriend and get her phone number. "So do you come here on your own?" That's nearly as bad as *do you come here often?*

"Mostly yes." Her knee is touching the outside of my leg. It's electric. Even Meghan didn't have this effect on me.

I'm not sure what *mostly* means so I decide to go for it. "Do you fancy a coffee after?"

"I can't today. Sorry. Some other time though?"

"Great. Sure. I'm Jamie." I offer her my hand.

"Carly." She touches mine lightly. I lift it to my lips and kiss the top of it, just above her knuckles so that she's in no doubt I fancy her. She giggles again. I *really* like her.

It's only mid-afternoon when I return to the car, thinking about what a good day it's been so far. I feel more than a twinge of guilt for being happy Mum. But then, I'm cut back down to size. As my phone signal returns outside the gym, a flood of text messages from Iain light up my phone.

I'm at the police station now.
There's been another tweet.
They're doing something.
They know where the tweets are coming from.
Call me.
Where are you?

I don't know what to do first. Check Twitter or ring Iain. My stomach growls, all sickly. I've not eaten for hours. I've been too on edge. I can almost hear your voice Mum. *Trust you, Jamie. How can you think about your stomach at a time like this?* I shut my phone inside my glove box, I can't face it all just yet. I want to think about art college, feel normal and look forward to something for a change – just for half an hour and then I will return to reality. I grab my wallet and stride across the leisure park to TGI Friday's. They've got an 'early-bird' offer – a steak and a pint.

We all came in here for Auntie Liz's fortieth, do you remember Mum? I'd turned down a lad's night to come. I wasn't chuffed when I learned Iain and Claudia would be there but decided I could cope. I found out there'd be a fair few others there too. I did my best to avoid sitting near them but whilst I was at the loo, everyone had shuffled about a bit, leaving me sat next to Iain with Claudia opposite. Nice. Not.

Iain spoke to me a bit. I'd just started my crap job at the insurance company, so he was asking about that. Pretending like he was interested in me or something. Claudia just sat there with her usual face on. You and she didn't speak at all. I think you'd given up. Everyone else seemed to be having a good time and if they sensed the atmosphere between us four, they didn't let on.

Iain asked me if I fancied a day at York, rally driving, soon. I didn't really know what that was all about. *Not with him* particularly, but if he was paying … Claudia really saw her arse then. "You never do anything with *me* Dad. *Anything."*

"Why, do you want to go rally driving?"

"If it means you don't take *him.* He's got his own dad."

Stupid cow. "No worries Claudia. I'm not after yours. In fact, if I never saw either of you again, I wouldn't give a toss."

"Jamie. Stop it. It's your auntie's birthday." You piped up then.

"Well let me swap places with someone then. I'm not sitting with these arseholes."

"That's enough Jamie." Uncle Si stood up. "Have a bit of respect. Swap with me, before you spoil everyone's night."

We had another drink and then the meal came. Everyone settled down and I started to have a better evening now that I was sat with Auntie Liz and her goddaughter who was quite fit. I looked across at Claudia. She didn't have a meal.

"Are you OK Claudia?" You asked her.

She ignored you.

"She doesn't feel well," said Iain.

"Then why did she come?" You were trying to keep your voice low but I could hear you, three places away.

"Because she felt fine before we set off."

I watched as you glared at Claudia. Usually you put up and shut up. But the wine must have helped you to feel braver. "She wants to ruin the evening," you had said. "Just like she ruins *everything."*

"That's enough Anna." Iain pushed his chair back with a scrape. "We're not coming down to your level. We're going. Come on Claudia."

"Look. I'm sorry. I didn't mean -"

What are you apologising for? I thought to myself. She's a miserable cow. You're right.

"I'll ring you tomorrow." Iain rose from his seat.

"Don't bother," you replied.

Claudia stood up. Iain threw twenty pounds onto his plate. "I'm sorry about this everyone. But my daughter comes first." Then with a final glare at you, they headed off. I knew you were about to cry. You shot to the loo and Auntie Liz ran after you.

I'm sat three tables away from where we were that evening. Just looking across at that table makes me shudder. I give my order to the waitress. She's petite with long, dark hair. (nudge, wink). After I have ordered, I add, "Maybe you could write your phone number down for me?" I'm feeling braver than normal today. I don't know what's got into me.

She flashes a diamond-clad ring finger at me. "Sorry, already spoken for."

Gutted. Everyone around me is settling down. I'll be left behind if I'm not careful. Although with my new-found money and art college place, I should be fine. After I've eaten, I nip into Tesco Express for more beer and some essentials – ready meals, pizza, chocolate, cake, etc. I've always dreamed of my food shop being like this but can feel you frowning at me as I pay. I lug my bags to the car and drive home, singing along to *Don't look back in anger*. Oasis rocks.

I've unpacked the shopping before I remember the phone in the glove box. *I'll have to deal with it now.*

It's dead. Whilst I wait for enough charge to switch it back on, I open a beer. I'm getting as bad as Dad. I guess I feel on edge all the time Mum. I never know what's coming next. You'd probably tell me to drink chamomile tea. I remember you making me a cup before my driving test. It tasted like gnat's piss. No thanks.

I can hear your voice, warning me not to turn out like Dad, holding him before me as an example of how not to be. You would mean well but I sometimes used to hate you for doing it. My divorcing parents, always at war and me, never knowing whose side I should be on. I guess my loyalties were with you Mum – you were the one who'd brought me up.

CHAPTER TWENTY FIVE

Which is why Iain, when he came along, was as bitter a pill for me to swallow as seawater, especially when he started to get his feet under the table. Dad backed off and left you alone after you met Iain and I felt really pushed out. He was your future. I was your past. You were both acting, you and Iain, like I was in the way. You wanted me to move out. It was a crappy feeling.

I'm on Twitter now. I click through.

@artistanna123 If *they are not stopped, they will do it again. Someone else will die. Why should they live when it's their fault I'm dead?* #cuckoo #beforemytime

Stacey's retweeted with a 'shocked' emoji and added *who needs Coronation Street?* The post has twelve 'likes.' Probably messed up weirdos. Someone I don't know had typed the word *macabre* and another, *sick*. I don't know what *macabre* means - I Google it. Then I write *Do one, all of you.* As I press the tweet button, my phone rings. Iain, of course. "I've been trying to get hold of you for ages." His tone isn't as abrasive as it normally is when he rings me. "The police have been round to see me and they've told me what they've found so far."

"What have they said?"

"They've got Twitter to reveal the IP addresses of all the tweets so far. They're all different."

"What do you mean?" I'm wandering up and down the lounge as I speak to him. Since you died Mum, I can't sit still. I can't relax. I'm wired all the time.

"They're all libraries. Nine different libraries. All local. Your mum's library card has been used each time to log into the network."

"Really? What does that mean?"

"The police have asked if she ever lost her purse or her bag. I don't know anything about that – *do you?* I think she'd have mentioned losing her *purse*, if she had."

"Nope. Not to me either."

"So they're saying that the person behind the tweets is probably someone who knew her well enough to be able to get hold of her library card before her …" His voice trails off.

"Death?" I finish. Everyone's so scared of using the 'd' word. I decide to ignore the accusatory tone in his voice when he said *'someone who knew her well enough.'*

"They're quite interested in that hashtag cuckoo thing. They're saying it could be a family link – we were on about that the other day, weren't we?"

"A family link? *What family?* It's hardly a family."

"I know it's hard for you Jamie. It is for me too."

"*Hard.* It's much worse than *hard.*"

"So, which libraries are they on about?"

"They're all local. Hang on. I've written them down. There are the big ones; Leeds Central, Harrogate, York and Skipton. Then five smaller ones; Burley, Pudsey, Otley, Ilkley and Horsforth."

"I wonder why they're all different."

"So whoever it is can cover their tracks, I guess."

"What happens now?"

"The police are checking the tweet times against CCTV at all the libraries so it's just going to take a little longer. Anyway, they're on it."

"I'll let my Uncle Si and Auntie Liz know."

Chapter Twenty Six

It's one of those nights when it's too hot to sleep. It's nearly two in the morning and I'm staring at the wide-open window yet again, grateful for the slivers of light the garden lamps offer. I leave them on all the time now. I've always hated the dark. You did too, didn't you? Now, because I'm alone in the house, it feels like it could suffocate me.

I hear an owl in the distance and the old lady two streets away is still calling for her dog who died two years ago. You said it was one of the saddest things you ever heard and reported it to the authorities, worried about her being out, alone, in the middle of the night. You worried about everyone.

I wish I could stop thinking. My mind won't shut down. Round and round it goes like the Scalextric you once bought me for my birthday. I turn over, slamming my head into the pillow. Another sound is competing with the owl for attention, a low humming sound. I lay, frozen for a few moments. Then a scratching sound, like a cat at a scratching post. I sigh in the silence and jump as there's a thud. *Someone's in the house.* I click my bedside lamp. I'm sure I hear a splintering of glass then some banging. It sounds as though the doors of the kitchen units are being opened and closed again. I sit up, knowing I'll have to go and investigate but not daring to. If you were here Mum, you'd be down there by now, protecting us. You wouldn't have thought twice about it – that's what you were like. I'm sat here, panicking. *Bloody coward.* My tracker is saying my heart rate is 108. Told you I was scared.

There's silence for a few moments and I steel myself to go downstairs. I press three nines into my phone, ready to hit call, then yank my pool cue from its case. I creep down the stairs in the darkness, avoiding the stair that creaks. As always, I close my eyes against the memory that haunts me every time I go up or down the stairs. You, broken, at the foot of them.

As I stand in the hallway, where you lay dead, adrenaline is coursing through my body and I'm struggling to control my breathing. I hear another sound, this time a rustling that sounds like papers being leafed through. *Be a man*, I say to myself as I snap the lounge light on. I race towards the kitchen door, holding the snooker cue aloft and burst in.

All is as it should be. I flick the light on and laugh out loud in relief as I notice what will have probably caused the noise. A fox or something. In the garden, the wheelie bin is overturned and the contents are strewn across the lawn. There's nothing to explain the glass or the door bangs though. Maybe it's next door. It's really rattled me. I open the fridge and have a huge swig of milk. You'd bollock me if you were here. *Pour it into a glass Jamie. No one wants your germs on the bottle.* Ra-ra-ra. At least I'm not drinking beer. Although it might settle me down if I did.

I wake early the following morning, surprising really, to say I've been awake half the night. I'll be glad when I start college and have purpose and routine in my day again. I'll go into the gallery later. I need to get my brain into something and I want to be more involved, especially if I'm taking sixty per cent of the profit – I need to physically earn some of it.

The house is cold this morning, despite the sunshine outside. Downstairs greets me like a lonely punch in the chest. I'm sick of being on my own. You used to do my head in Mum, and Iain even more, but right now, I'd kill for a bit of company and banter. I grab a muffin and my keys – there's no point hanging around here.

I'm sitting at the lights when I notice Dad coming out of the library. His hands are full of leaflets and books. Yes, I did use the words *Dad* and *library* in the same sentence. I beep the horn and he looks startled. Then he notices me and points to a parking space over the road, which I head towards. I can never parallel park when someone's watching me. He's laughing at me when I eventually get out of the car. "You made a right meal of that son!" I jump a little as he claps me on the back, having stuffed all his books under one arm.

"What have you got there? You've never read a book in your life, have you?"

"I told you I was going to sort this business out. And I am. The library is pretty good actually. I've got some books out on writing a business plan, getting some more finance and doing some advertising."

"Sounds like you're on it."

"Sure am. They run free courses on it all too so I've put my name down."

"Cool." I am genuinely shocked. I thought, he'd take that **twenty** grand and piss it all up. At least he *has* bought a van and finding him here shows he's taking it seriously. I doubt you'd believe it though!

"Well without you, son, I couldn't be doing this."

"Without Mum, you mean?"

"She'd never have given me anything. She took the lot when we split up. I was forced to kip in the car in the beginning. Don't you remember – she wouldn't even let me get my head down on the sofa after we'd split up."

"Yeah. Yeah." I've heard his sorry rendition too many times. I used to attend his pity party. I often tried to reconcile you with this woman he told me you were, but I could never match them up.

"Are you going to treat your old man to some breakfast then?" Dad pats his paunch. "Since you're the one with all the money."

"You can't have spent that twenty grand *already!*" I bet he's going to come at me for more. He's hinted at it enough.

"A fair bit. I've bought a van and a load of new gear, haven't I?"

"You just need to put them all to work now."

"I am doing. Stop being a smart-arse Jamie. It doesn't suit you." His jaw is clenched and he looks like he hasn't shaved for days. "I can't just launch a business. Some thought has to go in first."

"Sorry – I wasn't being -"

"Yes you were. You're definitely your mother's son at times. I don't care how much money you've got in the bank, if you want me and you to spend time together then you show me some respect, right?"

"Yep." I'm suddenly desperate to make amends. "Where do you want to go for breakfast then? There's a Wetherspoons over there."

"It'll do, I suppose."

Dad orders an extra-large, full English. I know I'll struggle with a bacon sarnie. My appetite's still shot. I need to start pumping some iron in the gym. Build myself up a bit.

"So has Katherine got over herself yet?" The tomato sauce bottle 'farts' when I squeeze the sauce out and it still makes me laugh. Dad smiles too. I think it's the first time I've seen him smile since I bumped into him.

"How old are you?" He takes the bottle from me and slathers sauce all over his food. You used to go mad about the amount of sauce Dad and I got through. I watch him as he shovels his breakfast down. The sight and smell of the grease and all that red sauce is making me feel nauseous. His breakfast looks as though someone has bled all over it. Instantly, I'm transported again to that vision of you, laid at the bottom of our staircase. I don't think it will ever leave me.

"Things are still a bit strained. With Katherine I mean." Dad wipes sauce from his mouth onto the back of his hand. *Ugh!* "She was jealous of your mother before, but now, it's gone to a whole new level."

"What's she got to be jealous of?" I don't get it. I really don't get it.

"Apparently I talk too much about her and the tweets are driving her mad too." He stabs at a sausage. "She thinks that now your mum's gone, we should be getting on with our lives. I wish she'd understand that me and your mother used to be married."

"She's jealous of *me* too." I probably should shut up and change the subject. I might be a bit lonely but no way do I want Dad coming to stay with me again. He gets stoked up easily and I don't want to add fuel to his Katherine-shaped fire.

"Me and your mum had our differences." He chews, slowly. "Big differences, as you know. I hated her at times. She had her life sussed, whereas mine, well, you know." He takes a slug of his tea. He's worked up. "I resented her hugely, especially when she turfed me out. Then her business went on to be successful. And her art."

"I'm going to be as good as she was." I speak to the table, rather than with conviction. "I've been offered a place at art college. Do you remember I mentioned it?"

"Good for you son. Anyway, it was *me* that got your mother to where she is, I supported her and never saw a penny. She made a bomb out of that damn awful *Toxic Marriage* painting."

He's not interested in me at all. He wouldn't care whether I did well at art college or ended up in the gutter.

He continues. "I guess it's true what they say about Karma. In a roundabout way, I'm being paid back now. Shame it had to happen *this* way though. That she had to die, and that."

It was bad enough when he talked about you when you were still here, but now? Well, it's just plain wrong. I really want to change the subject. "I've joined a gym, Dad. Virgin Active. It's the business."

"Good for you."

"You should come with me sometime. I've got some guest passes. Do you fancy it? There's a spa bit and everything."

"Nah, it's not for me."

"You used to be into fitness, didn't you? I remember you cycling all the time."

"Never mind all that." He lines up his knife and fork in the centre of his plate. "What's the latest with Iain and the police? Any developments yet?"

"You could say that."

He doesn't hear what I just said because he's talking over me, as usual. "Someone will end up being done for wasting police time." He laughs like a drain. I'm not sure what is so funny.

I stare at him. "They're actually taking it really seriously, you know."

"Go on." I've got his attention now. "What do you mean?"

"Apparently the tweets are being done at a few different libraries. Whoever is doing it might have known Mum. It's her library account that's being used. The PIN number and everything.

"Bloody hell." He plucks his phone from his pocket. "I'm gonna let Katherine know. She thought it was a hoax – a load of shite – I always knew there would be more to it." As he presses the buttons on his phone, he says, "Don't libraries have CCTV? Surely they'll be checking that?"

"That's what we're waiting on."

"The tweets have changed, talk of her being pushed and stuff." Dad takes a noisy slurp of his tea. "It can't be your mum that's behind them – I don't believe in all that - spooks and stuff. But they *are* getting worse."

"I know." And your broken body slips into my mind once more. You're twitching, in the final throes of life. Blood is seeping from your mouth, ears and nose.

"It all wants getting to the bottom of anyway." Dad piles sauce-

CHAPTER TWENTY SIX

splattered napkins on the top of his plate. I only see blood smatterings. "I've said this all along. You let me know as soon as you hear something, do you hear?"

"Yep." I'm not going to confide in Dad about it, but once again, I feel an awful sense of foreboding, of dread. I just want the whole thing to go away.

As I walk back to the car, I notice a familiar figure in the window of Costa Coffee. I slink behind a wall and watch for a few moments. There he is, large as life. Iain, with a woman. He's holding her hand across the table. The woman is angled away from me so it is difficult to have a go at recognising her. All I know is that it isn't Stacey as this woman is brunette and Stacey is blonde, like Claudia. *Maybe she has dyed it.* I keep watching. No, this woman is thinner than Stacey. Iain lifts the woman's hand to his lips. It's far more than a friendly gesture. *Bastard.*

As I wrestle with the urge to march in and lamp him, my anger gives way to shock as the woman turns her head. There she is, one of your best friends. Sarah. You'd be gutted Mum. *How long has he been seeing her?* I wonder if you ever suspected anything before you died. She seems to be looking straight towards me. I duck down. I'll work out how to deal with it later.

Chapter Twenty Seven

The art gallery is manic when I get there. I've spent the journey trying to convince myself that it's just friendship between Iain and Sarah. Or if there is something happening, maybe it's only just started. Although that is still bad. Your fiancé and your best friend.

Dawn is busy explaining the story behind your now infamous *Toxic Marriage* painting. She trails off a little when she notices me.

"This is Anna's son," she announces. My cheeks are on fire as her group burst into applause. After the usual condolences about your death, they speak to me as though I'm some sort of celebrity. I tend to respond with the same stock answers now. *Some days are better than others. Yeah, I miss her.* On and on and on. No one can bring you back and no one can ever say anything that will make me feel better. What does lift me is when one or two people from the group ask me about my own work as an artist. It's the first time I've been asked about *my* art, apart from at my college interview.

As I detach myself from the group, a woman catches my arm. "You must miss her dreadfully." Then, in a more guarded tone, she adds, "I follow her on Twitter. You must know about the tweets?"

"Yes. We're looking into it." Clearly she's digging for more but she's not getting it from me.

"Is there anything you want me to do?" I ask Dawn as she breezes

CHAPTER TWENTY SEVEN

past me, leading her captive audience to another part of the gallery.

"There are a few bits and pieces you could help with actually," she says. "But it's stuff I need to show you first. Perhaps you could do a bit of filing in the office until I get the chance to go through things with you. Bear with me one moment," she says to the group. "If you could just be discussing this picture here. It depicts the relationship between a man and his home. Perhaps you could talk about the emotion behind the piece."

I follow her into the office where she unlocks a filing cabinet and thrusts a pile of papers into my hands. "They're mainly receipts and purchase orders. Oh Iain's forgotten these." She moves a pile of books from the top of the cabinet to the edge of a cupboard near the door. There are six books with *Landscapes for Beginners* at the top. *Iain's learning to paint!* He muscled in on our lives and now he's elbowing his way in on the only thing I'm interested in. I'm going to be the artist, *not him.*

Half an hour later, I'm still filing and feeling resentful about it. I own sixty per cent of this business and I'm being treated like an office junior. *Everyone must start somewhere. It's the way to learn – bottom up.* Your voice again, bollocking me.

My phone flashes on top of the filing cabinet.

Anna Hardaker has followed Stacey Price who has 258 followers. I click through it and my breath catches in my throat when I realise that you've tweeted again.

@artistanna123 *My paintings still hang where they hung. Others have cashed in on my life. How does your conscience let you sleep at night? #cuckoo #beforemytime*

I dial Iain's number. The very least I can do is interrupt his little afternoon meeting. "There's been another tweet," I announce flatly, without any preamble. "And whoever is operating my mother's Twitter account is now following your ex-wife too."

"*What?* Let me have a look. I'll ring you back when I've reported it to the police. It needs to be added into their investigation."

"Sorry if I have interrupted your afternoon. I'm sure you have better things to be doing." I hope he detects the sarcasm in my voice. I end the call before he has chance to reply.

I can't think straight enough to do any more filing. All I want is normality. To go to work, or now, college, find a girlfriend, move to a new house (yes, I've decided.) I just want to live an ordinary life instead of one filled with ghosts, regrets, fear and bloody tweets. I throw myself into the office chair and look over your office. This spot is where you spent many hours. I feel as though I have hijacked your life in some way – the life you were supposed to be living, the one that somehow, I'm going to have to try and live on your behalf. You used to be proud of me and I *will* make you proud again. We didn't get on too well in your final months, but that was down to Iain. I jump as my phone rings.

"Right, I've let them know the latest." Iain sounds out of breath. "But in the meantime, they've let me know more. They've got CCTV footage on four of the tweet locations so far. They've identified the same person at all four libraries on the different occasions."

"Who is it?"

"They wouldn't tell me over the phone."

"Would they say whether it was a man or a woman."

"Nope. But they want me to go in and have a look at them tomorrow and help with identification. Hopefully this nightmare can end, once and for all."

"Can I take some paper and oil pastilles home with me?" I ask Dawn.

"Yes, of course you can but I'd have thought your mum would have tons of that sort of stuff stashed at home."

"I'm not going home tonight."

CHAPTER TWENTY SEVEN

I can't face another night like last night. Lying awake, hearing and seeing things. I jump in the car and head south on the motorway. I have no idea where I'm going but my spinning mind escorts me to North Wales in the middle of nowhere. And as luck would have it, there's a room available in the first bed and breakfast I come across.

The view from the window is breath-taking. I'm relieved to be here, away from the house that I can no longer relax in. It's a rubbish phone signal and no one knows where I am. I'm going to do what you would do Mum. I sprawl out in the cushioned window seat with my huge sketch pad and oil pastilles, intent on capturing the scenic landscape stretching away from me. *I can really do this!* I copy the cloud formation whilst showing the approaching storm and the darkness that's sneaking in behind the fleeting sunshine. My fingers flick back and forth over the page. I'm at peace and I know that from now on, I'll always paint and draw. Whether I make any money from it, or not.

I'm overcome by a feeling of melancholy as I look over the luxurious, yet confining bed and breakfast room, then back at the picture I've created. There's an air of menace about it, something I've shown, without meaning to. It's just where my head is. Maybe the calm before the storm. Tomorrow we will find out about these pathetic tweets and for whoever it is, the shit will hit the fan. But for tonight, I'm out of it all. Nothing and no one can spoil this feeling of freedom.

Chapter Twenty Eight

I've dragged myself back to reality and am in the supermarket. I was tempted to stay another night. It would have been perfect if I'd had a girlfriend with me. I'm so sick of being on my own. I must keep living, whatever happens. I'm sure that's what you'd be telling me to do. I can't stop checking my phone. Iain will be ringing any time soon with news from the police station. My breath catches when I notice Meghan is working and despite every bit of me wanting to avoid her, I decide to brave it and go to her checkout. It was her who messed up, not me.

"I'm sorry about what happened," she mutters as she scans my stuff through, avoiding my eye. "It's just, me and Connor, we had unfinished business. I did like you Jamie, it's -"

"Look, it's fine." I sling my purchases into a carrier. "I'll live."

I'm pleased with myself for going to *her* checkout and I'm thinking *her loss* as I walk away. I'm not so pleased when I notice Katherine sat outside the supermarket with a bag of shopping and her head stuck in a book.

"Oh hello Jamie, are you OK? I'm just waiting for your dad to pick me up."

"What are you doing around here? Isn't it nearer for you to go to Asda?" I hope she's not going to make a habit of it, turning up near where I live, that is.

CHAPTER TWENTY EIGHT

"I had to drop the car at the garage. I've just picked up a bit of shopping and called into the library. What are you up to?"

"Killing time whilst we wait for the CCTV results. Has Dad mentioned it to you?"

"Vaguely." She turns away from me, seemingly scanning the car park for Dad. "It's none of my business really."

"Well, Iain's gone into the station to have a look at the CCTV footage. He should be ringing me any time."

"Are you going to hang around until your dad gets here?"

"Nah. I saw him yesterday."

"Did you?" Her eyes narrow. "He never said anything to me about it."

"We just had breakfast. It was good to catch up."

"I wonder why he never mentioned it. It's not that long since you last saw one another."

Her voice goes right through me and I can't stand the look on her face. "I've got a ton of stuff to do. I'll catch you later."

My phone's ringing as I turn onto the main road. I can't be arsed pulling over so decide that whoever it is can wait until I get home, even if it is Iain. I'm in a foul mood after seeing Katherine's reaction to my having breakfast with Dad. And I must admit, that having seen Meghan, I feel really cheesed off that things didn't work out there. The overwhelming, familiar darkness cloaks itself over me as I pull onto the drive.

Betty comes scuttling over. "Iain's been looking for you. He says he needs to speak to you urgently."

"How long ago was he here?"

"Oh, a couple of hours now."

Right on cue, my phone beeps. *I need to speak to you asap.*

I feel a bit nervous to be honest. *What's he found out?* I think I might need a beer whilst I ring him back. There's a pile of post on the mat

– all crap. I really want this *'will stuff'* to go through and not have everything hanging over me. All this grief is supposed to get easier with time, isn't it Mum? It's been over three months now. For me it gets harder every day, not easier.

I put the shopping away whilst swigging my beer and then head back to the car. I'll drive over to Iain's, discover what's been found out and we will take it from there. He doesn't want to tell me by text by the looks of it.

I'm on autopilot for much of the journey. I drive past where Stacey lives and resist the urge to go and put her windows through. Instead, half an hour later, I'm pulling up outside Iain's house. He and Claudia are shouting at each other. I can hear them from the street.

"It wasn't stalking. I was trying to help." Claudia's hysterical, clearly not wrapping her dad around her little finger as well as she normally does. She sounds like an eight-year-old. I can hardly make out what she's saying, she's in that much of a state. I can hear Iain in a much lower tone. I crouch behind the bins to listen. I'm better knowing before I go in, what I'm dealing with.

"Don't make me go Dad. Please!" *Go where? What is going on?*

"I can't! I'm scared! Can't they just talk to me here?"

She must be talking about the police. *What's she done?* The stupid cow. *It must be her!* You once told me *never* to trust Claudia. You said I should always watch every word I said. *Don't offer her any more weapons for her arsenal.* I laughed at you, and said you were being well melodramatic. You said that the less either of them knew, about *anything*, the better.

You'd go mad if you ever discovered that Iain was imparting information to Claudia and her mother. Not that you ever had any secrets really. You just didn't want them being able to meddle in your wedding plans, your arguments, your former relationship with Dad, finances or anything to do with you, really. It was *your* business, you

CHAPTER TWENTY EIGHT

said, and rightly so.

In the early days, I remember you trying hard with Claudia, to the point where it used to sicken me. You were once banging on about always having wanted a daughter (*as well as me or instead of me Mum?*) You'd said you could have the next best thing. *Iain's daughter.* Someone to go shopping with, for coffees with, to do meals with, that sort of thing. I thought you were weird, saying that.

You'd always take great care with birthdays and Christmas, making sure you bought her something you'd heard her talking about. With me, you just shoved money in a card.

"I'm so ashamed of you." I can hear Iain again. He seems to have moved closer to the window.

"Please Dad. Don't say that! Don't ever say that."

"Why did you do it Claudia? Did you think it was funny?"

"I couldn't live with the *knowing* anymore."

"Knowing *what?*"

"I can't tell you Dad. I'm in enough trouble with these tweets."

Little bitch. It *has* been her tweeting. The police were right. They said it would be someone who'd known you and could get access to your library card. I remember as well how Iain had said something about the cuckoo hashtag having a family reference.

I suddenly recall about three weeks ago when I noticed Claudia had parked (*in your sodding car Mum*) in the central library car park. After I had quelled my initial idea to cut her brake lines if I could get away with it, (only joking Mum!) I then wondered what the thick cow would be doing inside a library. After all, she came out of school with one GCSE and can barely hold a job down. Far easier to run to Daddy with an outstretched hand.

"Before I take you to the police station Claudia – I want to hear your reasons for what you've done."

There are a few moments silence. I'm getting cramp in my legs, here, behind the bin. And it stinks – I can't stay here much longer. I pull my t-shirt over my nose and awkwardly pull my phone from my pocket to check Twitter. I'm shocked to see your account *still* hasn't been taken down. *I didn't fall, I was pushed. If they are not stopped, they will do it again.* Then I notice another one's been added, three hours ago.

@artistanna123 *Karma. Your time is nearly up. You're going to get what's coming to you and I'll be watching. #cuckoo #beforemytime*

Karma. Dad used that word earlier too. Everything's so screwed up. Stacey's 'liked' the tweet. Normally she retweets or adds a comment. Perhaps she knows that her sick daughter is behind it all. Maybe she's involved too. I rise from my hiding place. I shall knock on the door – play dumb. Claudia opens it. Her hair's wild and her face is streaked black.

"What are *you* doing here?" She backs away from the door and stands beside Iain.

"You wanted to speak to me?" I ignore her and look at him.

"You should have let me know you were coming." The usually placid Iain looks stressed and dishevelled.

"You said it was urgent." I've got the upper hand here. They don't know that I know.

"It is but I can't go into it right now."

"I want to know what's going on. Is it something to do with my mother?"

"Look. I've got to drop Claudia off somewhere, but I shouldn't be too long."

"So what am I supposed to do?"

"Wait here. Make yourself a brew. Stick the telly on. We'll talk when I get back. I'll be as quick as I can."

"No! Dad! Please! Don't leave him *here. Not in our house!* And don't make me go. I can't – I'm really scared!"

"What's wrong with her?" Told you I was going to play dumb Mum.

CHAPTER TWENTY EIGHT

Iain takes hold of Claudia's arm. "Come on." Then to me, he says, "I'll try not to be long. I'll tell you what's going on soon."

I wonder if he's going to have to drag Claudia kicking and yelling to the car, but she volunteers herself in the end.

"You wait," she mutters as she passes me at the doorway. I curl my fists inside my pockets, wondering what crap she's got stored inside her evil little brain now.

After they've gone, I help myself to some toast and a glass of milk in a bid to stop the churning in my belly. It's hunger or anxiety – probably both. Then I spend twenty minutes or so wandering around the house, looking at things with new eyes. Iain's already been spending. He's replaced the sofa and the TV. He's got a well decent surround sound and an Apple Mac sits proudly on the coffee table. Yeah. He's cashed in alright. It's a similar story upstairs.

I see he's kitted his room out with new furniture. There's a picture of you together on his bedside table, at someone's wedding, I think, and several of your dresses hang in his new wardrobe. I wonder if he'll get rid of them. Probably when some bird demands he does. Like Sarah. Or maybe Stacey. He was quick enough to want to bag up your stuff at our house, I'm surprised he's not done the same here.

I look in Claudia's room. She hasn't done badly out of you either, Mum. A Dyson hairdryer is on the floor with its box beside it and there's a ton of shopping bags around. H&M, New Look, Miss Selfridge. She's not even unpacked them yet. I sit on her bed and glance around. I've not been in here before. *Why would I?* There are a few framed photos of her with her parents as she was growing up and a large one of Iain and Stacey on their wedding day. *Talk about living in the past!* He was supposed to be marrying *you* soon. I look closely at the picture of Stacey's more youthful face and realise how much I hate her. It's a shame that car didn't drive over that ugly head of hers. Like you've always said, she's poison. Her mission was to split you and Iain

211

up and get him back for herself.

There were a few rows between you and Iain, due to Stacey's constant phone calls and texts to him, and even 'tagging' him in on things through Facebook. Then there were all the things she needed 'fixing.' Add to that Claudia's meddling to alienate *you* and bring *them* back together, it's a miracle you didn't split up. I once asked Iain why they'd divorced. Stacey had had an affair. And yet, she still wouldn't let him go. It must have driven you insane Mum. And I'm still wondering about his relationship with Sarah. I don't think I can hold back from asking him.

I'm not hanging around here, I head back to the car, knowing who I'm visiting next. I'm so pumped that I arrive at my destination with little recollection of the journey. There's a vacuum blaring through the open windows as I stride up the path. Stacey's next-door-neighbour eyes me curiously from where she kneels, weeding or whatever. I ignore her and knock at the door. *No answer* but the vacuum silences. This time I thump on the door. I can sense someone at the other side. She can probably see me through the spyhole. I try the handle.

"Do one Jamie. I'm not opening the door to you. No way."

"I want to talk to you." I can feel tension throbbing in my jaw. I look to my right. The neighbour has got to her feet and is stood, arms folded, watching. I resist the urge to tell her to get lost.

"I've got nothing to say to you. Go away." Stacey's voice is muffled.

"Well I've got plenty to say to you." I thump at the door again. "Open this bloody door. Now."

"Yeah, I'm *really* going to do that." Her voice has a mocking edge. I spot a milk crate and throw it below the wide-open kitchen window, I can now lean through it.

"Get out," she shrieks. She narrowly misses my head as she throws a large plant pot at me. That would've hurt.

I respond by hurling glasses, one by one, from the draining board,

CHAPTER TWENTY EIGHT

back at her. She screams and runs from the room. The woman from next door has come to her aid and is tugging the crate from under my feet. I should have just jumped straight through the window, instead of messing about. I lower myself back to the ground. By now the neighbour is on the phone. I grab the crate and hurl it at her.

As I drive off, there's blood running down the side of her head. I'm going to get lynched for this. I don't care anymore. Everything is fucked anyway. Claudia's been tweeting. Pretending she's you. Stacey was probably in on it as well. I can't go home after this. The police will lift me there, for certain. Shit. I should have kept a lid on myself. I'll go to Dad's. I ring him but he's not answering. No change there then. The only parent I could ever count on was you Mum.

As I drive, I wonder what's going on at the police station. I imagine Claudia crying and being pathetic in an interview room and think about what possible reason she could be giving for being the person behind all those tweets. *Impersonating a dead person.*

Surely, it's some sort of fraud? Iain won't be allowed in the interview room; I wouldn't have thought. He may have gone back home by now, to talk to me, but more likely he'll be sat in that green waiting room, all calm and matter of fact. Nothing can rattle Iain's cage. Apart from a few tears at your funeral and when we scattered your ashes, I've hardly seen any reaction from him. All poker face and stony eyes. He'll get Claudia the best solicitor money can buy. *Your money.* They make me sick.

Chapter Twenty Nine

A police car crouches like a cougar outside Dad's house. There's no one in it. They must be inside, speaking to Dad and Katherine. Dad's van is on the drive. *Phillip Hardaker. (Proprietor) Reflections Window Cleaning Service.* They must be looking for me after what happened at Stacey's. Although I don't think Stacey would know where Dad lives. So how could *she* have sent them here? Perhaps the police are telling Dad about the tweets. *But why?* It's nothing to do with him now.

I reverse out of the cul-de-sac and park my car around the back of the *Jug and Barrel*. An all-day breakfast and a pint will sort me out. I've hardly eaten lately. A man can't operate in these circumstances with no food inside him. No one bats an eyelid when I walk in. I don't know what I was expecting. *A wanted poster*! Or someone pointing their finger, saying *look, it's him!*

I order my meal and a beer and settle down, unnoticed and insignificant in the corner. I glance around the room. Normal life continues even if mine is ruined. Men in work boots banter over an after-work pint. Sky Sports News blares through the speakers. I wonder if there's a match on. Footie season should have started by now, though I've never really followed it. I watch a crowd of girls, they're about my age – in fact a couple of them are quite fit. They're huddled around a high table, intermittently giggling whilst watching a

CHAPTER TWENTY NINE

neighbouring table of office boys. Out of the corner of my eye, I notice a bang tidy lass walking towards me.

"Bit late for breakfast," she says as she slides the plate in front of me.

I smile and thank her. Fit as she is, I can't be arsed with conversation though. I need to think. I bolt my food down without really tasting it. Another thing you used to bollock me for, Mum. I'm going to have to speak to Iain. I try to focus my thoughts. I can't. My head is jumbled and I've a searing pain at one side of it. I sit for a while, massaging my temple and sinus area, willing it to go away. I had a migraine a few years ago and it was awful. I thought I had a brain tumour and it made me throw my ringer up. *And it's going to happen again.* I jump up and search frantically through my blurred vision for the bogs. I don't see them so I rush towards the exit, my mouth full of putrid spew. But instead of getting outside, I barf at the side of the group of girls. My barely digested all-day breakfast slides across the wooden floor towards them.

"Ugh," they collectively screech, jumping away from the table.

"Too much to drink," I hear one of the workmen say.

I think about explaining, apologising, but no words will come. The pain in my head is excruciating. I stagger out of the building. No way can I drive. People are staring at me as I make the walk home, probably looking as though I'm drunk out of my brains. If only. I feel like this pain's going to kill me and I consider ringing an ambulance or something. But then worry that I'll just get locked up in a police cell after what happened this morning. I don't know how long it takes me to get home or how I even find the way, but I have to stop and puke a few more times as I go.

By the time I get home there's nothing left inside me and I'm crying my eyes out as I fumble for the front door key. I'd do anything to have you on the other side of this door Mum. You'd give me painkillers, a flannel, water. You'd look after me, you'd care. I'm sobbing as I get into the hallway. I half wish Betty has seen me and comes over. In the semi-darkness, I find some strong painkillers you were given when you hurt your back last year. I get an ice pack from the freezer and down a pint of water. I re-fill it, feeling slightly better. I hope I can keep it down as I head back through the lounge and up to bed.

I pull my blind down and get under the duvet, fully clothed. I bury my head under the pillow, soaking up the tears. I don't think I've ever felt this bad. Ever. It's not just my head. I physically can't stop crying and it's hurting my chest. This is what a broken heart must feel like. I hope it *is* just a migraine I've got and not something more sinister. Maybe if I fall asleep, I won't wake up again. It would probably be days before anybody found me, rotting in my bed. *Who'd come to my funeral?* Hardly anyone, I reckon. I want to stop crying. I miss you Mum. I miss Meghan too. I wish Dad would turn up. I can't remember if I locked the door after me. I try to relax. Breathe a bit deeper. Wait for the pain to leave me.

The room is pitch black. My belt is digging into my waist. I press the backlight on my watch. 3:34am. I put my hand on the side of my head. The pain has completely gone, though my eyes are sore from all the crying and my throat burns from the puking. I lean towards my bedside table and down half the pint of water. I'm beyond grateful that the pain has eased off.

I'm ravenous now. I brace myself to get out of bed in the dark and go downstairs. I snap the landing light on outside my room. If I can't see the shadows, perhaps they will go away. The light bulb pops as soon as I've turned it on. *Shit.* The whole lights circuit will have tripped. *Where the hell is the fuse box?*

I feel my way down the stairs in the darkness, trying to quell the rising panic in my chest as I cross the area in the hallway where your lifeless body once lay. I know this vision will never leave me and I've

CHAPTER TWENTY NINE

made the best choice in deciding to move. I'll get settled into college first, wait for probate to go though and then I'm out of here. I look up at a white box in the hallway. *The fuse box.*

That was easy enough.

I drop some bread into the toaster and pour another glass of water. Whilst I'm waiting for the toast, I recall the altercation with Stacey. Surely the police would have come after me by now? Maybe she hasn't even reported it – perhaps she's too much to hide? She *must* have been in it with Claudia – at least I know now *who* has been tweeting. Screwed up, sick bitch. What I want to know now, is *why*? As I lean against the kitchen counter, slowly chewing my toast, I nearly choke as Claudia appears in the kitchen doorway.

" What are you doing here? It's four o'clock in the morning!" My chest is thudding. "I can't believe they've let you out."

"You should try locking your door." She walks towards me and gently takes a piece of toast from my plate. "I'm starving. They didn't even offer me a cup of tea."

"You never answered my question. What are you doing? *Here?*"

"I've told them *everything*." She gives me a strange look as she emphasises the word *everything*. "And I'm going to tell my dad next."

"Tell him what? Where is he?"

"He went home earlier. To talk to you, *remember*. He'll be here soon. I rang him before I got in the taxi." She takes another bite of the toast and slides herself up onto the breakfast bar stool – crossing one denim-clad leg over the other and cocking her head to one side. She shakes her hair down her back and stares straight at me. I guess she doesn't look too bad to say she's spent most of the night at the police station. I bet most lads fancy the pants off her. I, however, *hate* her guts.

"Why did you pretend to be my mother, Claudia? Tweeting from the grave." I cross my arms and take a step away from the counter I've been leaning against.

"I wanted people to know the truth." She smiles. "And to lead the police to Anna's murderer."

"What are you on about, you're warped, you are! When are you going to butt out of my life?"

"Sooner than you think." She's still smiling.

I walk up to where she's perched on the stool. She brushes crumbs from her lips and shrinks back. "I saw what you did."

"I didn't *do* anything."

"I was here, hiding. On the afternoon your mum died. I've told the police. I'm going to tell my dad. I'm not scared anymore."

"You're out of your mind. Mental slag. Who's going to listen to *you* after what you've done?"

"It was *you*. I saw you push her as hard as you could when she was balancing on the banister. She didn't stand a -"

I grab her by the throat and ram her backwards against the wall. A few hours ago, I felt like I was dying, now I've got the strength of a bodybuilder. Her arms flail out to break her fall but there's a crack as her head connects with the wall.

"You're deluded. I've had about as much as I can take of *you*." I crouch astride her, grab a fistful of her fringe and ram her head against the wall again. I want to knock her out. She's squirming beneath me like an eel.

"Get. Off. Me. Stop." Her voice is a croak and her eyes are rolling in her head. Venom is still coursing through me like an after-rain torrent down a hill. I sit heavier on her and am shocked to find my hands around her neck. *What the hell am I doing?* Yet I can't stop. Something has come over me and I need to shut her up forever. I tighten my grip on her neck. The fight is draining out of her. Her eyes start to bulge and I squeeze harder. I've got her now. Just another minute.

Chapter Thirty

"Get off her!" The stool crashing onto my head is enough for me to let go. I jump up to face Iain. Claudia is gasping on the floor. Iain grabs me by the throat and forces me back into the lounge, pushing me into an armchair. "Don't move," he orders as he towers over me. Claudia crawls into the lounge and leans against the wall still panting. Just a few more moments and I would have finished the job.

"What the hell were you doing to my daughter?" He grabs me by the t-shirt, two hands. I smell his coffee-laced breath. "I always knew you were a wrong 'un."

You'll think I'm disgusting here Mum, you always told me never to spit. What's a man to do when he's held by the scruff? I give it all I've got.

"You dirty little bastard." He lets go but punches me hard in the face. My head's forced back into the chair. *Blow me.* The man's got a punch on him. He grabs a cushion to wipe the spit away. "Fucking animal," he mutters as I get to my feet. He punches me again, at the other side of my face. Blood splatters out as I'm thrown back to the chair. "I said stay there, you little scrote."

OK. OK. I'm not moving, not if I'm going to be met with a punch like that each time.

"You alright love?" Still stood over me, he turns to Claudia, panting like a bitch on the ground.

"He nearly killed me! Thank God you came when you did!"

"We need to ring the police."

"Not yet. There's something I need to tell you first." Her voice is hoarse. A whisper.

"About the tweets?"

"Yes, I did them. It's true. But I had good reason. I was scared. Really scared."

"Of what?"

"Him. You."

Tears are pouring down her pathetic, skinny face. I'm going to hear what she's got to say and then I'm going to make a run for it. I'm not waiting for no police. I've got money. I can get well away from here. Abroad if I have to.

"You were scared of *me? Why?*" He's still stood over me but looking at Claudia. I look past him to the hallway where I can see my trainers and my wallet on the second stair. Sweet.

"I shouldn't have been here Dad. I wanted to break you and Anna up. I'm sorry."

"Been *here?* When?"

"The day that she died. I borrowed your key. Let myself in. There was no one in when I got here."

"I'm listening." He looks at me. So am I. I feel sick again though.

"I was going to leave something in her room, so you'd think she was carrying on with another man when you came around later."

"Like what?"

"Pants, a condom, a note. That sort of thing."

"Was Anna having an affair?"

"I don't know. I don't care. I just wanted to stop the wedding. I hated her. You knew that but you were *still* going through with it. You didn't give a toss about my feelings, did you?"

CHAPTER THIRTY

"Just for the record, she hated you as well," I say, though Iain's blocking my view to her. "You can give her fucking car back and stop spending her money. You grasping, scrounging little waster."

"Have you told the police all this?" Iain's as practical as ever.

"Yes. They're going to arrest him, I think."

"Who? Me? No, they're not." I try to pull myself up by the chair arms but Iain, once again, pushes me back and turns again to Claudia.

"So you're in Anna's bedroom, trying to stage some kind of affair. Bit lame, but go on."

"Then they come back. Anna and *him*." She points in my direction. "It was a Tuesday afternoon when I thought she'd be out teaching her class. That's what she was supposed to be doing – I'd checked. And *he* should have been at work. She points at me. But instead, they came back here, screaming at each other. Anna was shouting at Jamie to leave her alone. Said she was going to get on with the painting and he should go to his room to calm down." She rubs at her neck. "I was like, shit, I'm going to get caught here." She shifts from the floor into the armchair, her hand not leaving her neck the whole time.

"Then what?" Iain looks down at me with so much hate in his face, it takes me aback.

"I could see through the crack of the door. Anna had got up onto the banister where she was balancing to paint the high bit of the landing wall." She points upwards as she speaks. "Jamie was ranting, telling Anna she was old enough to be a grandma and there was no way he was living with a screaming brat in the house."

"Go on." I wish Iain would get away from me. I need to make a move shortly.

"They were arguing like hell Dad, about you and money and all sorts. All the time she kept painting. He kept telling her to stop and listen to him. She had one foot on the banister and the other against the wall. And she told Jamie he had to find somewhere else to live. And that's when he pushed her."

"She's lying. I never pushed no one."

"Shut it, you." Iain looks from me to Claudia, his expression unreadable. "You've told the police this?"

She's whimpering again. "Yes. I climbed out of the back window. I was so scared and I couldn't tell anyone what I'd heard and seen 'cos well, look at what I was trying to do." Snot's dripping off her nose. *I hate her.*

"He was getting away with it and I couldn't let that happen. I couldn't live with what I knew. The longer it went on, the worse it got." She's still rubbing at her purple-coloured throat. "I know I'm in trouble too, but I feel better now it's out."

"I think you've been punished enough," Iain says. "As far as -"

Whilst his gaze is averted to Claudia, I kick him as hard as I possibly can between his legs, feeling his bulge on the top of my foot as I connect. He bends double, groaning, and it's his turn for his eyes to bulge. Bingo. Iain *does* have responses! Quick as a dart, I'm on my feet, making towards my wallet, trainers and jacket. I burst through the front door, into the night. "Shit." I suddenly remember. *No keys.* I could have collected my car if I'd remembered. Got away quicker.

"Jamie!" Iain's voice echoes out, but when I look around, he hasn't come after me. I'd outrun him any day of the week.

I tap my jeans pocket as I keep running. *Thank fuck I picked my phone up.* I'm running towards Leeds Bradford Airport. If I can't get a flight straight out, I'll book one from my phone. *No. I haven't got my passport! What am I going to do?* Then I remember you saying that you went to Cate's fortieth in Dublin using your driving licence when your passport had expired. I'll do that. I keep running, thankful to have a plan of sorts. I've got money. I can start again, which is what I wanted to do anyway. I can't live in that house without you Mum.

Iain may come after me in the car, I suppose. With that in mind, I get

CHAPTER THIRTY

off the main road. *Please help me get away Mum.* My life is over if they catch me, especially after what I've just done. The sky has brightened a little and has become a dark purple instead of inky black. I need to get to the airport whilst I've still got the dark. A police car screeches by, in the opposite direction, followed by another one. I stand in the shadows at the edge of a field. Maybe they're on their way to our house. I keep going. I've only got about another ten or fifteen minutes to run before I get to the airport. I can see the lights in the distance and a plane's just taking off. I hope that I can get straight on one and out of here.

I keep going. I'm in a farmer's field, probably standing in God knows what, whilst knowing that the cover of darkness will soon dissolve. My heartbeat thuds through my entire body as my arms keep pumping me forwards. I'm powered by adrenaline. I can see the airport sign now. Nearly there. I take a gulp of air and power on. Then hear the single whirr of a police siren. No! That's not far away either. Peering into the clearing, I spot an unmarked police car, its headlights dipped.

Have they seen me? I'm not taking any chances. I'll hide till they've gone. Nimble as a squirrel, I'm up the nearest tree, grateful for my childhood tree-climbing expertise. You used to go mad at me when I returned home, bark and moss stained, scrapes on my knees and holes in my jeans. *Money doesn't grow on trees,* you'd screech or *if God meant you to be a monkey, that's how he'd have made you!*

Fuck. Fuck. Fuck. They really are looking for *me.* I see two of them in the semi darkness, poking at undergrowth with sticks and shining torches. I think they've got a dog with them. I grip the branch I'm balancing on, hardly daring to breathe. Hopefully they'll give up soon and I can get to the airport. My chest hurts as they come closer to me. They're so close, I can make out what one is saying into his radio.

"Yes Sarge. We're on foot. Sighting of suspect running off road. The dog's picked up a scent. We'll have him shortly."

Don't look up. Don't look up. I'm praying silently. Shit. He's got a dog alright. At his side, is a huge German Shepherd that I'd not like to be on the wrong side of. They take a few steps in my direction. I feel like I'm slipping. Snap. Suddenly I've lost my perch and I'm hanging by my hands to an adjacent branch, the dog is under me on its hind legs, stretched to its full height as it barks madly beneath me. If I lose my grip, I will be dog food.

"Looks like we've got you son." One of them shines the torch into my face. "I'll call the dog off, then you can come down. Zena. Down girl." The dog returns to his side.

I'm losing my hold on the branch and my shoulders are killing. I fall into a heap at their feet. The dog is growling. I've had enough. I'm knackered, hungry, thirsty and can taste a mixture of bile from hours before and blood from where Iain smacked me in the mouth. Mum, you'd be gutted if you could see me now. This was never how it was meant to be.

"Jamie Hardaker I am arresting you for an assault occasioning actual bodily harm against Claudia Price. You do not have to say anything, but it may harm your defence if you do not mention when questioned, something which you later rely on in court. Anything you do say may be given in evidence. Do you understand?"

"Yes." It crosses my mind to run but one look at the teeth-baring dog tells me there is no point.

"When we get to the station there's another matter we'd like to discuss with you whilst you're under caution."

Bang goes my little trip to Dublin. I'm going to get screwed for what I've done to Claudia. It's serious shit. And possibly Stacey and her neighbour yesterday too. But as for the other shit Claudia's spouting about you Mum, well, the police will eventually see how much she hates me. Her, Iain and Stacey probably want me out of the way so they can get their hands on *everything*. What it boils down to is her

CHAPTER THIRTY

word against mine, I hope.

"Turn around Jamie. Face the tree. PC Winchester is going to cuff you before we take you in. When you've turned around, place your hands behind your back, wrists together."

I feel the chill of the cuffs around my wrists and the hard snap of them being locked. "Argh – they're too tight."

"You'll get used to them. This way please." PC Winchester or whatever his name is, turns me by the shoulder in the direction of their car.

The other one speaks into his radio. "DC Harrison here. We're bringing Jamie Hardaker in for questioning. Is there an interview room free at Weetwood?"

Pause. Beep. Crackle. "Yes. I'll put the engaged sign up."

"There is? Good stuff. Can you alert the CPS that we're on our way, so they've got someone ready on this?"

I'm scared Mum. This is the stuff of TV dramas. I've never been handcuffed in my life. It hurts. I've never been arrested before either and I don't know what to do. I reckon I'll need to ask for a solicitor or something.

"Get in the back," says Harrison. "My colleague will sit with you."

I look at the dog beside him. I used to like German Shepherds. This one looks savage though, with its huge teeth.

"Don't worry." He must sense my fear. "She's in a cage in the back." He opens the door and I get in, beaten. The sky is pink as we progress to the police station, passing the pub where you used to buy us a carvery when you couldn't be arsed cooking. Then, the Asda where I used to help you with the food shop when I was younger. I haven't helped you for years. I never helped you carry it from the car or put it away. I feel guilty now. We pass the crematorium where we had your funeral. It could be *any* car journey. Until we pull into the car park of Weetwood Police Station.

Chapter Thirty One

"I am Detective Chief Inspector Stephen Harrison. I will be conducting this interview with my colleague," he gestures across the table.

"Police Constable David Winchester."

"PC Winchester will be jointly conducting the interview and taking notes." He points to me next. "Can you confirm your full name and date of birth please?"

"Jamie Phillip Hardaker. 29th June 1994."

"Thank you. You have chosen to be legally represented by a Solicitor from Rowlings, Finn and Mason. Can your representative please confirm his name?"

"Yes certainly." He clears the frog in his throat. "Martyn Browne."

I've had to wait an extra two hours in a stinking cell until he got here. I was tempted to forgo a solicitor to get this over with faster, but common sense was screaming at me that I'm in far too much shit to try and swim out of it by myself.

"Right. It's 9:16 am on Wednesday 11th July and Jamie Hardaker has been arrested following an allegation of Actual Bodily Harm against Miss Claudia Jade Price at around 0400 hours earlier this morning, Wednesday 11th July. This took place at his home. Jamie, could you please confirm your address?"

"7 St David's Road, Farnley, Leeds."

CHAPTER THIRTY ONE

"Thank you. Before we start the interview, I will remind you of your rights. You do not have to say anything, but it may harm your defence if you do not mention when questioned something which you later rely on in court. Anything you do say may be given in evidence. Do you understand all that or do you need anything explaining to you?"

"I understand." *Let's just get on with this.*

"As we've just mentioned, you've chosen to be legally represented, so if at any point during the interview, you need to speak privately to your solicitor, please let us know. We will pause the recording and leave the room."

I'm relieved I waited for a solicitor to be honest. This is as bad as it gets Mum. He's from the same company that's been handling your will, but from the criminal department. It was the only solicitors that I knew the name of when they asked me if I wanted one. He seems sound. He spoke to me in the cell and has advised me to do a *no comment* interview until we find out what they've got on me.

If it's just Claudia chatting her poison, I might be alright. Hopefully she's in the same amount of trouble as me over the tweets, and the police, courts or whoever might understand I went for her because I was upset about her pretending to be you.

"Right Jamie." Harrison leans towards me. "We'll start with what happened this morning. The altercation with Claudia Price which took place at your home at 7 St David's Road. What time did she arrive there?"

I look towards Martyn, hesitating, feeling a little ignorant. "No comment."

"Right." He looks at his colleague before continuing. "Next I want to ask you for your version of events leading up to where Claudia's father, Iain Price, found you, as he put it, on the verge of strangling her."

Shit. *Would I really have strangled her?* I would never have thought I was capable of it. I don't know really. Who knows what would have happened if Iain hadn't stopped me? I was well wired. I've never hated a person so much. I remember the feel of her bulging neck against the grip of my fingers and grit my teeth. "No comment."

"Can you explain who you were running from this morning? And why we found you hiding up a tree?"

"No comment."

"Have you any idea why Claudia Price might have spent the last two months logging in to your mother's Twitter account, trying to provide leads to the supposed killer of your mother?"

I want to say; *can't you see this is why I hate her so much?* But obviously I can't speak. "No comment."

"Are you aware that Claudia Price is alleging *you* killed your mother?"

"No comment."

"Do you know that she is saying your mother was *pushed* to her death, rather than it being accidental, as has been previously assumed?"

I look at Martyn again. He sits, staring forward. He's having an easy time of it and is probably charging a hundred pounds a minute. "No comment."

"Can you tell me, in your own words, how your mother, Anna Louise Hardaker, died on Tuesday 16th April, earlier this year?"

"No comment."

Martyn raises his hand slightly and clears his throat. "Forgive me for interrupting but I thought we were here following allegations of Actual Bodily Harm, not to discuss the circumstances of Jamie's mother's death? Can you clarify this please?"

So he does speak!

"It's all relevant and interlinked." DC Harrison runs his finger down some notes then looks at PC Winchester who nods. He hovers a finger over a button on the voice recording equipment. "This interview is concluded at 9:50 am."

CHAPTER THIRTY ONE

I watch as he slides two tapes out of the machine, then as he puts them into boxes which he writes on and seals. "We'll be back in a moment," he says. They stand up together, leaving me with Martyn and his braces and shiny shoes in the green, airless room. Everything is different shades of green. The walls, the table surface, the paintwork and the plastic chairs that are bolted to the floor. Maybe the colour green has some effect on whether people tell the truth when they're being interviewed? If they hadn't taken my phone off me, I'd be Googling it. I recall when I was recently here with Uncle Si, I wish I could go back. Claudia and Stacey aren't worth the trouble I'm in. I should have left it.

Martyn's voice cuts into my thoughts. "It sounds as though they haven't got enough to charge you with yet. We'll stick with the 'no comment' arrangement unless they come up with something different."

He's about your age Mum and wearing a very expensive looking suit. When I get through all this, I'm going to treat myself to a suit just like his. Slim fit obviously as I'm starting to look like a coat hanger. Right on cue, my belly growls.

"Because there's a witness to the actual bodily harm, they may well have you on that one. Tell me, did you assault her in the manner mentioned?"

"She was pretending to be my dead mother. I wasn't thinking straight."

"We might be able to argue mitigating circumstances but prosecution is likely here, once they have the forensic evidence to back up the witness statements. We'll have to see what happens. But what about the other matter?"

"What other matter?"

He's looking straight into my eyes which makes me uncomfortable. I've never liked prolonged eye contact. Apart from with Meghan or something when we're - *for God's sake, reality check!*

"*Did* you push your mother to her death Jamie?"

He's supposed to be on my side yet I'm feeling like he's interrogating me. I open my mouth to respond but the two policemen suddenly re-enter the room. "Right Jamie." DC Harrison resumes his seat and the other one stands behind him. "For now, we're releasing you, pending further enquiries." Relief pools in my chest and I let a long breath out.

"You must agree to reside at your home address and surrender your passport. Part of your bail conditions will be to not make any contact, directly or indirectly with Claudia Price or her parents Iain Price and Stacey Price. You must also report here, at the station, every day. Do you understand?"

I nod. I've never been so relieved in my life. *I'm getting let out!* "Can I have my things back?" I just want to get out of here. They even took the laces out of my Nikes.

"In a moment. We may recall you at any time to answer further questions that arise as a result of our ongoing enquiries. Do you accept this as part of your bail conditions?"

"Yes."

"Good. When you are ready, please come into the reception area where we'll return your property and get you to sign a couple of things. After you've left, if you decide there's anything you'd like to tell us, please get in touch." He pushes a business card across the table, then he and his colleague follow each other from the room.

As I get to my feet, Martyn is plucking a form from his briefcase followed by a pen from the top pocket of his jacket. It's not just any pen Mum, it's a posh silver one. He uses it to cross a couple of places on the form.

"This is so I can continue representing you," he explains, "and put in a bill for Legal Aid. They should cover some of our costs, however you may have to be responsible for some of them too."

"*Really?* How much?" Shit. I know what solicitor's fees are like.

CHAPTER THIRTY ONE

"It depends on how your financial situation pans out and what comes to light with the charges." He clicks the buttons on his briefcase. "Before I leave, is there anything you'd like to tell me?"

I shake my head.

"Well, if you think of something, you've got my number."

I'm beyond grateful to exchange the odour-infused police station for the afternoon sunshine. My eyes ache in the sudden glare as I try to orientate myself. I remember that my car's in the pub car park from when I became ill yesterday. *Yesterday.* It feels like a lifetime ago.

Chapter Thirty Two

To use another of your expressions Mum, I'm like a cat on a hot tin roof for the next couple of days. *What's Claudia said? What have they got on me? Am I going to get done for nearly throttling her?* I hate her with every fibre of my being. She should never have turned up at our house. *Smug cow.* She's lucky her dad got here in time. I'm glad really, if I'd killed her, I'd have never got bail. At least I've got a chance of things being dropped. She should get done for impersonating a dead person or wasting police time, or something. And as for her saying I pushed you, well it's just her *saying* it. And it's her word against mine anyway.

After three days, the not knowing is doing me in. Without much consideration about what I'm about to do, I find myself in my car. I go to Dad's and there's no one in. I get a sense that there's been no one there for days. His van's there and so is Katherine's car. But the blinds are tilted so they're nearly closed and a light from the upstairs landing can be seen through the hallway window. All the stuff in the garden has been put away in the shed. I ring him. Voicemail.

I ring her. She answers. "We're just having a few days away Jamie."

"Can I speak to my dad?"

"I'm not with him at the moment."

"When will you be with him? Where are you?"

"I'll get him to call you when we get back home." She sounds flat.

CHAPTER THIRTY TWO

Who does she think she is? His receptionist.

"I want to speak to my dad." The phone goes dead. I feel like smashing it on the floor.

I get back in the car and point it in the direction of the A62. I'm off to Iain's. I need to know what's going on. What Claudia thinks she's got on me. I feel sure the police would have been back by now if they were going to be. I just want to get on with my life, move to a new house, put this shit with Claudia behind me.

When I arrive at the house, I can hardly recall the journey. All I know is that I've got here quick. It's about eight in the evening so there isn't much traffic about. I feel so lonely Mum. I'm shaking as I walk to the door. I'll probably get the door slammed in my face. All I want to do is get them off my back, call it quits and all of us forget about each other.

I hesitate before knocking at the door. When I finally do, I freeze when I see Claudia's silhouette behind the frosted glass. Shit. There was no car outside. I contemplate running off but she's swung the door open before I can. Her neck is covered in bruising. I feel pleased that I've reduced the stupid cow to this state, whilst being ashamed, all at the same time.

"Dad," she says in a voice I've never heard as she backs away from the door. *She's scared of me.*

Iain appears behind her. "Go back in there love." He steps in front of her and she runs inside. He turns to me. "What the hell are you doing here?"

"I-I want to know what's been said. No one's telling me anything. Just tell me what you know then I'll be out of your hair for good."

"You'll be out of my hair now. I'm telling you nothing." His mouth is set in a hard-straight line.

My nerves become anger at the way he looks at me. "Why not? I've a right to know what's going on."

"You've a right to nothing lad. After what you've done. To my daughter. To your mother." He starts to close the door. I wedge my foot inside the door frame.

"What do you mean, *to my mother?* You don't know shit mate."

"Do one Jamie. Before I call the police. Move your foot."

"I just want to know what they've got on me. I can't live like this anymore."

"Tough. You've brought it on yourself. Move your foot."

"Tell me. Agh!" He opens and slams the door on my foot which I immediately pull out of the way. "Tell me what's going on. Tell me, you arsehole." I beat my fists against the glass of the door, feeling all my fight drain out of me. "Tell me." Claudia's ranting and wailing inside. "I'm calling the police," Iain shouts.

I scarper. As I start the car up, I feel like driving it at full pelt into a brick wall. I've had enough. I've really had enough. I need a pint. Or ten. So that is where I head.

I feel as though everyone is looking at me as I enter my local, as though they all know that I'm on bail. I stay there till closing then drive home. You'd kill me Mum. Drink driving was one of your biggest no-no's. Especially after Dad. I've had it anyway so adding drink-driving to the rap sheet won't harm.

Despite what I've drunk, I feel strangely sober when I get home. There's no sign that anyone's been here, looking for me. Iain must have been bluffing when he said he was calling the police. I put the telly on, just wanting to hear human voices after an evening of staring into pint glasses, hoping to find the answer to my misery in the bottom of them. I can't face going up to bed. To the silence and darkness of my bedroom. I swing my legs up onto the sofa and tug my jacket over myself. Tears leak down the sides of my head onto the cushion and part of me hopes I'll never wake up.

But I do. Again and again. By 6:20am I admit defeat and stand from

CHAPTER THIRTY TWO

the sofa. I must get up too quick as I go dizzy. I look again at the space where you ended up. Particles of dust swarm in the early morning sun that is streaming through the window. If Iain had called the police, they'd have come for me by now for breaching my bail. Suddenly I get a strong sense that everything is going to be alright. A weird feeling of peace washes over me and I let out a long breath.

A flicker of excitement dances in my belly as I remember that I'm starting college in a few weeks. September was always your favourite month Mum – you said it was kind of like a new year. You got your new students and said there was an energy around that only exists at this time of year. You loved Autumn too. See, I knew you in a way no one else did. Not Iain and certainly not Claudia.

I flick the kettle on and push some bread into the toaster. I'll go and buy some new paintbrushes today, have a blast at the gym and call into the art gallery. I wonder if Dawn has heard about all the shit and know I should probably go and explain things. I take my breakfast into the garden, like you always used to do on sunny days. Four days have passed since my arrest. Maybe I won't hear anything else.

The garden is overgrown now. I haven't touched it this summer. You'd be gutted if you could see it. You wouldn't be able to get your lawnmower through the long grass. It must be well over a foot high and it's going brown. Your carefully planted shrubs are barely visible for the weeds. There's certainly no way you'd be able to sprawl out on your sun lounger with a book if you wanted to. I can remember you planting bulbs out in April, about a fortnight before you died, just as the days were starting to warm up. It was the long weekend at Easter. You wanted me to help but I couldn't be arsed, as usual. They're all coming up now Mum, behind the weeds, that is. This was your garden. I guess I should sort it if I'm going to sell the house. I can't believe how wild it's gone in three months.

When I buy my bachelor pad, it will not have a garden, sack that.

I don't come out here much – this was your domain. Hanging the washing out, feeding the birds, painting in the sun, eating breakfast at your bistro table. This is your house Mum. Now you're gone, I feel like an imposter. Like I don't deserve for you to have given it to me. I mean, what twenty-five-year-old owns a three-bedroom terrace with a garden, half a business, a van and a hundred and twenty grand in the bank. Well more like a hundred now that Dad's got his hands on some of it. But most lads will kill for what I've got. The doorbell goes, jolting me out of my thoughts. I don't feel like talking to anyone. I ignore it. It's probably Betty and I really can't be bothered at the moment.

"Jamie." An unfamiliar voice sounds from the driveway. Then a noise. A radio. A police radio. *No!* "Jamie Hardaker."

There's two of them in our back garden Mum. I have a feeling this is not going to be good, though maybe it's just because I broke my bail conditions.

"Jamie Hardaker. We are arresting you in connection with the death of your mother Anna Louise Hardaker. We will also be re-interviewing you regarding the recent incident with Claudia Jade Price. You do not have to say anything, but it may harm your defence if you do not mention when questioned something which you later rely on in court. Anything you do say may be given in evidence. We will let you secure your home before we take you to the station. Do you understand what is happening?"

"Yes." I'm gutted. I can't believe they're back. "The front door's locked. Let me put some shoes on."

It's the same two coppers as before. Harrison follows me into the kitchen and watches as I slip my feet into my trainers. I reach for my phone and wallet and slip them into my pocket.

"Time to go Jamie," he says softly, with handcuffs in his hand. "If you could just face the sink whilst I fasten these onto you. Just until we get to the station."

CHAPTER THIRTY TWO

It's like a bad dream. I hold my hands in the required position and watch as he locks the back door behind us and slips the single key into my pocket. My tea is still steaming on the garden table. My toast will have gone soggy and cold now.

As we squeeze past my car on the drive, I notice Betty watching. "What's going on Jamie? Are you alright?"

I keep my eyes fastened to the ground. I don't want to look at that puzzled expression on her face. I allow myself to be guided into the rear of the police car and then look at the sunny exterior of our house as we pull away. I hope it's not long until I see it again.

Everything is taken off me again when we arrive at the station, right down to my belt and the laces in my shoes. They obviously think I might hang myself. No matter how bad things are, I wouldn't have the guts. As they slide my wallet into a polythene property bag, I ask them to take out the contact card to ring Martyn. I think I'm going to need him here this morning.

"Certainly," Harrison says. "You also have the right to let someone know of your detention here. Is there anyone you would like us to contact?"

I think of Dad then immediately dismiss it. "No." My guts feel heavy. *You* were my emergency contact Mum. Now you've gone and I've no one. I haven't been in touch with Auntie Liz or Uncle Si. I guess they'll find out soon enough about all that's going on.

"I'm going to put you in a cell again whilst we wait for your solicitor," Harrison tells me. "Hopefully he won't be too long."

I allow myself to be led towards the cell, not that I've a right lot of choice. I sink onto the concrete slab, topped with a skinny mattress as the heavy door clanks and I'm being locked in. I look at the metal toilet in the corner and shudder. *Is this what prison is like?* I hope Martyn is not going to be long. I stare at the barren stone walls before dropping my head into my hands. It's no wonder they take belts and laces off you in here. But I'm surprised by how calm I feel, considering. I lie on the mattress. Curl into a foetal position. Try to ignore your face crowding my mind. Pray that I will get out of here soon. I will myself to be rescued by sleep until Martyn gets here. I don't want to wait, don't want to think and don't want to remember. I must drift off because the next thing I hear is the metallic thump of the lock turning again as Martyn is let into the cell. I sit up and rake my fingers through my hair.

"Can I get you anything Jamie?" Harrison calls over Martyn's shoulder. "A drink? A sandwich?"

"Just some water, please." To eat is a resignation that I won't be out of here anytime soon.

"I'll bring some to the interview room. I'll give you a few minutes with your solicitor first." The door clangs behind him.

"How are you doing?" Martyn perches beside me on the mattress, hitching his trousers up first.

"I can't believe they've lifted me again. Have they told you anything?"

"No. But they *must* have *something* on you. They do need specific grounds to re-arrest. They won't give anything away, I wouldn't have thought, prior to interview."

"Why not?"

"They won't want you to have the chance to prepare anything. They will be hoping to catch you *on the hoof*. But you'll get the chance to put your side across."

"Will I get out after the interview?" The alternative is unthinkable. I've kept calm so far but I need to know what is going on. I'll be knocking myself out against these walls if they don't let me go. And I mean that Mum.

"It depends on what they want to re-interview for. And what evidence has come to light. I recommended a *no comment* interview last time, simply because we didn't want to give them something they hadn't got."

"So what do we do *this time?*" I'm saying *we* as though his head is on the block as well.

"Take it as it comes. It may be that it's just a few further questions about the incident with your stepsister – Claudia, isn't it?"

"She's not my stepsister. She's nothing to me."

"Well. Whatever. Or they might want to question you in relation to your mother's death. In which case, we need to see what evidence they've got, if any, before we respond."

"There's no evidence they could possibly have about my mother's death. I didn't do anything. She fell from the banister – I've told you."

"Well, OK. Let's see how it all goes and remember that we can ask them to leave the room if we need to discuss anything. If you're not sure how to respond to something, make sure you ask me first."

"Cool," I say. It's anything but.

"Is there anything I should know before I tell them we're ready?" He stands. I notice how sharp his trouser creases are - my trousers always end up with tramlines when I iron them. "Anything you would like to tell me?"

"No." I stand too.

He looks back at me as he knocks on the cell door. "And Jamie?"

"What?" I follow his gaze to the clenched fists at my side.

"Stay calm. I'll get you through this with the best possible outcome."

"Thanks." As I follow him and Harrison through the booking in area to the interview room where Winchester is waiting, all I can think about is the slipping away of my big chance at art college. It's all Claudia's fault.

Chapter Thirty Three

We sit in the same places as we did four days ago. Hopefully this will be the last time I have to sit in this hellhole of a room. Maybe they just want to give me one more chance to talk, and then they will have to let me go. *But why would they have arrested me?* They must have *something*.

A beep of the recording equipment signals the beginning of the interview. "The date is Sunday 15th July and the time is 11:40 am. I am DC Harrison and my colleague is PC Winchester, who will be taking notes. We are interviewing…" He gestures at me.

"Jamie Hardaker."

"Also present is his legal representative, Martyn Browne from Rowlings, Finn and Mason." Harrison's voice is gruff and croaky today as though he's coming down with something. That might make him want to get the interview over with sooner. I'm desperate to get back home. I just want to get on with my life now. I don't ever want to see Iain or Claudia again. Not ever.

"Right then Jamie. We've arrested you for the second time in relation to the incidence of actual bodily harm, with intent, against Claudia Jade Price on Wednesday 11th July. You are also here to be questioned about your involvement in the death of your mother, Anna Louise Hardaker on Tuesday 16th April."

"She fell. I wasn't involved." I can feel tension pulsing through my

CHAPTER THIRTY THREE

jaw. Nothing feels real anymore. I can't believe they want to quiz me about your death. *Haven't I been through enough?*

"You'll get the chance to have your say shortly Jamie." Martyn frowns at me.

"You were read your rights at the point of arrest, but I've got to go through them again. You have the right to remain silent but that and anything you say might be used in evidence. Do you understand your rights, or do you need them explaining?"

"I understand." I should do by now.

"We have now collected statements from Claudia Price and her father, Iain Price in relation to the incident that took place at your home on Wednesday 11th July, your home being 7 St David's Road, Farnley, Leeds. Miss Price has also been physically and forensically examined by a police doctor. We have enough grounds to charge you with Actual Bodily Harm with Intent. Do you have anything to say?"

I look at Martyn who nods at me as if to say I'm alright to speak rather than *no comment*. "Isn't what *she* did going to be taken into account?" Hell. *I'm going to be charged.* I expected this really. No way would Claudia ever let what happened go.

"What do you mean?"

"Tweeting as though she was my dead mother. Taunting me. Turning up at my house."

"You'll get your chance to build a defence for the charge against you in relation to Miss Price, Jamie. Everything *will* be heard and considered carefully in court, probably in front of a jury, depending on how you plead."

I look at Martyn. *Shit.* They're talking juries and pleading. I'm well in the shit.

"We'll discuss it soon Jamie." Martyn writes something down.

"For now, the Crown Prosecution Service have agreed the charge against Claudia Price." Harrison continues. "And as we have enough evidence to bring it against you, we're going to focus more on the other matter first."

"Will I be allowed home until I go to court?" My voice has gone all high-pitched. *Oh my God!* I might end up back in that cell. I really will just knock myself out against the walls. Who needs a belt or shoelaces?

"That's for the court to decide," Martyn explains. "I'll put a case together for bail. For now, just answer the questions Jamie. And remember, if you need to speak to me privately, we can stop the interview."

"Or the Crown Prosecution Service might decide to remand you," adds Harrison. "A lot will depend on the rest of the interview."

I swallow hard. Mum. Mum. Mum. If you can hear me, wherever you are, please get me out of this.

Harrison continues. "You were asked on Wednesday about your involvement in your mother's death back in April. At the time it happened, we attended the incident, and it was concluded that her death was a result of an accidental fall down the stairs." He pauses and looks at his notes. "We were led to believe that she'd slipped from her position on the banister whilst decorating. A post-mortem was carried out and there was no evidence to suggest any foul play."

"That's what happened. It was me who found her, and I rang 999." That image of you once again fills my mind.

"Before we begin questioning you further about this Jamie, is there anything you would like to tell us?"

I shake my head. I'm going to see what he has to say. He can't possibly have anything on me. Not for this. I accept what happened with Claudia, but not this.

"Can I remind you that this interview is being recorded?" He's a dick, this DC Harrison, a proper dick. He talks to me as though I'm an idiot. "For the benefit of the tape, can you answer the question out loud please, rather than just shaking your head? Is there anything you would like to tell us before we begin questioning you in relation to your mother's death?"

"No," I reply. I'm starving now. I hope to God I get bail for this Claudia shit. I'll be going straight to the pub.

"Right," he continues. "In that case, I'd like you to tell me exactly what happened on the afternoon of Tuesday April 16th, the day of your mother's death."

"I'd been out. I'd a half day from work as I'd been paid. I got home and found her."

"What time was this?"

"I'd been into town. Got some trainers and stuff. Been for something to eat. Probably about three."

"Ok. So then you found her. Where?"

"She was lying at the bottom of the stairs and she had her painting clothes on. She'd been decorating and was doing the staircase at the time. Afterwards we found a footprint on the banister where she must have been balancing to paint a high bit. It looked like she had lost her balance and fallen right from the top." I shiver, even though the interview room is stifling. The landing wall still shows your final brush strokes. I didn't have the heart to finish it off. I had washed the brushes and roller before Iain could take it upon himself to. "She should have waited for me to do it or got hold of a proper ladder. But that was my mum. She always wanted to do stuff herself."

"So you're telling me she was already dead when you found her?"

"Yes." Martyn is scribbling things down and so is PC whatever-his-name-is. Why are they bothering to write things down when they're recording me? Doesn't make sense. A rush of sweat rolls from my armpit down the side of my body beneath my t-shirt. I've got to get out of this oppressive green room. The walls are closing in on me. "Can I have some more water please?"

"Sure." Harrison presses a button on an intercom. "Sorry to bother you Sarge. When you've a minute, can you bring some water in for our interviewee please?"

"And for me, if that's OK?" Martyn adds.

"Make that two Sarge. Now, where were we? Yes, you were saying that your mother was already dead when you came home. How did you know?"

The image will never leave me Mum. It was like you'd been crumpled. Your head was stuck out at a weird angle and your eyes were slightly open. Glassy. I remember your hair moving in the breeze of the door when I opened it. "It was her neck," I eventually reply. "I knew straightaway she was dead." Heat stabs at the back of my eyes. It kills me, remembering.

"Where exactly had you been?" Harrison asks. "Prior to finding your mum, I mean?"

"Leeds. Shopping. Like I said."

"Can you remember which shops?"

"Quite a few. I can't remember. JD Sports maybe. I usually look in there."

"How did you get home?"

"I was in my car."

"So after you found your mum like that, what did you do? Thanks Sarge. For the benefit of the tape, Sergeant Johnson has just entered the interview room with some water and is now leaving."

I watch him, wishing I could follow him out. Instead I take a glug of the water, run it around my parched lips with my tongue and feel its chill slip down into my empty stomach. "I ran out into the street. I was a right mess. Shouting for help, running around. It's a blur now." For an awful moment, it feels like the water is going to come back up. Nausea creeps over me like a rash. I swallow. "Betty, our neighbour heard me and came out."

"Are you OK Jamie? You've gone very pale."

CHAPTER THIRTY THREE

"Yep. I'll be fine." I take another sip of water. "It's just, you know. Having to think about my mum like that, on the day ..."

"You alright to continue?"

"I guess so. It's so hot in here."

"I know. Anyway, moving forward a bit, what were your thoughts when the tweets started to appear through your mother's Twitter account?"

My nausea is subsiding slightly. *So far, so good,* I'm thinking. They're possibly just wanting my version of things. Checking *my* facts against Claudia's load of crap. The assault thing against her, fair enough. *But this – no.* "I was confused. And a bit freaked out to be honest. There were things in them that nobody could have known about. Like Mum being pregnant."

"Did you have any idea who could be behind them at the time?"

"Not at all. You've probably got it on record that I came with my uncle to report them to you. My head was all over the place. I even wondered if it was my mother's ghost." *Did I just say that? In a taped interview?* Well I suppose it's the truth. I *did* think it a bit.

"Why do *you* think Claudia was orchestrating this campaign of tweets? Now that we know for certain that she's behind them." Harrison has his hands clasped in front of him on the table and is twirling his thumbs round and round each other. Irritating.

"Cos she's a psycho. And so's her mother. They can't stand me and I can't stand them. They hated my mum as well."

"So it's fair to say none of you got on?"

"Very fair."

"And you can't give a reason as to why Claudia was behind the tweets?"

"To cause trouble. She likes to be involved with things. Especially if it's drama or someone else's misery."

"And how were you feeling about the suggestions that your mother was *pushed* to her death, rather than falling to it?"

Is this man for real? "How do you think I felt? She fell – she wasn't *pushed*. I found her. I've already told you."

"Claudia Price has told us something else."

"Well whatever she's said, she's lying." I should have throttled her whilst I had the chance. I knew she was trouble from the very first time I laid eyes on her. Hairs had literally stood up on the back of my neck. Jake, next door, had joked about foursomes with you and Iain. *Sick bastard.* He said I *must* fancy her, at least a little bit, but I really didn't. "Claudia will be wanting to stitch me up. I've already told you that she disliked me from the first time we met and even more as time went on."

"Why do you think that was Jamie?"

"I guess she was jealous. Probably about her dad or something. She liked him to be with *her*, not us. She was always slagging my mother off behind her back."

"I guess the stepfamily dynamic can be a difficult one." Harrison takes a tape from inside his folder. "For the benefit of the tape, I'm about to play an audio recording, taken from the mobile phone of Claudia Price at the time of her recent interview."

"Eh? What's that got to do with anything?"

"It's a recording of an altercation at your home, 7 St David's Road, Farnley, between you and your mother, Anna Hardaker, shortly before her death on Tuesday 16th April."

My hands are tingling. I've gone really, really hot. I stare at him as he slides the tape into another tape player and presses play. I feel like I can't breathe. I think it's one of those panic attack things.

"Of course things are going to change Jamie. That's life." It's your voice Mum. It feels so weird hearing it again, three months on. Eerie, yet comforting. God, I miss you.

"You haven't even thought about me, have you? Just you and that

CHAPTER THIRTY THREE

dick!" It's *my* voice now. I sound awful. Almost like my dad with all that anger inside me. I'm ashamed. *I don't get this. How's it come to be on Claudia's phone?*

"What am I supposed to do whilst you're all playing *happy families*? If you think I'm putting up with some screaming brat."

There's a clatter and the sound of you clearing your throat. "You're twenty-four years old Jamie. Perhaps you should be thinking about finding your own place. Most lads your age aren't still living at home."

"Oh well, this just gets better." I'm shouting at you now. I'm sorry Mum. I feel guilty. "So you and the dick get married, spawn some shitty, puking brat that will probably be born retarded at your age, whilst I get kicked out onto the street?"

"Jamie. You can't talk to me like this. Who the hell do you think you are? You're getting more and more like your father." I can hear the paint roller going back and forth, back and forth. "My life doesn't revolve around *you,* you know." I can recall how irritated I felt when you didn't stop what you were doing and talk to me. You kept on rolling the fucking paint onto the fucking wall whilst telling me to fucking leave.

I still don't understand what this conversation's doing on Claudia's phone. Did she have something rigged up? My blood is flowing cold around my body. *I know what is coming.*

"So why haven't you told me about this before?" My voice again. "The brat, I mean."

"It's your brother or sister, you nasty little sod. I didn't tell you because I knew how you'd react." There's a bit of clattering. I can remember you climbing down to load your roller with more paint.

"Well I think it's sick."

"*What's sick?* Look Jamie, I don't have to put up with this."

"The *baby* thing. It makes my skin crawl. We were alright as we were, before *he* came along and you turned into a slag."

"What did you call me?"

"You heard."

"I want you out of my house."

"I'm going nowhere."

"Yes you are. Pack your stuff and do one. I've had enough of you."

"You can't just kick me out."

"Watch me."

"I've got nowhere to go."

"Not my problem Jamie. Go to your dad's or something. I don't want you here anymore. I'm not putting up with being called a slag from my own son."

"You kick me out and I'm no son of yours, you slag."

"Pack your stuff and leave. NOW! I'm not going to tell you again."

"I've already told you. I'm going nowhere."

"Yes you are. As soon as I've finished this, I'm ringing Iain and *No!*" There's an eardrum-piercing scream, several seconds of banging and a cracking sound. Then deathly quiet for a few seconds before my voice cuts in.

"Mum! No! What have I done? Oh my God. Oh my God. Oh my fucking God. She's not moving. Oh fuck! Mum!"

Harrison presses a button on the machine. Everyone's expressions are unreadable. I close my eyes. "Have you anything to say Jamie?"

My mouth is dry. I'm done for. I've had it. I take a sip of my water. You've had the last laugh here, haven't you Mum. You always did. Or should I say, *Claudia* has. "I didn't mean for her to die." My voice is a whisper. "It was an argument. I'll never forgive myself."

"But yet you led everyone to believe she'd fallen, and you've carried on regardless for three months since, and, from what we've been told, you've certainly been enjoying the fruits of the inheritance money you've been left. Hardly the behaviour of someone who *can't forgive himself.*"

CHAPTER THIRTY THREE

"I haven't had it all yet. Is this what it's all about?" I glance at Martyn. He's not meeting my eye. Probably pissed off with me for not telling him everything. *"Money?* Does Claudia think she's not had enough? She's got my mum's car, you know. And what I want to know is where that recording came from." I'm in no position to be arguing and calling the shots but I want to know.

"Claudia has admitted to being a few feet away from you as you argued," Harrison explains. "Behind the door of your mother's bedroom."

"I don't understand."

"She's been frightened to come forward up until now for fear of being in trouble. She knows she shouldn't have been in the house."

I can't take it in. It still doesn't make any sense.

Harrison carries on. "Claudia was behind the tweeting 'campaign.' She couldn't live with knowing what had happened to your mum. She needed to let someone know that it wasn't an accident."

"It was. I didn't mean for my mum to fall. You can tell from the tape. I shoved her but I didn't mean for her to fall."

"You'll get the chance to defend that. When it goes to court, I mean."

You'd taken me to a cafe Mum. Normally we'd have been at work on a Tuesday afternoon, but I'd had a bit of a cold and you obviously wanted to speak to me. I'd had hot chocolate and a slice of chocolate cake. You'd balked at the price. *Fourteen quid for two cakes and two drinks!* You did say, however, that you'd missed us doing things like this and that we should do it more often. Then you said you wanted to talk to me about something. You wanted to tell me about the baby before I worked it out for myself. Before you started to 'show.' You seemed happy, almost *glowing*. I wanted to punch the smile right off your face. Go back to how things used to be.

"So whilst we were in the café, Claudia let herself in at our house?"

"Yes."

"Why was she recording? How come I didn't catch her?"

"She said she'd decided to record when she heard you both walk in, arguing. She thought she might be able to capture something that she could play to her dad. Something she could hold against your mum."

"Like what?"

"I've no idea." The interview room is so quiet, I feel like everyone will be able to hear my heart thumping. I'm truly, truly *screwed*.

"How did she get out? I never saw her."

"Through your bedroom window. Apparently, she jumped onto the shed roof and out of the back gate."

It's an escape route I often utilised as a teenager. "You sound like you're on her side," I say. "Does she get off scot free with *everything?*"

"You need to worry about your own outcome, not Claudia's." Harrison's voice hardens somewhat. "Jamie Hardaker. I am charging you with Actual Bodily Harm with intent against Claudia Jade Price on Wednesday 11th July. I am also charging you with the murder of Anna Louise Hardaker on Tuesday 16th April. You do not have to say anything but anything you do say may be used in evidence."

"What happens now?" My voice is barely audible. All energy has seeped from me. I really have had it. I'm going nowhere.

"You'll be formally charged at the front desk. Then you'll be returned to the cell."

"Till when?"

"You'll be in front of the Magistrate's Court in the morning. That will decide whether you'll be bailed or remanded in to custody whilst you await trial. In the meantime, you'll stay here."

"Here!" I can't believe it. "But I'll crack up! Can't I go home, just for tonight and come back in the morning?"

"Sorry Jamie. It doesn't work like that. It's for the court to decide."

"Can I have a few moments with my client please?" Martyn places his pen on top of his notepad.

CHAPTER THIRTY THREE

"Interview concluded at 12:52." I watch in dismay as Harrison labels and packages the two tapes before leaving the room.

"Right Jamie." I feel the weight of Martyn's hand on my arm. "It's just one night. I'll do everything I can to get you bail tomorrow."

I can't reply. I sit, reality sinking in, my head in my hands with tears dripping down to my chin and splashing onto the table. I don't know if I'm crying for me, crying for you, the life we should have had or the life we'll never know. I know it's my fault, but I can't help blaming Claudia too.

As I'm led from the interview room, back to the cell, I'm done. I want to go to sleep and never wake up. I want to be with you Mum. I want tomorrow's bail hearing over with but at the same time, I never want tomorrow to come.

Epilogue

K*iller Son Caged*
 Son of 'tweet mum' ousted by 'stepsister'
 A twenty five-year-old man yesterday pleaded guilty to the charge of manslaughter, after appearing at Leeds Crown Court.

Jamie Phillip Hardaker had inherited the lion's share of his mother's estate after her death in April of this year. Artist and Arts Coach, Anna Louise Hardaker, aged forty one, was the sole proprietor of a thriving business, *First Impressions Fine Art*. She was best known for the construction of her 'Toxic Marriage' painting which invited widespread acclaim.

Anna had been three months away from marrying her fiancé, Iain Price, also forty one, and was reportedly in the early stages of pregnancy. It is alleged that Hardaker pushed his mother to her death whilst she was painting the staircase at their home in Farnley, Leeds. It was suggested that Hardaker was primarily motivated by financial greed, coupled with jealousy over his expected half-sibling.

Judge Lakin, presiding, said the case highlighted the problems of resentment and jealousy in second-time families, where fractured families are forced to bring their 'baggage' and merge their lives under one roof, often against the will of the children. He added that this is a sad example of a culture where one in three marriages will end in divorce. We have moved away from the 'nuclear' family, he said, to a situation where the stepfamily is the norm. Statistics also show that the step family dynamic fails eighty three per cent of the time.

He acknowledged that it was a 'moment of madness' in which Jamie had robbed his own mother of her future and consequently, his own. He had been about to embark on his own art career after becoming the largest shareholder of his mother's estate but was instead led weeping from the dock. He will return for sentencing in October and will also be sentenced in respect of a charge of Actual Bodily Harm, brought against him by his would-be stepsister, Claudia Price.

Hardaker was brought to justice by Claudia, aged twenty three, who was behind a social media campaign to lead police to Anna's killer. Although reprimanded for not coming forward earlier, her fears and apprehension were said to be justified. Speaking outside court, Iain Price, (Claudia's father and Anna's fiancé said,) "I applaud my daughter for ensuring the truth came to light, in a situation where it would have been far easier just to let things lie. This truth will never bring back my beautiful and talented fiancée or our unborn baby, but Jamie, the perpetrator of this, is now being punished and the woman who was meant to be my wife can rest in peace. I take comfort that Jamie has been robbed of his future too."

Phillip Hardaker, ex-husband of the deceased, and Hardaker's father was at the hearing with his second wife. His only comment was that *he had washed his hands of his son.*

Reading Group Questions

1. What do you think the significance of the title, 'The Last Cuckoo' is?
2. What are your thoughts on the use of 'second person narration?' (Where a character is addressed directly as 'you.') What effect does it have?
3. Research has shown that eighty per cent of 'second time' families fail. What factors might contribute to this? How can they be overcome?
4. How does the emotion of *jealousy* manifest itself in this story?
5. Throughout the story, Jamie is treated in a variety of ways by others, as he works his way through the grieving process. How do people respond to him? Is this typical of society?
6. The smell of acrylic paint makes Jamie cry. Why is smell so evocative? What smells evoke emotion both in the story and for you?
7. Is there any truth behind the stereotypical 'mummy's boys' and 'daddy's girls?'
8. What are your thoughts on Claudia? To what extent does she redeem herself at the end of the story?
9. To what extent can Phil be blamed for the events in this book?
10. Why does a person's art seem more valuable after their death?

READING GROUP QUESTIONS

Can you think of examples of this?
11. How much does money cause family division within this story?
12. What are your thoughts of Iain's fidelity?
13. What forms of domestic abuse are there in the story? What are the effects of this?
14. Does Phil *love* his son?
15. Might a successful relationship between Meghan and Jamie have changed the course of the story?
16. Does the story evoke any emotion in you, as a reader? How are you left feeling at the end of it?
17. What do you feel will become of the characters next?
18. This novel has used an unreliable narrator. What is this and what effect has it had on you as a reader?
19. How would the scenes involving Claudia look, if written from her point of view?
20. Given Jamie's imprisonment, what should happen to Anna's estate?

Before You Go

I hope you have enjoyed this book. I would be hugely grateful if you could take the time to leave a review by revisiting Amazon. In doing this, you are making an enormous difference to my career as an independent author.

You might also be interested in joining my 'keep in touch' list, so I can keep you posted of my news and forthcoming publications. When you join, you will receive a free copy of my short story collection, *How to get Away with Murder*. This is available by visiting www.autonomypress.co.uk.

I would also love it if you would consider joining my advance reader team, by going to my Facebook page (Maria Frankland, Author, Poet and Creative Writing Teacher,) where you can read a free copy of my novels two months before publication and receive freebies and special offers.

'The Last Cuckoo' was my debut fiction novel.

If you would like to read my next novel 'The Man Behind Closed Doors,' you can get your copy by visiting Amazon. Below is the opening chapter to whet your appetite. Thanks again for supporting my writing career. I hope you'll keep in touch!

The Man Behind Closed Doors - Chapter One

His fingers probe her wrist and he gulps bile, retching with the stench of blood hanging in the heat of the June night. "My wife's been stabbed!" Paul slithers down the front of the cooker next to where Michelle is slumped on the tiled floor, amidst blood-splattered cupboards.

"In the chest. I don't know." He's gabbling into his phone. "Michelle Jackson. Yes, there's a pulse. No bubbles from her mouth. The knife's stuck." Reaching up, Paul drags a towel from the worktop, bringing a shower of cutlery down. He wraps the towel around the impaled knife, his chest thumping. She goes limp. He feels for a pulse again, his blood-soaked hands smearing against her wrist. "Paul Jackson. Summerfield Holiday Park, Filey. I don't know!" He hauls himself back up and glances out of the window. "There's a silver Ford Focus outside."

He strokes the hand on which Michelle wears her rings, then lets it flop back to the floor. *This isn't happening.* He glances back at the lounge. "No, nothing's been taken ... Emily, stay in there. Close the door. Daddy'll be there soon." Avoiding the seeping blood, he rises and lurches towards Emily's bedroom door along the hallway, broken glass crunching under his feet. "Yes, I'm still here. It's my little girl. Six years old. No, I don't know what she's seen."

"Daddy!"

"I'll be there in a minute."

Paul peers around Emily's door. He decides not to go in, covered in her mother's blood. Her room is in semi-darkness so hopefully she can't see it. She peers at him above the pillow she is clutching to her chest. "It's alright, it's going to be alright, Daddy's here. Mummy's going to be fine. The ambulance people will be here any minute. Emily?"

She says nothing. Probably in shock.

He wants to go to her, comfort her but to cover her in blood isn't the best course of action. "What happened? Tell me," he tries to disguise the urgency in his voice

She is trembling. He should go back to the kitchen but can't bear to. What if Michelle has died? She didn't look good. No, he's best staying with Emily. He can pretend for a moment that his wife isn't half dead a few feet away.

"Come here girl." Carla, their Spaniel, slinks from under the bed and cowers at Paul's feet. "They're coming!" He pulls back the hallway curtain in response to the shrieking sirens, before darting back to his wife. Michelle has slid further to the floor, her hair fanned around her. He kneels at her side.

"Mr Jackson?" Within moments, two paramedics stand at the cottage doorway into the kitchen. "If you could move aside for us please." They approach Michelle and squat either side of her. "Mrs Jackson, I'm Joel, a paramedic for the ambulance service and this is my colleague, Marvin. We're here to help you. Can you hear me?" His gaze flicks from Michelle's ashen face to Paul's. "What's happened here?"

"I found her." His own voice sounds alien to him. "Emily, stay in your room." He notices the door twitching along the hallway. "I'll be back in a minute." The red-haired paramedic pulls items from his bag and cuts Michelle's blouse open with scissors.

"You found her?"

"I don't know what happened, we had a row, I left her to calm down, and then I came back ... this is how I found her!"

Paul leans against the door, watching as they inspect the protruding knife. Becoming faint, he crouches against the wall. He has never seen as much blood in his life. The voices of people gathering outside swim around him.

"We need to stem this bleeding then we can move her." Marvin tugs a radio from his belt and Paul notices how freckly his face is. "I'll let control know what we're dealing with. This should be left in situ." Marvin points to the knife.

Paul follows Joel's diverted glance back to the door where two police officers now stand, one male, one female. "Mr Jackson?" The man crosses the threshold towards where Paul slumps. "I'm DC Calvert and this is my colleague, PC Bradshaw". The weight of his hand rests on Paul's shoulder. "I need to take a few details from you."

"I need to be with Michelle. How can I leave her after what –"?

"Let the paramedics do their job. She's in good hands." He frowns at one of them. "Remember this is a crime scene." He gestures towards the medical equipment littered around them. "Make sure the weapon is bagged, as soon as you're able to."

Calvert glances towards the door where another police officer has appeared out of the darkness outside. "Put the cordon round," he commands of his colleague.

"Sir."

"And when you've done that," Calvert continues. "Don't touch anything. I want you to radio through. We need the forensics down here. Tell them we're dealing with an aggravated assault with a weapon."

"Sir."

"My daughter!" Paul gestures towards the bedroom. "She's in there. I can't leave her – she's only six." He looks in turn at them all. "She was asleep." He's aware of their possible judgments of him, yet their expressions are not giving anything away. "I should never have left her!"

"PC Bradshaw will take care of your daughter whilst we talk to you." Calvert nods to his colleague.

"What's her name?"

Paul is marginally reassured at the voice of the female officer with a blonde ponytail poking out from under her hat. "Emily." Paul sees her now, she's opened her bedroom door and stands, shivering in her pyjamas. He wants to scoop her up and make it all better. "Will it take long…your questions, I mean? I need to see to my daughter and go to the hospital with my wife." The female police officer walks towards Emily and Paul feels the anxiety rising in him like vomit.

Calvert turns to him. "An officer will go with your wife. I'm going to read you your rights and then we'll head to the station. We can record your interview and then depending on the outcome of that, we'll have you straight to the hospital. I'll drive you myself."

"Are you arresting me?"

"Yes. Paul Jackson, I'm arresting you on suspicion of attempted murder. You do not have to say anything, but it may harm your defence if you do not mention when questioned, something which you may later rely on in court." His voice his robotic. This is something he's clearly said countless times already. "Anything you do say may be given in evidence. Can I have your mobile phone please?" His tone becomes more *conversational*. "You'll get it back after the investigation has been conducted."

"Attempted murder? But" Paul's attention is averted to the paramedics as they manoeuvre Michelle from the floor to the stretcher. He cannot tear his gaze from her face, and he wonders if he will ever see her again.

Available from Amazon

Acknowledgements

First and foremost, I'd like to thank my husband, Michael for his unwavering support of my writing career. For encouraging me and being the first to read what I've written.

I would like to thank my talented book cover designer, Darran Holmes, who has worked so hard to bring my book cover vision to fruition, and also to Sue Coates, the photographer who took my 'author photo.'

A special acknowledgement to my beta readers, Sheila Young and Ali Standen for their early feedback on the story and to Steve Whitaker, (Literary Correspondent for the Yorkshire Times) for the wonderful and detailed critique he took the time to give me. This was then followed with feedback from my wonderful Advance Reader Team.

I am also grateful to Leeds Trinity University and my MA in Creative Writing Tutors, Martyn, Amina and Oz. I have always been a writer but the Masters degree enabled me to make the transition from aspiring writer to professional.

Thanks to my sister, Allison Brown for her eagle-eyed proofreading skills and to the rest of my friends and family for being so excited about the arrival of my first fictional novel, especially Jane, who has travelled the journey alongside me. We have come a long way from scribbling away when we should have been doing our uni essays in the kitchen.

And finally, to you, the reader. I really hope you enjoyed it.

About the Author

Maria Frankland has been no stranger to turbulent times which have provided raw material for her novels and poetry. The domestic thrillers she writes shine a light into the darkness that can exist within family relationships.

She is proof that life begins at 40 after escaping an unhappy marriage, then pursuing a long-held dream of writing professionally and using her teaching experience and Masters Degree in Creative Writing to coach other writers in the craft of writing.

She is a 'born 'n' bred' Yorkshirewoman, a mother of two and has recently found her own 'happy ever after' after marrying again.

Still in her forties, she is brimming with enough ideas to keep writing novels for the rest of her working life, and is dedicated to motivating and inspiring other aspiring writers to follow their dreams too.

You can connect with me on:
- https://mariafrankland.co.uk
- https://twitter.com/writermaria_f
- https://www.facebook.com/writermariafrank
- https://autonomypress.co.uk

Also by Maria Frankland

The Man Behind Closed Doors
What could be so bad that a six-year-old stops talking?

Domestic violence isn't only perpetrated by men. Ask Paul Jackson who is on remand, accused of stabbing his wife, Michelle.

As he reveals his reality behind their troubled marriage, it seems that only his six-year-old knows what really happened. But she's trapped in her own world of silence. Out June 2020

Don't Call Me Mum
An out of control son. An outcast mother.
Is it ever acceptable to dislike your own child?

Tom is hyperactive, with severe behavioural issues. In infancy, he screams all night.
As a toddler he is destructive and fearless. At school, he is disruptive and lacking in concentration.
As he grows, so does the havoc, reaching a crescendo in his teenage years. In her quest for support, Sarah consults every specialist available, only to be met with blame and indifference.
This compulsive story of an outcast family, challenges the *'I blame the parents'* view. It is a 'must-read' for any parent who struggles and feels alone.

Described as a 'page turner,' readers have commonly said that *they are unable to put it down.*

Left Hanging
Within a marriage can be the sweetest, or the darkest place to be.

Ed and Kerry Huntington-Barnes have an idyllic life, with their five-year-old twins, successful careers, a luxurious house and an affluent lifestyle. Yet the secrets they're harbouring force their separation.

Kerry is fighting her own demons, amongst which is the knowledge that she is the wrong gender for her husband to ever truly love her.

Parallel to this it the death of a local man, Russell Lawson, which affects both Ed and Kerry in different ways. Will his widow Davina, and the other shadows that surround their separation and Russell's death, destroy their lives, and their sons' lives even further?

This is a story that portrays the darkness that can exist inside marriage and the hatred that can linger amongst families that are supposed to love each other.